GOOD RICH PEOPLE

GOOD RICH PEOPLE

ELIZA JANE BRAZIER

THORNDIKE PRESS
A part of Gale, a Cengage Company

LIBRARY OF CONGRESS CIP DATA ON FILE.
CATALOGUING IN PUBLICATION FOR THIS BOOK
IS AVAILABLE FROM THE LIBRARY OF CONGRESS.

ISBN-13: 978-1-4328-9494-8 (hardcover alk. paper)

Published in 2022 by arrangement with Berkley, an imprint of Penguin Publishing Group, a division of Penguin Random House LLC.

Printed in Mexico
Print Number: 01   Print Year: 2022

To my dog, BB

There is blood in the fountain turning the water an eerie rust color. I call someone to drain it.

I meet him at the gate and lead him down the stoop into our courtyard. Our courtyard is designed to be an oasis, a reprieve from the realities of the world. It is dappled with palm fronds, sprinkled with hothouse flowers.

I lead him to the fountain. It gurgles, desperate, like a person drowning. I stand over it, see my gray cashmere tinged dark in my reflection. "I want you to drain the fountain."

He steps forward, almost timid. His face wavers in the murky pool. "What is that?" He reaches with his hand, dips a finger so it undulates the surface, then brings it to his nose.

"How should I know?" I cross my arms. "I just want it out."

"It smells like blood." He shakes the water from his hand. His tool bag slips from his shoulders. It hits the ground with a crack. The tools rattle together. The sky is blue and glazed with clouds and there is blood in the fountain and I want it out.

"I don't know what it is."

"This is your house, isn't it?" He unbuttons each sleeve, rolls them slowly past his elbows. "Got a wall around it." He tips his chin at the walls on all sides, high walls, the kind you can't see past.

"I don't see what that has to do with anything."

He snorts.

"It's not my house, as a point of fact. It's my mother-in-law's house. Margo. She lives above us, see? With the pointed roof." I indicate the tower, whittled to a point like a thorn crown. You can see it from our house. You can see it from almost anywhere.

I once climbed the stairwell all the way up to the top of the tower. Graham told me it was useless. *It's decorative,* he said, but I wanted to see it. I reached the top. It was tight, a narrow box, and you couldn't see anything, not our house, not the city below. The windows were angled and the glass was too thick and you could not see anything above or below.

I still shiver sometimes when I see it. I still think it's watching me. It looks like it sees everything.

"You live here." He sits on the edge of the fountain and reaches into the water. Blood seeps into his rolled-up sleeve. He stretches deeper.

"Just because I live here doesn't mean I know every little thing that happens here. It was probably an animal. There are animals everywhere in the hills."

He grasps around for a moment, searching for something, then grunts, removes his arm from the water, shakes it out. Little droplets sting my flesh. He has a 4.7 rating on Yelp. I thought I could trust him. I should have known better. He was probably rated by middle-class people. Rich people don't waste time giving out ratings. They rate everyone the same.

"You really think that I've had someone murdered, don't you?" I perch carefully on the edge of the fountain, close enough to smell his backwater scent. "And I've called you here, because I know you'll never do anything about it. Because even if you can see it, even if you can say it, you can never believe that someone you know could kill another person."

His skin crinkles as he tries to look at me

but is blinded by the sun. "I don't know you."

"No." I flick the water with my index finger. "You don't."

LYLA

I get so bored sometimes, I think I will do anything to stop it. I decide to make Graham dinner. He blames me for what happened.

We don't have anything in the kitchen except Moët — dozens and dozens of bottles that Graham's mother, Margo, keeps giving us, daring us to celebrate.

I decide to make spaghetti because it's European and I think I can manage it on my own. The housekeeper got spooked and left, so we've been ordering in. I need to hire someone before Margo does, but I like how our house looks with a little dust. It looks like people actually live here.

I go to my closet to choose an outfit for the market. Everything in my closet is shades of gray. I've always wanted a signature color. Margo's is white. Graham's is blue. He says it's a power color. All of my underwear is blue.

I select a gray cashmere top and gray cashmere bottoms. Not the same shade of gray, because I don't want to look like an insane person. I accessorize with the exact right amount of diamonds and the hot pink gator Kelly bag I won in a game with Margo.

I stop to check my reflection in the full-length mirror. Sometimes I am scared by how beautiful I am. Every inch of me is buffed and primed. My face hangs exactly right. My muscles are taut and organized. I am scared because I don't want to lose it: the shaped nails, the tip of my nose, the sapphire glow of my eyes. I am sad because I want everyone to see it, but I don't want to see them. I want them to know how lucky I am but I don't want them to have access to me. It's a real problem.

I pass through the living room on my way out. It's Monday and light is streaming through the wall of windows, onto the travertine dining table, the gold bar chairs, the carved silver accents. The house is decorated to Graham's taste because I don't have any. I acquired his taste the day we got married. It was easier that way. Marriages fail because people are different. I want to be the same. Look the same, feel the same, have the same appetites. I want to cross the stars for us.

I pass through the courtyard on my way toward the gate. The flowers stink. The fountain gurgles uselessly, like a body choking on its own blood.

Our house looks like a handful of glass tumbling down a hill. Our front facade is modern, stoic, but when you step inside, the house stretches, open-plan, back and back forever, until it reaches a wall of windows. What you can't see from inside is the structures, the plinths underneath that hold it up, allow for the illusion of those never-ending floors.

In the hills, people will build anywhere. The more perilous the precipice, the more insecure the foundation, the more they *need* to build something on it. It's a challenge, a victory of money over matter.

Our house is built on the edge of a cliff.

And underneath it, between those concrete plinths, is a hidden guesthouse. It was built to hold up the house above. Margo once used it to store her exotic shoe collection, but now we use it to store a person.

I exit the gate and lock the door behind me. I can see Margo's tower above, chiseled to a point. Margo's house is like a castle, with all the requisite wars and rumors of wars. Graham says one day we'll live there, when he inherits everything, but I have no doubt that Margo will live forever to spite me.

I sometimes wish we would move somewhere, start our own life with our own money. But there is a little-known fact about people with money: They are beholden to people with *more* money. So although Graham could afford his own house and his own life, his mother has *more* money. His mother has money that makes our money look poor.

When you're rich, you can control everything. Except the richer.

Graham is afraid of losing his mother's money. Maybe even losing his mother — who knows? So we live in a glass house beneath her fortress, in a tidy alcove in the hills above Los Angeles, the ugliest and most beautiful city in the world, depending on where you're standing.

There is a little village square with a market just three blocks away but I have to drive. The streets in the hills are narrow and uneven and there are no sidewalks. Only mad people walk in LA. For my birthday, Graham gave me a gray Phantom. It's terrible to drive in the hills. I've scraped the back end four or five times and cracked the rear lights but Graham won't fix them

14

because he thinks it's funny.

It takes me ages to get it out of the garage and even longer to navigate the narrow streets of the hills because inevitably cars appear going the other way and I have to honk until they back up. People are such assholes.

I finally make it under the stone archway that signals the village. It's designed to look like a European enclave, all stone streets and storybook architecture. It really just looks like an abandoned fairy tale.

When Graham and I first moved in, we walked to the village market together at dusk to buy a bottle of red wine. The memory itself has very little to offer — it was dark and we were holding hands — but what I remember is not the night itself, but the promise of the future contained in it, how I thought that we would do this again, perpetually: walk beneath the arches in the semidark, kiss in the stone corner of the vintage boutique, pretend we were a couple out of time. I remember saying, *This is so magical. It's like we're somewhere else. It's like Disneyland!*

Now I drive beneath the arches and I think, *We never came again.* Not once. Graham works. We order everything in. If I ask him to go for a walk, he says, *Are you kid-*

ding? Rich people don't walk. Their shoes aren't designed for it.

I get to the market and find handmade pasta, but the sauces are all wrong. There is a clerk beside me filling the shelves — a teenager with a constellation of zits from his ear to his throat.

"Excuse me?" I hold out the priciest pasta sauce. "Why is this so inexpensive? Is there something wrong with it?"

The attendant looks flummoxed, like he has never been asked such a question. "Uh . . . I'd have to ask."

"Do you have anything more expensive?"

He blinks. "Uh . . . you could buy two?"

"You should make it from scratch." A familiar woman approaches from farther down the aisle. I've probably seen her in the neighborhood. I turn to face her. She has three necklaces around her neck, so I know she's crazy. One is a star, one is a circle and one is a cactus. I've seen the star necklace before, but it's a popular design.

"Me?" I can't believe she's talking to me. Her under-eye area is clogged with mascara dust. She has wrinkles but she is probably younger than me. She just doesn't have a good doctor.

"It would be more expensive if you bought all the ingredients separately." She crosses

16

her arms. She carries a shopping basket, but it's empty.

I set the pasta sauce back on the shelf, stamp my foot, throw up my hands. "I have no idea what's in pasta sauce!" I say, like nobody does.

"I can help you" — she shifts her hip — "if you want." She purses her chapped lips. Those three necklaces glitter with menace. But Graham would be so impressed if I made my own pasta sauce. Even more impressed if I had someone make it for me.

The corner of my Kelly bag is digging into my side, so I adjust it. "Oh, would you? I would so appreciate it." She nods eagerly. I indicate my cart. "Would you mind? It's so hard to carry a bag *and* push a cart." I frown.

She hesitates, face closing. She doesn't know what it's like having to carry a Kelly bag everywhere. It's not like I can just put it in the cart!

She sighs and swings her plastic basket into my cart. I follow her to the produce section. She finds me the priciest tomatoes, precut garlic, red onions. It's a good thing I'm there, because one of the onions looks dirty and I make sure she swaps it out. As she shops, she explains to me how to mix everything together. Of course, I don't pay

17

attention. I hate listening to people when they talk.

"Got it?" she asks when all the ingredients are in my cart.

"No," I say blithely. She shifts from foot to foot. "I'll never get it! We used to have a housekeeper who did all this, but we had to let her go," I lie. "She was very religious." That part is true. She suggested we were all going to hell. I privately thought hell couldn't be worse than Margo. At least in hell you don't have hope.

"I could help you," the woman says, "if you want." She adjusts her empty basket. "I'm actually looking for work."

I find myself considering it. She seems to know her stuff, and I do need to hire someone before Margo does. It looks like I would be doing the woman a favor. Her hair is knotted. Her eyes lack sleep. Her nail beds are dirty and uneven. She'd be very lucky to work for us. There are far worse places to be.

Her necklaces remind me of something, but I can't remember what.

Maybe it's someone I used to know.

Or maybe it's me.

LYLA

My new housekeeper helps me unload the bags and carries them to the gate. As I unlock it, my eyes shoot automatically to the tower. I have to remind myself she can't see us.

My housekeeper notices. "That's a big house. Who lives up there?"

"Margo. She's Graham's mother. Graham is my husband." The key sticks and I have to fight the lock.

She sets down the bags and helps me. "I'm Astrid, by the way."

"Oh." The name is too pretty for her. "Lyla. But you can call me Mrs. Herschel." It's dangerous to be on intimate terms with staff. Not just for me.

The gate groans as she unlocks it. "It's a beautiful gate," she says.

"Thank you. Graham got it from some monks or something." I hate the gate. It's some elaborate wood-carved delicate thing.

It always seems on the verge of snapping, and the lock sticks.

She readjusts the bags and follows me into the courtyard. She stops at the fountain. "What a nice water feature."

"It's loud." I was always taught to never take a compliment well. It's rude.

She gasps when I open the front door. Most people do. To the untrained eye, the house looks like it is floating. Guests are always careful when they take their first step out on the floor. My housekeeper is no different. She steadies herself on the side table. "This house is stunning."

"Yes, it's a work of art. But it's a terrible place to live. Maybe people aren't supposed to live in works of art. The kitchen is this way," I say although she can see it. Everything but the bedroom and the bathroom are open-plan. The floor is segmented by modern furniture, a fireplace we never use. At the wrong angle it looks like a game of Tetris sliding toward the glass.

The view is the most spectacular, so clear that it sometimes seems the mountains are inside with you, the trees and the houses all close and collected.

"When will your husband be home?" she asks as she sets the bags on the kitchen counter. The setting sun pierces the glass.

She raises a hand against it. Her face is blue and yellow.

"Not for another hour. Can you finish by then?" I say. She nods. I set my bag on the counter and lean in close. The sun catches in my eyes but I let it. "I need to ask you a favor."

She nods, but I wait until she croaks, "Okay." There is a fuzz of sweat along her top lip. I can tell she is uneasy. It's something about this house that does it. People feel themselves falling. It took me ages to get used to.

"Don't mention to my husband where we met. Let's pretend you're an old friend, someone I can trust. I can trust you, can't I?"

"You just met me," she says, which proves her trustworthiness.

"Exactly." I straighten my spine. "I can't trust anyone I *know.*"

I sit on a bench at the kitchen island and watch her cook because I don't have anything else to do. It's soothing actually, the way she knows just what to do and when. It's like watching a witch cast a spell, a pinch of bay leaves and a sparkle of salt. I am not used to seeing people do things with their hands. There is something so earthy about it. Her necklaces glint and twist to-gether.

"Where did you learn to do this?" I imag-ine taking cooking lessons but what would be the point when you can hire someone better without lifting a finger?

"My mother taught me." Her voice is monotone. She's in a cooking trance.

"We used to have a tenant who cooked." I sigh into my knuckles. "You could smell it rising up all the way from down there." I indicate the yard beyond the glass, which is blackening by the minute.

"A tenant?"

"Yes, we used to take tenants in our guesthouse. It was our way of giving back. We would find someone *in need* and try to help them. This world can be so inacces-sible." I have repeated this spiel so many times, it comes easily off my tongue, but my nose crinkles, my tongue sours.

"Used to?" Her eyes tip up, catch mine, then flutter down.

"We stopped after the last one. It turns out it's very draining having a stranger practically underneath you. You end up wrapped up in their lives. Besides" — I stand up, walk across the floor to the point in the glass where you can see the house down below — "it's so hard helping people, you know. Some people just don't want to be helped." I see the roof peaking out from below, the porch and the fence around it. I remember nights on that same porch, how loud we would laugh, knowing our laughter would rise up. "There's a little guesthouse right there. It's a terrible place to live. It's very dark and cold. I told Graham we ought to keep the help down there. Would you want to live there?"

"No. I mean, no, thank you." Her jaw is set in a funny way.

"No." I run a finger down the glass. "Neither would I."

The pasta sauce is simmering pleasantly when I hear Graham come through the gate. I know it's him by the way he shoves it, like he hopes it will snap back. I peek around the glass and see him hesitate over the fountain, catching his reflection.

Graham is one of the few people I know who is more attractive close-up than he is at a distance. Far away he could be any other handsome, well-dressed man. Up close, his appearance feels like a threat.

He finds what he is looking for and walks toward the door, briefcase swinging easily beside him. The new housekeeper is gone, like the best help, invisible. I gave her a

23

bottle of Moët to take with her.

I can see the scent hit his nostrils as he walks through the door, spring in his step. "What the hell is that?" he says, lips teased into a smile.

"I made dinner."

He swings his briefcase onto the table by the door. It clangs against a decorative silver tray. "*You* made dinner?"

"Well, I hired someone. Obviously"

"Thank God." He undoes his top button. "I don't want you cooking."

He pauses at the mirror. Graham is doomed to be beautiful, or everyone else is doomed for him to be. True beauty is always confused for goodness in a man and deceptiveness in a woman. Graham looks like a saint. He dresses in three-piece suits in shades of blue so dark, they're near black. His suits are so perfectly tailored, it looks like he was made for them. He is so clean that he makes you want to wash your hands.

"And I found a housekeeper." My voice hits a high note, too eager to please. "Two in one."

He loosens his tie. "What a woman." He strides to the kitchen and wraps his arms around me, like tentacles. I can smell him.

Graham smells nothing like he looks. You would expect him to have a crisp, clean scent — newly minted cash soaked in lemon verbena. Instead, he smells like hot testosterone, like something feral, like the kind of man who would hack down the door with an ax to save kittens from a burning building. I don't know what to do with his smell. There is nothing more confusing than being sexually attracted to your husband.

He steps back, fixes my hair. He hates when my part is uneven. Then he leans in close so he can whisper in my ear, "If you think this is going to make up for what you did, you have another think coming."

Lyla

The sun has set by the time we sit down to eat. We are so high up that you can see three or four stars, even with the city lights down below. I try to find them every night. Tonight, I find only three. They make me think of the housekeeper's necklaces.

Graham is groaning over her dinner. "This is actually superb, you know." He spins the spaghetti neatly on his fork with a spoon. He has immaculate table manners.

"You're welcome." I've lost my appetite.

"Well, you didn't make it, did you?" It's like this every time. The game ends, and he recedes.

"You're being mean."

"Why do you think that is?" My fork scrapes the plate.

"It's not my fault, what happened."

"It absolutely is." He dabs his lips with a linen napkin. "You warned her."

I twirl my fork in the pasta. Margo hates

when things go wrong. She likes to think she can control everything: the light, the mood, the weather and especially people. "It was her choice. It's no one's fault but hers." It's trite and it sounds it. The kind of phrase that's washed of color by overuse.

He shrugs, angles his hips so he can spread his legs, getting comfortable. I know he agrees. They're his words slung back at him. We gave her a choice, but she created her own option, one we had never even considered. "Well, you'll have your chance."

"What does that mean?"

"There's another one moving in this weekend."

My chair jumps. "What?"

"Margo's idea. The best way to get over someone is to get someone else." He stuffs pasta into his mouth, relishing this. He dines on discomfort. He swallows it whole.

"Why do we need another tenant? Can't we just take a break? Have some time to ourselves for a change?" He looks bored by the proposition.

My relationship with Graham has always been a throuple: me, Graham and boredom. It was there the day we married, warming itself in the backseat of the Rolls-Royce as we drove down a lane of sparklers, silver cans rattling in our wake. It was on the

27

private island on our honeymoon swimming circles around us in the bathroom bleach blue water. It was waiting for a turn, every time he took me to bed. It is especially present at anniversaries and birthday parties and holidays. Anytime we are expected to be happy, our third raises its head.

It was Margo herself who sat me down one afternoon and told me how to get rid of it, or at least get it out of our bed.

We were sitting in the second tier of her garden, having a tea. She peered at me over her fine bone china cup, eyes echoing his. "My son has needs," she said. "We are not like ordinary people, the kind of people you're used to associating with." Margo was always sure to sneak a dig into any of our conversations. "We have more money. We get more bored. If you want to keep him and keep him happy, he needs amusement. He needs amusement above all else."

Margo and Graham need the tenant. They need someone to dominate. Other rich people have nannies, dog walkers. That's not enough for them. They need tenants and their tenants need to be special. Exceptional. The game is more entertaining that way. If they don't have their tenants, they will find their entertainment elsewhere. They will play their games with me.

28

"Margo had an idea how to make it interesting," he says. I brace myself. "She thought you could take a turn."

My back stiffens. "But I don't want to take a turn. I don't want to play." I have accepted this little anomaly in Graham, but it's not for me. It's his hobby. He doesn't insist I play golf. I don't invite him shopping.

"It's not really about what you want." He spins his fork. "You need to prove yourself." I want to argue but I have to be careful. Graham often uses Margo as a scapegoat. This might not be her idea at all. It might be his. More probably, it's both. It's not important who thought of it first. They share blood and sometimes a brain. "You need to show her that you deserve to be here."

I don't meet his eyes. My neck is hot. "I married you. I sacrificed my life for you. My family doesn't even speak to me —" He flinches. He hates when I mention them. "I accept you. Graham. I accept you; don't you understand? When no one else would." He doesn't have a monopoly on manipulation.

"That's not enough. She wants you to embrace us." He sucks a speck of sauce off his pinkie finger. "Does this have crack in it?"

I don't want to play. It's different when

29

it's them, when it's something I see at a distance. Something I am aware of, but can easily ignore.

I got too close to the last one. There was something about her I liked: an innocence, a hopefulness, like she expected the fairy tale was in the castle, when it's always in the woods that the princess learns what *really* matters.

"What do you want?" I shove my plate forward, finished. I don't know why he likes it so much. It tastes like something out of a can. "What is it that you want from all this?"

He leans back in his chair, stretches his taut stomach. "I want what everyone wants: to be entertained."

"But when is it going to be enough?"

He swallows so hard, I can see it. I think I detect a sadness behind his eyes. But maybe his eyes are just beautiful; maybe that's the sadness. Everything is shallow with Graham: his looks, his thoughts, his actions. And there is something so attractive about that, the lack of depth. No hidden parts. No secret baggage.

But I think it hurts him sometimes, his shallowness. The way nothing matters. This pain is the thing I love most about him, because it is the thing we share: the dread, the fear, that nothing matters. Or worse, that it does for everyone else but us.

I get out of my chair and go to him. I bring his head to my stomach and he lets me. I brush his black, black hair. He's like a predator I have caught, a monster I can hold in my hands.

I bend my knees, try to slide onto his lap.

"Don't." I freeze. He fixes the hair I brushed out of place. "There's nothing more vulgar than trying to seduce your spouse."

I wobble in place for a second, uncertain. Then I stand. Graham sets his jaw and overlooks me as I clear his plate. Then he goes to his chair at the end of the floor, the one with armrests that look like wings. He puts his socked feet on the ottoman and scrolls through the news on his phone, announcing all the bad things that are happening like they make him feel better.

"Stock market's fucked! That fire's at one hundred thousand acres! Another hurricane!"

And that night, we lie down in bed together, like we do every night and we will every night forever. He lets me touch him for the first twenty minutes, stroke his hair, follow the tight, muscled lines of his body with my fingers, smell the musky scent that oozes from his neck. Then he scoots away, gets down to the business of sleeping. I slide to my side of the bed to worry.

His breathing pattern slows as I gaze up at the ceiling, the tiny light fixtures like pinpricks. My stomach churns with thoughts of the game, my turn. I don't want to play. There has to be some way out of it. Maybe I can prove myself to Graham another way. Maybe I can make him love me, finally.

He whimpers in his sleep. He always has bad dreams. Almost every night, a light squeal escapes his lips; his eyelids flicker. I used to ask him what he dreamed about. "You were crying," I would tell him. "You were crying in your sleep." But he always claimed not to remember. "I never dream anything," he said. "I never have dreams."

I brush the soft hairs on his neck to comfort him. He seizes on a sigh, then goes quiet.

Sometimes I ask myself why I stay. But I have known money long enough to realize that it always comes with strings attached. And I have known the world long enough to know that at its core, it's a game. Either you play or you are the one being played with.

LYLA

The housekeeper arrives as promised, early the next morning. I go out to let her in. "I'll have to make you a key," I say, leading her into the house. I have ordered in breakfast because we don't have anything in the cupboards. She puts the food on plates.

Graham doesn't even notice her. He has been raised not to see help. He allows me to kiss him at the door, distracted. "Margo is going to forward you the e-mail."

I want to protest but instead I nod. There must be a way to get out of this. I ask the housekeeper to clean but she doesn't have any products.

"Everyone brings their own!" I say, exasperated. "We don't have cleaning products; we only have Moët!" I give her money to buy some at the market. "Make sure you get bleach. And buy groceries, too. Just whatever normal people get. But better."

By the time I sit down on the sofa with

my laptop, I am already rattled.

I open my e-mail account to find a single new message. Margo has forwarded the new tenant's paperwork to me. She's cc'd Graham. She leaves no message of her own, no hint that this is anything other than an ordinary rental.

I read the new tenant's plucky e-mail:

Hi!

My name is Demi Golding and I'm looking for a quiet, peaceful place in the city.

Look elsewhere.

It's just me!

This is a must. Margo does extensive research to make sure there won't be interference.

"We want people who won't ask for outside help," she once said. "People determined to make their own way in the world. *Bootstrappers*" — her tongue twisted with disgust — "who work so hard to get ahead that they don't have time for anything else."

I make $350,000 a year as a Director at Alphaspire.

I lose my breath for a second. She makes more money than Graham.

My credit score is 801. It's very important to me that I have a good relationship with my neighbors.

You've come to the wrong place. You couldn't be more wrong. Margo would say it was her fault. That she was asking for it. "There is nothing more debased than climbing the ladder!"

One last thing! Shoe closets are a must! I'm a bit of a collector.

Us, too. But not shoes.

I am still hoping for a way around this. A deus ex machina. But in the meantime, I'd better prepare. I crack my knuckles and open a new tab.

I google "Demi Golding." Her LinkedIn profile confirms her name and her position. She got her start at a small school in a bad neighborhood, then went to NYU, got her master's at Columbia. There is no picture. She doesn't have Facebook or an Instagram. She is too busy for social media. Too ambitious to exist. I wonder if she's pretty, but I doubt it. If she were pretty *and* smart, she wouldn't work for a living.

I set my laptop down, pace the floor. Three hundred and fifty thousand dollars a year. What would I do with that kind of money? Then I remember we have far more. We.

I stop at the edge of the floor, so close to the glass that I can see my breath on it.

Margo has never chosen a tenant like this, someone so accomplished. She wants me to lose.

The game is simple, in theory, but in practice it always gets messy. The tenant is the pawn. The landlord is the player. The family is the audience. We observe from a distance, talk it over at private dinners.

It started long before I came, with Graham's nanny. According to Margo, "She had some high-minded ideas. She thought we were *family*." By the time Margo was finished with her, she did not think that.

And so the games began. Chefs, housekeepers, drivers, were all fair play. Anyone who Margo felt wanted to rise above their station: an overly familiar comment, a criticism or — worse — a compliment was reason enough to say, *Game on.* But after a while, it seemed silly to hire someone just to crush them — after all, it's hard enough finding good staff. And it was too easy. Margo was even a snob about the people she was a snob about. So she started taking in tenants.

When Graham was old enough to get wise to it, Margo let him play, too. They started taking turns, trying to top each other.

The most important rule was no interference — not because anyone was afraid of losing but because rich people can't deal with any conflict they didn't create. In fact, it's almost impossible to "lose" the game because the players have all the advantages, and the tenants have no idea they are being played with. It's very much like hunting. You don't walk into the forest and punch a deer in the face. You have a gun, a deer stand and a bloated sense of your own virility.

It should be easy for me to win. But I've never wanted to play. And I'm still rattled from the last one. The one that went wrong.

Margo blamed me. "You'd better clean this up," she said once they removed the body. I was still shaking. Graham had an arm slung over my shoulder, drifting from comforting to casual so quickly, it unbalanced me. "After all, it is your fault."

I made the mistake of calling the housekeeper. The second mistake in Margo's book. The first was "interfering" — the worst crime you can commit. My job was to watch. My job was to say nothing. My name is "Complicity." And now she wants me to play. And now she wants me to lose.

Margo has never liked me. She said I tricked Graham into marrying me, like it was a bad thing. She tried for ages to get rid of me, but now she has resigned herself. She can't let me go. I know all about her and Graham. She has to keep me around, as long as Graham wants me.

I'm not deluded enough to think my husband loves me but I accept him, when not many would. I let him play his games. I let him be entertained. And now he wants me to play with him.

The housekeeper returns with bags of supplies. I don't want to be here when she cleans, so I leave for a walk around the reservoir. It's a big wild lake hidden in the hills. Most people don't know it's there. It has a chain-link fence around it, so even we can't access it. Wealth is all about access. There are circles of wealth like there are circles of hell and we're all trapped in our particular punishing privilege.

I wasn't always rich. I was born rich. I was raised rich. But for seven months before I met Graham, I had nothing. My dad lost everything. Or rather, it turned out he'd had nothing for a long time but we were all too preoccupied to realize it. I was forced to shoplift designer bags, sell family heirlooms, steal credit cards. I almost had to get a job. It was inhuman.

I dated a lot of rich guys but none were as rich as Graham. From day one I could see there was a darkness in him, something I thought we shared. He was fucking me in the bathroom of a luxury hotel when he noticed the security tag still on my dress.

"Did you steal this?" he growled.

"I reappropriated it," I snapped back.

On our first date, he took me to dinner at Sunset Tower. After twenty minutes, he excused himself to go to the restroom and never came back. I was disappointed, but I wasn't done. I bought a bottle of Veuve Clicquot on his tab and finished it on the roof while I plotted.

I didn't hear from him, but in my mind the game kept running. I started to see him in everything I couldn't get, reflected in the glass at every designer store, the glint of the mansions on the hill, the roar of V12 engines. I was determined to make him mine.

I found out where he lived. I stole a car, and one morning when he was pulling out of his garage, I hit him so hard, it set off his air bags. I left the stolen car at the scene so someone else would take the blame. Then I showed up in his hospital room and tossed him the hood ornament from his busted Phantom.

He smiled at me for the first time with his perfectly symmetrical dimples. "You are so fucked-up."

I sat on the edge of his hospital bed and said, "Takes one to know one."

We were engaged in a week. It's not every day you find someone as fucked-up as you are. Even Margo seemed to like me. I have since learned that she is her happiest, her most glittering, with the people she is most intent on destroying.

The night before we were married, on the drive back from our rehearsal dinner, Graham said to me, "By the way, Margo told me not to marry you. She says you're a con artist."

At the time, I thought I had been making inroads, had even convinced myself she was happy about the marriage. She did invite four thousand people. "Maybe I am a con artist," I said, "but I'm not conning you."

"She doesn't think you're conning me," he said, rolling down the window of the chauffeured Royce. "She says you've conned yourself into believing you actually love me."

I was taken aback. "But . . . what do you think?"

"I think Margo was married six times." He shrugged again, let his hand dangle out the window.

I felt grateful that he didn't care what she thought. I felt ungrateful that he had felt compelled to share it at all. But that was what Graham did: whatever he wanted. He never thought about things like consequences, because there never were any for him.

Maybe Margo was right. Maybe I did marry him for his money. Maybe I did con myself into believing I was in love with him. But somewhere along the way I did fall in love, with his beauty, with his sadness, with his changeable indifference to me. When he is good, he is very, very good. His dimples show. His eyes glimmer. He makes the sky fall down laughing. When he is entertained. He is like all the good things in life: forever *just* out of my reach. He is so twisted up in my survival, it hardly matters whether I ache for him or his money. I still feel the pain.

I want him. I need him. I can't imagine a life without him, but even if I could leave, if I could talk myself out of love and money, there is no doubt in my mind that Margo would *annihilate* me. Not only would I not get a penny, but I would be lucky to walk away.

So I circle the lake, and I think about Demi. I think about what I would do if I did play the game. As I walk, my eyes keep searching for a break in the fence, a way in. I can't help it. There is no place more beautiful than a place you can't get to.

LYLA

As I turn the corner onto our street, I see Margo walking her dog, Bean. Her eyes meet mine. It is too late to escape.

She waits for me at the peak of the street, absently tugging on Bean's leash. Bean grins as she pants peacefully beside her. Bean is the happiest dog I know. When I see her with Margo, I often muse that Hitler's dogs loved him, too.

Bean is Margo's whole world. I think she loves her even more than Graham. She buys her toys and treats, a doghouse that's a scale replica of Margo's own house. Biggest of all, she walks her three times a day. When you have as much money as Margo does, time is your most precious asset. Margo spends half her day walking Bean.

"Lyla." Margo's plastic surgery isn't perfect. If you look closely, you can see her original face.

"Margo."

At one time, she was more beautiful than Graham, but her beauty read as artifice. She has black hair, blue eyes with a violet tint. Like Graham, she has dimples when she smiles, and they deepen when she smirks. "Where did you come from? Not wandering the streets, I hope."

"I went for a walk around the reservoir. I was planning my first move."

"How quaint. Have you read the e-mail?" Bean is sniffing a piss stain on the ground.

"Of course."

She crosses her arms. She is dressed in all white, her signature color, and with her piled black hair and her violet-tinged eyes, she looks like Elizabeth Taylor's stand-in. "What are you thinking?"

It's a test. Everything with Margo is a test I can't pass. I want to tell her that she wants me to lose. Instead I say, "I don't understand why someone like that would want to live here."

Margo flinches, so I know I've scored. "Everyone wants to live here, dear."

"Not everyone."

"Well." Her lip fillers stretch. "You're still here." She slides the leash through her fingers. "Can I give you some advice?" I want to say no but I also need help. My mind is a fog of panic. "Figure out what she wants. Then give it to her."

"I thought I was supposed to ruin her."

"Oh, Lyla." She clucks her tongue, flicks the lead's handle back and forth. "Haven't you noticed? Giving someone what they want is the worst thing you can do to a person." She thinks she is being clever, talking about me. "How is Graham? Are you taking care of him?" she says like she knows I can't.

"He's fine."

"He was very upset about the last girl." He didn't seem upset to me, but she often acts like he confides in her when he never does me. It's another thing about Graham that drives me wild. I am sure that he needs my help, that I could save him, if only he would let me. If only he would come to me and not to Margo.

"I know," I lie, and she loves it. I have walked right into her conversation trap.

"But you won't let him down this time. You'll keep him entertained." The word is nasty on her tongue.

Bean jumps forward suddenly, barking at a phantom in the trees. Margo jerks her leash so the chain rattles, but Bean ignores it, lost as the predator, lost in the prey.

LYLA

That afternoon, I go to meet my friends. I hate them but you have to have friends. Today we are in Mitsi's garden because she is throwing us all an un-birthday party. She ran out of real things to celebrate, so she has started creating holidays.

Her garden is California pastoral. It's lush and stuffed full with a variety of plants but they're spiky, they're desert and tough, so the garden is beautiful but treacherous. An aloe plant scrapes my leg as I follow her staff up the red tile path. At the top of the garden, where Mitsi and my friends collect, the view opens up and you can see the hills and the gray fog of downtown Beverly Hills.

All the women are crammed artfully around a table with so much decor, the servers can hardly find space for the plates: There are fine china teacups and Fabergé eggs. The egg at the center of the table is cracked open and stuffed with gold dust.

Everyone is doing gold dust this year.

I brought a whole case of Moët. Her staff sets it on the gift table.

"Thank you so much!" Mitsi exclaims. Mitsi's expression is always tinged with the disappointment of discovering that she has her mother's face after all. She is not beautiful, so everyone likes her the best and wonders about it: *There's just something about Mitsi!* She's not competition. She makes you feel like you're winning.

"You brought that last time," Posey says, sipping her Veuve. Posey is just pretty, but so stylish that she can afford to be an asshole. She has a way of dressing like she should be hanging in the Met. Today she wears some thick draped thing — the kind of dress an artist would use to study folds — with a matching scarf tied around her head. She looks ridiculous and gorgeous at the same time, which is the most attention-getting kind of gorgeous.

"It's not a real party," I snap back.

"These are from my real birthday," Mitsi says, indicating the frothy white garlands crisscrossing above our heads. "I'm always trying to reuse. I almost wore this dress before."

"It looks stunning!" Peaches walks in behind me, carrying a cut-glass vase of

47

hothouse flowers. "Where should I put this?"

"Anywhere!" Mitsi gestures to the over-crowded tables. "It's beautiful!" Peaches searches for a place, then finally hands the flowers off to the staff, never to be seen again.

We all arrange ourselves around the table. There are twenty of us, but only three who matter: the wives of Graham's old school friends. Everyone is wearing pastels except me. I'm wearing my signature color.

"You know," Posey says, sitting next to me. "I really admire your commitment to *gray.*" She makes "gray" sound like "drab," and I question my whole existence.

We go through the charade of a tea party like a pack of twelve-year-olds. The staff pours tea and serves cakes. Everything they serve us changes colors, smokes or has to be set on fire. This usually involves a lot of awkward waiting as they struggle to get it right — *It worked upstairs! Sorry. This will take just a second!* And then, once everyone has moved on, it happens in a flash — *Oh!* And everyone gasps or offers halfhearted claps. We are required to "squeal" over something once every ten minutes. When you're rich, there is no work harder than being impressed.

48

These women are a good reminder of what's waiting for me if I ever leave Graham, if he ever leaves me. It's impossible to be good in the world — even the good things you try to do, like saving someone, for example, can have terrible consequences. That leaves two choices: evil and mediocrity. I watch these women gasp at tea cakes and think: *This is mediocrity.*

I have never felt more alienated in my life, until Posey leans over the table and says to me, "How are things with Graham?" She dated Graham all through school. She got his best years, the years before he learned how much he could really get away with.

"Fine," I say. I don't mention that he, Margo and I are all participants in a silly but dangerous game, or that it's my turn, or that I am still hoping for a chance to back out. This is the trouble with friends. You have to lie so much to keep them, rearrange the fabric of who you are to please them. It's exhausting.

"Isn't his *real* birthday around the corner?" I don't know why she bothers asking. She knows it is. Every year she shows up at his party in a dress that would make Scarlett O'Hara blush. "Do you have anything planned?"

"Of course, I do." I've been planning Gra-

49

ham's birthday since Christmas, when we sat beside the fire at Margo's and Graham — drunk and smoking like a chimney — complained bitterly: *Fucking Christmas. I'd rather be crucified than have to unwrap another goddamn sweater.* Graham is quite funny when he's drunk. Never intentionally.

"What are you going to do?" Posey's eyes glitter with challenge.

I glance at the other women, but they're wrapped up in watching a server pour liquid nitrogen over a swan, revealing an egg underneath. "We're going to play a game."

Posey leans back in her chair, drums her fingers on the table. "What kind of game?"

"A shooting game. With real guns."

I was trying to shock Posey, but Mitsi overhears and gasps. "Real guns? What are you going to do, kill people?" All of the women here are slightly in awe of Graham.

"Real guns but fake ammunition," I say. "It's called Simunition. It's what the police force uses for training. I'm having it made special with gold dust, so when you shoot someone, they turn gold." I pinch the gold dust on Mitsi's table and flick it in demonstration. "It's going to be spectacular." I'm actually very proud of my idea, although I know it will be lost on these women. It won't be lost on their husbands, who always act up for weeks after one of Graham's parties. *I hate to tell you this,* Peaches once told me. *But after Graham's parties, Henri always threatens me with divorce.* Graham's parties bring out the worst in everyone. It's a real skill to throw a party that good.

"Fabulous." Posey grins with all her teeth. She likes the threat of violence. I suppose there is a reason she dated Graham.

Mitsi inhales slowly, less sure. "Graham is so *masculine,*" she decides. That's one way to put it. "I'm glad Mark isn't so masculine."

"Women like games, too," Posey says. She pinches a finger full of gold dust and blows it across her dress so it looks even more fabulous. I wonder what would have happened if she had married Graham. Would she have played the game? Would she have stayed? The truth is, I don't know her, and she doesn't know me. That's why we're friends.

"It must be very hard for you," Mitsi says, "keeping up with him." She meets my eyes and my chest aches.

"I'm not afraid of Graham," I volunteer, which is not what she was saying at all.

LYLA

When I get home, the housekeeper is gone and the house is spotless. I have this uneasy feeling. I go to the cupboards and count all the bottles of Moët, just to make sure she didn't take any.

Graham doesn't return until after sunset. There are so many windows that the dark crowds in, punctured with little lights from the houses along the hills. There are only three stars in the sky.

"Did you read the e-mail?" I am standing in the living room when Graham crosses the long floor. He perches on the arm of the sofa beneath me, looks up at me.

"She makes three hundred and fifty thousand a year," I say without thinking.

"She sounds impressive." Graham is always impressed by money. He slides the tie from the back of his neck and it tugs his collar open. It releases his scent, enticing me.

I step forward until I am straddling him. I run a finger down the inside of his open collar. I kiss him, and he kisses me back. I let my hand drift down toward his pants. I kiss him again, but when I find him, he's soft.

Sex has always been sporadic in our relationship. It was his wedding present to me. A surprise gift that came with commitment.

I remember our wedding night exactly, how he laid me down on the bed in our suite at the Beverly Hills Hotel, just like he was supposed to. How he glistened with perspiration, how he looked at me like he loved me, just like he was supposed to. But he couldn't have sex with me. He couldn't. And I told him that it was okay, that it was understandable. *You're tired. It's been a long day.*

And he went out on some phantom errand, to get fizzy water or something, and he came back hours later. I was lying in bed watching *Real Housewives*. And I switched the TV off and he climbed in beside me and he said, "I'll make it up to you. I promise I'll make it up to you."

We haven't had sex in almost a year. I know this is true but I can't believe it. I have this alternate reality in my head where we have sex the normal amount. It protects me from the truth: that even though I have sacrificed myself to be the same, we are not.

I have trawled through Reddit posts of other people with similar problems. I never post myself; I don't need to. There are people out there who understand sometimes you're in love with someone who won't sleep with you. The replies from people who *don't* understand suggest visiting a doctor. Who are these people? If I even hinted to Graham that there might be something wrong with him, he would never look me in the eye again. And even if I could somehow convince him to go, I'm afraid of what a doctor would reveal. That everything is fine. That the problem is me.

If you want my professional opinion, you're not sexy enough.

"I've had a long day." His voice is almost pleading. His animal scent mixes with the leatherwood shampoo in his hair as I press my cheek against his neck. I know it's not my fault, but it can't be *his* fault. I've been told all my life that a man will have sex with anything.

"Dinner." His lids are hooded and he sets his hands on my hips and replaces me. He sets me back so he can stand, look down on me again.

"Graham." I want him so badly. I want to make him beg and weep and cry out. I want him to worship me. But he walks away into the kitchen and all I see are cashmere throws and white sofas. "It's okay," I say but he doesn't hear. I'm talking to me.

He opens the fridge, takes out a bottle of Moët. "Let's celebrate." He breaks the seal and pops the cork. "To Saturday."

Lyla

Demi moves in on Saturday. I go out right before she is supposed to arrive, so she will meet me coming back from somewhere. I want her to think I have a life.

Graham is away on one of his golf trips. He goes almost every weekend, comes back with complicated stories about breaks and birdies, which he recites like someone trying to pass a test.

"I thought you would want to see her," I said yesterday morning. He was leaving straight after work, so that was the last time I saw him.

He shrugged. "You can tell me what happens." That is a big part of the game: the story. It is always told over ornate private dinners, too many cocktails, expertly arranged views. It's recited like the winners write the history books. The others can't interfere with the game. They're supposed to wait for the story. In fact, they're not really encouraged to interact with the tenant at all. It can throw off the game. It's also part of the reason that Margo and Graham are so unhappy with me about what happened with the last tenant. I wasn't supposed to talk to her, let alone befriend her.

"You need to come up with a plan," he reminded me, kissing me once on either cheek, last on the lips. "Margo doesn't think you can do it." Of course she doesn't.

"She didn't think I could marry you either, but look how that turned out."

He tightened his tie in the mirror and walked out the door.

When I arrive home later that day, there is a large moving van parked in front of our house. Furniture is piled on the side of the street. I walk slowly, analyze it. Demi has unique taste.

There is a marble statue that looks like a woman but could be some kind of animal. There are two elaborately carved wooden structures, like towers. I think they might be bookshelves but I can't be sure; you couldn't fit many books on them. I don't know where she found them. Everything is unexpected. Nothing is functional. Her taste makes my skin feel tight.

Graham would detest it. He would call it

creepy and weird. He thinks anything that isn't classic is a sign of madness.

I stay in the courtyard for a while, organize the plants as the movers journey up and down the stairs. I am hoping to get a glimpse of Demi, but she's not here. Good move.

Finally, I go inside the house but I don't close the blinds, even though the movers can see inside.

The housekeeper is there. "Is that your new tenant?" she asks.

"No," I say. "It's her things."

Once they finish with the big furniture, they start with Demi's shoes. Her collection. They descend the stairs with boxes piled three high: Louboutin, Lucchese, Pierre Yantorny. It's like watching a processional, a funeral for shoes.

The housekeeper makes me tea and I sit on the corner chair, the one set so you can look out onto the street and not be noticed. It takes them three hours to unload everything.

"You're very curious," the housekeeper says.

I bristle. "So are you."

I try to find Demi in her furniture, the human inside the possessions. But all I can think about is how invaded I feel. It's like she is crawling inside my womb.

Lyla

She doesn't arrive Saturday night. I stay up late. I lie on Graham's side of the bed. Our bedroom window looks out onto the courtyard. I have lifted the bottom of the shade. I watch the space, clamped by nerves.

Sometimes I see shadows cross themselves, ferried along by headlights or security lights, a rush of wind through the trees, and I think: *She's here.* But she isn't. She never comes.

All of Sunday, I pace the floor. Occasionally, the housekeeper annoys me.

"You seem tense," she says.

Finally, I dismiss her. "It's Sunday. Shouldn't you have the day off?"

Graham comes home on Sunday afternoon. He doesn't mention Demi, but I know it bothers him that she's not here yet.

He sets up at his desk at the far end of the living room, the apex, so the entire view crams in around him. He pulls at his collar and rubs at his neck, releasing his scent like a scratch and sniff. I try to think of things to do that feel like actual things, but end up moving from the kitchen to the window, to the bedroom and back, like a thing trapped.

"Can you stop pacing?" Graham says. I can't blame him. I am annoying myself.

I perch on the sofa under the window that looks out over the stairwell that leads to the guesthouse. "Do you think she's down there and we just can't hear her?" The sound from below is not always reliable. It's something we've often wondered about. Sometimes we won't hear a thing for days, when suddenly a sentence breaks through, clear as a bell, like the person below is standing in the room with you.

"We would have seen her." Graham doesn't look up.

"Why isn't she here?"

"She probably has things to do. Like *everybody* does." His words are pointed, but I know I am not the reason he can't work.

"Do you think I should check? To see if she's down there? Just in case?"

Graham leans forward a little, peering below. "The curtains are closed; she's not there." Like it's that simple.

"But maybe she likes to keep the curtains closed. Maybe she doesn't like people seeing everything she does." I scan our wall of windows, but we are so high, only the birds can see inside.

He sits back, rubs his neck. "Lyla, you're obsessing." He doesn't say this unkindly. "Why don't you go for a walk or something? Try to think about something else."

"It wouldn't hurt to check."

Graham groans, goes back to his work. "She's not down there."

I prepare to go for a walk. I select the perfect gray outfit in case she's there and sees me, in case she comes in as I'm going out. I stop at the door to put on my shoes. Graham looks up, smiles at me.

"You're the prettiest girl in the world," he says. I feel an almost overwhelming spike of dopamine, but then it drops away, when it used to last and last.

And I want to run to him, to hold on to the good, but I know that if I do, he will immediately say, *I'm working, I'm tired. You're being silly now.* Not because he doesn't want me, but because he only wants me at the right distance: not too close, not too far. Like an abstract painting that only comes together in one spot marked on the floor in an empty gallery. His love is farsighted. If I get too close, it blurs.

I don't go downstairs to check if Demi is

there. Instead I take the same walk I take every day. On the way back, I find Margo and Bean parked outside a great white van. The windows are covered with old blankets. Bird shit runs down the side like blood.

"Where did that come from?" I ask.

Margo's chin jerks in my direction. "It's an eyesore. We'll have to pay to have it moved." Bean is sniffing frantically, clawing the asphalt. Margo never bothered to have her trained. She wanted her to be herself, so she often acts in the most animal fashion. She barks once and then rapidly, one on top of the other. "Bean!" Margo jerks her leash but looks a little proud.

"I don't think you can have it moved. You don't own the street."

"Don't be silly." Bean lunges. The collar catches her in the air. Bean whimpers and comes to Margo, who squats and makes a fuss of her. "That's all right, my darling girl, my vicious little girl." She stands. "This neighborhood is going to hell."

Margo owns half the neighborhood. There are other houses on our street, but I don't think people live in them. On occasion I will see someone rambling along the street, looking startled, as if they're not sure how they got there. But I never see the same person twice. That is what Margo likes about the neighborhood, what she likes about Los Angeles in general: *You will never find a city where people care less about what you get up to.*

"Have you met the tenant yet?" Margo asks, regripping the leash so she can tug Bean away from the van and toward the gate that leads to her garden.

"No. She hasn't arrived."

"You'll let me know every detail" — the gate screeches as she opens it — "as soon as she does."

LYLA

Demi arrives just after midnight. Graham and I are in bed, at the stage in our sleep pattern where we turn our backs to each other. Graham sleeps on the side closest to the gate, so when I hear her, I shift to his side and peer through the opening below the shade.

He gasps, awake. "What are you doing?"

"I thought I heard something," I say, knowing I heard her.

"Get your elbow —" I move it. "It's probably that silly woman living downstairs." He is half asleep, so I try to be quiet, but she is struggling to unlock the gate, turning the key this way and that, jangling the fence, swearing under her breath. Graham comes together; anger puts his parts in place. "Does she have to be so fucking loud?"

She is still struggling.

"The lock must be stuck. Should I help her?"

"It's late."

I start to get up when the gate screeches, then bangs limply against the wall. "Fuck." That's her, Demi, outside our house.

I see her move down the stairs. First, her shoes, curled black and witchy, as she swivels on the step and locks the gate behind her. "Fucking shit," she mutters. It sears through Graham. He yanks the comforter over his head.

She wears a big black coat, as if she's just come in from some terrible ice storm in the middle of Los Angeles. Her face is a smear beneath wild hair and then she's gone, down below to her guesthouse.

I lie back in bed with my heart pounding as she moves down below. I can't hear her footsteps or her words if she says any, but I catch the flush of the toilet, the bang of a closet door. We are so close. Her place is actually part of ours, the same house, on another floor.

Graham moans and punches an opening in his cave of covers. "I hate when they wake me up." Then he moves to my side of the bed and buries his head in my chest.

Graham is such a snob; it turns him on to think there is someone *literally* below him. If I kiss him when she's downstairs, he

66

groans like he wants her to hear.

All week long, I get glimpses, but they are quick. She leaves early. She comes home late. She never sleeps, and neither do we. I know I will have only a minute to catch her as she passes to make it seem natural and spontaneous. I wait on the patio for hours, and she arrives the moment I leave, like her watch is set to avoid me.

Graham checks in every day.

"Have you met her yet?" and "Have you talked to her?"

I run into Margo and Bean out on the street. "Where is your mystery tenant?" Like all of this is my idea.

By Thursday Graham is actually angry. The housekeeper has cooked another amazing dinner. No stars are out tonight. It's too cloudy. There is only a fog that smells like ashes.

"You haven't even met her. You're not even trying." Graham pouts, then licks his fork.

"I *am* trying. She's never here. That's what happens when you choose someone with a high-powered job. They work."

Graham frowns and puts down his fork. "It's no fun when it's your turn."

"I never wanted a turn."

"Margo was right." It's my least favorite

set of words, and he knows it.

I put my hands on the table. "What do you want me to do, Graham? Set a booby trap? Move in downstairs?" My neck is hot, like he's onto me. The truth is, I have questioned my intentions. Maybe I really am not trying. Maybe her watch isn't set to avoid me; maybe mine is set to avoid her. Way deep down, I don't want to do this. My heart is treacherous.

"I want you to get her to like you. You can do that, can't you?"

It burns and he knows it. "You want me to seduce a stranger."

"You're seducing *me*." He strings his fingers together, sets his chin on top. "Let's make things more interesting. Get it done and I'll fuck you."

The word pops a bubble in my brain. So much of our relationship is a tacit agreement never to mention the fact that Graham can fuck me only under certain circumstances, ideal conditions. Not temperature, a different kind of heat. His heel scrapes the floor as his legs shift under the table. "Seduce her, promise her the world and ruin her."

That is the game Margo and Graham like to play. They invite a bootstrapper to live in their guesthouse. Someone who has climbed the ranks, someone self-made, woman or man. Then they conspire to make them lose everything, but spectacularly: a sex scandal, criminal charges, fraud.

But first, the player befriends them. They get to know them. "Poetic justice," Margo once said, "is so much more satisfying."

"Annihilate her," Graham continues. "Her job. Her money. I want her to lose *every-thing*," he says, beautifully transfixed.

I have often wondered what it is about the game that draws them. Is it because they fear losing their place to upstarts, ordinary people whose history is not riddled with wealth? Do they think there's not enough room at the table? Do they want to keep the head count small? But I think their reasons are different.

Margo invented the game and she does it to prove her power, her control over every-thing: the light, the mood, the weather but especially people. It took me longer to work out what was in it for Graham. He's too perverse to be political, too muddled and uneasy with himself to be so specific. I think he plays the game because he can, because he is bored, because he has appetites and wants for nothing.

He likes the pageantry of struggle. He's

only ever suffered psychic pain. Pain you can see sometimes feels like relief.

LYLA

Graham has been gone all weekend on one of his golf trips. I'm alone in the house.

I try to think but can't, try to plot but there's a block. My brain is starting to sweat. I sit on Graham's chair at the apex of the floor and look over the house below: the porch, the roof, the trees and their twitch. I don't want to do this. That is the truth. I am avoiding the game, avoiding her. Graham's right: I'm not even trying.

If I wanted her, I would wait in the courtyard. I would bang down her door. I would send a desperate and demanding text, conjure some emergency, force her to meet me. Instead, I am making excuses. I am giving up.

Margo may have been lying when she said Graham was upset about the last one, or she may have been fishing. Because she knew I was.

Her name was Elvira. She had bright red

hair that turned black underwater. She cooked dinner for herself every night. I was circling the reservoir one afternoon when I ran into her, going in the other direction. "We should walk together," she said. "We're going to the same place."

I knew the rules, knew that I wasn't supposed to interfere, so I told her, "I prefer to walk alone."

She just smiled and said, "Me, too. We'll be perfect together." She walked beside me, not talking, as if alone, all the way home. Not the next day, but the day after, she caught me again, and then over and over and over. She waited for me to start talking. When I did, she talked back.

Every day when Graham was at work and Margo was above, we walked to the reservoir. Margo found out. She found out everything. She said it was a bad idea. Graham warned me not to get attached. But Elvira and I shared a wicked sense of humor, a belief that at its core the world was a joke only we got.

It was Graham's turn, and I watched her fall in love with him the way everyone did. Watched him turn, watched her love him more. They all did. They all do. They all love Graham even more when he turns on them, because they are sure it's their fault, something they did, something they can fix.

"How do you put up with him?" she once said to me, words tangled in a laugh, like his power was funny, how it caught you off guard.

"I don't know," I told her but that was a lie. I put up with him for the reason everybody did. Because beauty and money are God, and Graham is more beautiful, and has more money, than anyone I've ever known.

She just laughed, and I hoped she would win. I hoped he would lose, just this once. But I should have known better. I should have known that the closer the rich get to losing, the more spectacular their eventual win.

I wait for Demi but she doesn't come. I open a bottle of Moët and drink it. The longer I wait, the more my resolution wanes. I feel myself sinking into the chair, immobile, inert, as if drowning. I watch the trees twitch and quiver below. My feet meld with the floor.

I'm trapped. My life is the trap.

I awaken to the sound of feet pounding up the steps. My head thumps from the champagne. I reach for my phone. It is after midnight and she is at the gate, shaking it,

73

clattering it, trying to get in. I groan as I climb from the chair. This is not how I wanted to meet. This is not how I pictured it. This is not a winning moment.

I stop by the hallway mirror and press the wrinkles from under my eyes, run my fingertips over my hair until it lies flat.

She is rattling the gate like she knows what's coming. I am what's coming.

I switch the hall light on. The rattling stops. I walk across the cold living room. Beyond the windows the hills are blue, scattered with halogen lights. I steel myself up and open the door.

She freezes on the stoop, her hair a wreath of artful tangles. She wears a light blue puffer coat with a torn collar, torn jeans, dirty sneakers. She reminds me of the rich English girls Graham went to school with who wore scrunchies and did ketamine in Shoreditch.

"Are you locked out?" I say, then realize she is inside the gate. "Oh. You're locked in."

She steps back from it, turns to face me. Her skin is translucent around the edges, the way Graham's gets when he drinks too much.

"Sorry. I was just making sure it was locked." She speaks with a raspy voice and an almost complete lack of accent, like she comes from nowhere, everywhere. She is younger than I expected. And there is something about her. Right away I can tell there is something special about her, as if she is an ingenue on the cusp of fame.

"I'm Lyla."

Her face is round. Her eyes are wide, blackish in the dark and filled with something: thrill, like we have collided on a fast train. Maybe she is drunk. Maybe she's high. She never seems to sleep.

"We live upstairs, my husband, Graham, and I. But you probably know that."

I step forward, offer my hand. Her hand is hot and feels immediate, electric. Her eyes widen and her lips drop open. She gasps a little at the touch, so I know she feels it, too.

Her eyes drift down, unsure. She finally says, "Sorry I woke you up."

I say nothing. I just let her apology float between us, forever making her aware she owes me.

She stuffs her hands in her pockets. "I'd better get back down."

"It was so nice to finally meet you." I move toward her. She moves away. "We'll have to meet again sometime."

"Sure."

"Tomorrow."

She freezes, hovers off-balance on the top step, foot hanging down. "I don't think I can do tomorrow."

"I think you can."

She laughs once. But she doesn't refuse. She just lets her hanging foot drop, then follows it down the stairs.

I feel my blood pumping. As I close the door behind me, as I walk to the bathroom, as I prepare to go to bed. I lie on Graham's side with my heart pounding, throbbing in my ears, too tight in my chest. I can't fall asleep. My eyes keep popping open, as if sensing a counterattack. I tell myself it's the alcohol. It's not.

It's the thrill of the game.

DEMI

I wrangled an appointment at HELPING HANDS by pretending I was writing an article about their charity. I sit on a good chair across from a woman with a row of toys with bloated heads, still in their boxes on a shelf behind her, and I can tell she doesn't get it. She is helping people she doesn't believe exist.

"For a lot of people, it's a lifestyle," she informs me. "That's one of the problems we face. Habitual drug users, alcoholics, hippies. Especially in California. People look at it as a way of life."

"So, you're saying they don't want help?" Her office is big and bright, but there are two framed pictures on the floor unhung, as if she is afraid to get too comfortable here.

"You'd be surprised how many people don't ask for it."

I would not be surprised. I'd tried to get an appointment here myself, but moving through their website was like playing a video game with a looping glitch, every click leading you back to where you started. Only when I pretended to be a journalist, when I made it clear I didn't *need* anything — in fact, I wanted to *give* them press — did they message me back.

"How do people get appointments here?"

"Mostly through referrals."

"Who refers them?"

This stumps her. She runs her nails through the hair above her ear, making a glamorous scratching sound. I don't think she expected specifics. She seems unhappy that I am asking questions at all. During an interview.

"And you house people?" I press on. "You have housed people?"

"Yes."

"Where?"

"We connect people to our shelter network."

"Shelters? But that's not housing. Have you put anyone in a house?"

"A shelter is better than sleeping on the street."

"But if you stay in a shelter, you lose everything you have." I know I should leave it. My voice sounds sticky with self-righteousness. "They only let you bring a backpack. And you're not guaranteed a stay beyond the night you're there. The next day, there might not be room for you." People don't understand the time it takes, the effort, the mental strain, just to find a place to sleep. It's the hardest job in the world, not having a job.

Her chair whines as she leans back. "Who are you writing this for? What's the angle? Because I would like to talk about *helping* people. I thought we had an understanding that this would be a *positive* look at the homelessness crisis."

I am triggered, but I have to swallow it. I have to swallow it because I need her to like me. I need her to help me. But if I had to define one of the biggest barriers I have encountered, all the times I have needed help, it's this idea that I am being negative. That by being me, by being a person who has lived through and dealt with terrible things, I am "negative," the rain on everybody's parade.

This isn't about me, I tell myself. Except it is.

"I'm sorry." I bristle at the words. I'm so sick of being sorry. "I'm just trying to establish the specifics, exactly how you're helping."

She purses her lips. She is about to ask

79

me to leave. It's late, and she already moved this appointment twice.

Be likable, I order myself, but I don't like myself. How can I? I have been taught all my life to hate people in need. "I like your toys." I nod at the ballooned cartoon heads. "Do you collect them?"

"Oh, yes! I have over three hundred at home. I keep a rotating crew here. Keeps me busy." She frowns suddenly, like I have tricked her into revealing something she didn't want to reveal. She sits forward and I feel myself move back, hoping she won't look too closely. Afraid of what might happen if she really sees me. "Are you implying that we're *not* helping? That we'd be better off just doing nothing?"

Her expression drops. Her eyes drift down to my dirty sneakers, then up to my jeans with their naturally occurring holes in the knees, all the way up to my unwashed hair. Her nose pinches, as if sensing the six blasts of perfume I sprayed on in CVS with my eyes shut, like no one would see me if I couldn't see them. Then her nostrils flare like she can smell the dirt, the urine, the sweat and the sunburned skin I can't afford to clean away completely, that smell that people sense by instinct, that they avoid like death.

Human beings are animals and nature instructs them: *Stay away from the poor and the struggling. They will drain your resources. They will bring you down. They'll be first, and you'll be next.*

"No! Of course not!" My voice cracks. "I'm so impressed by what you're doing." What exactly are they doing? "I wish there were more people like you." Virtue signaling by directing people to a false resolution that looks good on paper or confirms what all rich people secretly believe: They *don't want help. I'm not helping, because* they *don't want it.* When the number one question every person who suffers from homelessness asks is this: *Where do you want me to go?*

I have seen three people die in the past three years, in totally preventable ways. And every time I thought, *This is the answer to that question.*

Where do you want me to go? *I want you not to exist.*

"Aww, you're so sweet to say that!" She beams, presses her hand against her cheek like I've blown her a kiss.

A single tear plucks my eye and I swish it away. "Do you know of any charities that house people?"

She shifts on her chair. She gets the look

people get. *Are you asking me for something? Are you bothering me?*

The truth is, I don't need to ask her. I already know the answer. I have never had a house of my own. As soon as I turned eighteen, I moved in with my first boyfriend in his trailer in Altadena. I stayed for a year until we broke up. I went back to Dad until I met another guy, moved to his place, broke up. Moved home. Then out again, like a calf that just wouldn't sell. Failure is just like success: It doesn't happen overnight.

I always helped with rent, but I never had a name on any lease. And I worked. God, I worked. Minimum-wage jobs that didn't pay overtime, didn't have lunches or breaks. I worked hard but I didn't have a car. I wanted to move up, but I kept being passed over, pushed aside, ignored. They always knew I was needy. I didn't have to tell them. At an elemental level, I repulsed them. So I jumped to another job. I even did night school and got a degree in web design. I worked tirelessly but I never moved up. I kept my head above water, but that never felt like victory. I kept going, but that never felt like success. I stayed alive, and that always felt like losing.

I used to dream that one day my life would change. I played MASH as a kid: *You got the mansion! With the husband! Three kids! Seven dogs!* But after a while, I stopped playing those games. I realized it was impossible. That the *real* world, like a seventy-five-dollar jacket or a new pair of shoes, would always be out of my reach.

And all of that led me here, but it doesn't feel like a genesis, a journey, a natural conclusion. It feels like a shock. It feels like denial. It feels impossible: that when I leave this room, I will have nowhere to go.

Her head bobs as the lights go out in the hallway. "We're closing. Thank you for coming. I'm sorry if I couldn't give you what you need." She slides a brightly colored pamphlet toward me. It shows two women shaking hands, a child laughing hysterically. "Helping Hands" and the logo, two enormous green hands reaching out. Where are those hands? Attached to the Wizard of Oz? "I just want to emphasize how important it is for us to spread a message of hope. We find that when people feel down about the situation here, they're less inclined to get involved." She's not wrong.

I nod. I keep my mouth shut. I don't say what I want to say, which is this: *I would do anything for a house. I would give you my hands. I would give you my heart, my courage, my brain, just to go home.* I would do anything, but my tragedy is: There is nothing I can do.

"If you do your research," she chides, "I think you'll see there have been some positive steps toward resolving the crisis. I think it's important, you know. Stay positive. Things are getting better all the time."

A tear escapes my eye, slides down my face. She is both polite and cruel enough to ignore it. "Thank you for meeting with me."

The pain in my feet starts as soon as I stand. She stays seated, so I know she doesn't want to shake my hand, doesn't want to touch me. Her eyes glaze over; she doesn't want to see me either. I suddenly want to thank her again, am desperate to, am desperate to do anything that will keep me in this room.

But instead I leave her office. I walk down the unlit hall to the door.

The biggest way I trick myself, despite knowing better, is by hoping. I tell myself I don't. I tell myself I'm too smart for that. And I never feel it. I never feel hope, the good part of it, swelling through me. I only feel it going, like I feel it now as I walk out of that brightly colored office, leave the pamphlet on the counter, not even able to put it in the trash like I should, in case someone else wants it, in case it helps someone else. In case someone out there still believes in disembodied helping hands.

DEMI

My childhood was not idyllic, not in the traditional sense, but it was mine. My mother died in childbirth, so my dad raised me. Some fathers wouldn't have, and I always felt special for that. I remember trips to the grocery store where my dad used to steal, usually steaks or salmon, always bottles of wine. I didn't see it as a crime. I saw it as a game and proof that he loved me. Our whole life was a game, a kind of dare: Can you survive? *Without a washing machine! With too-small shoes! You've got eleven dollars in your bank account and seven days to wait for food stamps: GO!*

All of our furniture was sourced from the side of the road, so we had two huge executive desks with rolling office chairs, a brass bed, a piss-stained sofa we covered with scarves and caftans. We collected furniture we didn't need, because anything free was too good to pass up. By the time I was a teenager, our studio was filled with armoires and dressers and dining room chairs stacked to the ceiling. The dressers were filled with electrical cords, old radios, headphones, drills and saws and tools we didn't know how to use. Anything that worked or could be fixed or figured out, my dad had to take. He wasn't a hoarder; he was a survivor.

I never knew we were poor. I thought everyone lived like this. Until one New Year's Eve when I was six or seven. I found out the way everyone does: by meeting a rich person. My dad went out to a local club called the Globe and brought two people back with him. The first was John and I knew him. He was a Rastafarian who looked like a Rastafarian, so people would acquire him like a piece of clothing, and that night a rich woman hung off his arm. She was high. Her eyes were swollen blue and her lips were so juiced, they were crooked on her face. She was wearing a silver gown, like snakeskin that slithered down her sculpted form. I watched her through the break in the drapes — our apartment was all one long room, the bedroom separated by a scratchy blanket hung to make a curtain.

It was late and I was trying to sleep. That is the most consistent memory I have from childhood: how much I wanted to sleep all the time but never could. And the woman was high and she stumbled past the curtain, threw up in our closet all over our clothes, then looked at me, said, "There's a kid in here," laughed and walked out.

Dad didn't hear, and if he had, he wouldn't have cared. He was always ridiculously accommodating to other people, especially guests, offering them things we couldn't afford to lose, like it was a game he was playing with himself. "Take this jacket. It looks good on you! Do you need a Walkman? We have three!"

So I just cried quietly. It stank of vomit and I wanted to leave. I wanted to go for a walk, which was what I did whenever I got overwhelmed by everything. I walked to trick myself into thinking I was going somewhere else.

But it was too late to go for a walk, so I lay there listening to them through the curtain. She went to the bathroom and snorted drugs off our toilet, and then she took a shit, but the toilet wouldn't flush because sometimes it got stuck. She fought it loudly for a minute and then I heard a crash. And she walked out of the bathroom and said, "Your toilet's broken," and a few minutes later, she called a car and dragged John out.

The next morning, I discovered that she had broken the toilet. She had dropped the tank cover into the bowl and left an enormous gaping hole. If we flushed the toilet, water would rush out through the hole, flooding the bathroom.

When things broke in our house, it was permanent. We couldn't afford to fix them. To his credit, Dad didn't seem pleased about this new challenge, but he also refused to demand, even beg, that the woman pay for the repairs.

So we pissed in a bucket and poured it down the sink, or we crapped in the toilet and used that same bucket and water from the bath — carefully applied — to activate the suction to flush it down. We did that for the rest of my life in that apartment.

That was the night I became poor. Because poverty is not just not having money. It's the way you see the world. It's out of your control.

There were people I knew with less money than me who somehow never believed they were poor. For example, my dad was never poor, but I was. We lived in the same house, ate the same food, suffered from the lack of the same things, but only I was poor.

I think about that woman in the silver gown all the time. I rage and obsess. Her dress that night was worth ten times what it would have cost to fix that toilet. It drives me crazy that a person like that can just drift into your fragile world and break it and never look back. I know it was an accident. I know she wasn't the real culprit — poverty was. Accidents happened all the time to everyone. But I still hate her.

People never understand, God, what it feels like from your side. That you are like the ghosts in that movie; you forget you're dead until someone tells you, until someone laughs at you, until someone says, *You have only one cup? That's your only jacket? You don't have a car? You never had your own apartment?* Like you are a magic trick: impossible.

DEMI

The sun has set by the time I leave the HELPING HANDS office. I am on Victory Boulevard in Van Nuys, and I gaze down it, one way and then the other. Then I start walking.

It's a strange feeling, knowing I have nowhere to go. I can't quite believe it. I still imagine my dad's apartment sometimes, shimmering in the distance, beyond the horizon. That if I walk far enough and fast enough, I can get home.

My feet ache but I won't stop. I have to keep going; that's the only way to win the game. Or at least to avoid losing.

I may be poor. It may be a stain that will never go away, but I am *not* homeless. I have lived for years in other people's houses. I have never technically had my own home, but that doesn't make me homeless, in the same way my dad was never poor.

I won't do it. I will find a way out. Even if

I have to walk all night, walk for a week. I will not be homeless.

It's not as hard as it seems to walk all night. At least it's always been easy for me. You just need to give yourself a destination — far but not so far it feels unattainable — and then you walk there. Once you arrive, you hover around for a minute: Maybe it's a park and you sit on a bench. Maybe it's a mall and you look at the storefronts. Maybe it's a beach and you stick your toes in the sand. And then, just as you are starting to deflate, at the exact moment before that deflation transforms to inertia, you give yourself a new place to go.

That night, after I walk from Van Nuys to Glendale, I continue toward The Grove in West Hollywood. It's closed, but I tell myself I've never seen it at night, and that's enough of a goal.

Once I arrive, it's locked up like a fortress and I tell myself, *Well, now you know they close it up at night,* and I decide to head to the beach to catch the sunrise. This is where I sleep, on my backpack on the sand, like a traveling dilettante. *I just flew in from Poland! Who doesn't sleep on the beach?*

Days pass and my trajectory becomes mercifully blurred. I move from Santa Monica, to Hollywood, to Venice. I find places to crash: lobby sofas in college dorms, laundry rooms in apartment complexes, meeting rooms in libraries, campgrounds, hiking trails, beaches. I find food in trash cans or abandoned on trays at mall food courts. Bathrooms are always a safe choice and I can spend hours in a stall: at a gas station, in a library, at a bar or a busy restaurant. One in particular at a beach bar in Venice is beautiful, with Jimi Hendrix posters and palm plants, and I sit on the mosaic tile floor and rest my head against the wall, fall in and out of sleep and dream that I live there, in a beautiful bathroom on the beach.

The most important thing is that I keep moving so homelessness can't catch me. If I focus on a goal, if I always have somewhere to be, I am not homeless. I am not anything. I am just between things, a passenger traveling between one life and the next — the past, like a train still roaring in my ears, and the future, on the other side of the tracks, if I can just get there.

The worst days are when I can tell people mistake me for a person suffering from homelessness, which doesn't make sense — why should things be worse because someone else thinks it? But their thoughts are contagious, the way they look at me, the way they move away, like I am bad meat sidling up beside them, and for a moment the spell breaks and I see things clearly.

When a hand covers a mouth when I'm stopped on the corner, waiting for the crossing light to change.

When someone gasps at me darting onto the street to collect three pennies.

When a woman passes and says in a high thread of a voice, so quiet it's like she's reeling it in as she gives it out, "Don't let it bring you down."

I do work here and there but it's very hard to get paid for it. I work a whole week at a hot dog stand in Venice but am asked to leave when they discover I lied about having insurance. I should have insurance. I qualify, but my dad messed something up when I was a kid and now I am forever blacklisted. *There is nothing I can do. I'm not authorized to change this,* when nobody is. And I am so tired now, so tired all the time that everything feels shifty and illusory.

I get to know people on the streets, and they get to know me. Michael under the 101 below Franklin, who catcalled me five or six times before he realized what I was and stopped.

I get to know territories that were invisible to me before. It's like a secret second world rises up before my eyes.

The tent community that lives on the turf islands in the LA River.

The meth heads on the sofas in the bushes outside the Franklin Community Center.

The swap-meet-style grottoes beneath the 101 freeway.

All my life I have avoided looking at people suffering from homelessness, and it is freeing, thrilling, to look. At the artful arrangements of reclaimed furniture, the cozy wall-less living rooms, the collected items on shelves that look like shops, the art, the wooden boxes of donated orange peppers.

There is a style to the streets that is part lost boy, part art college. Bare-chested men swaddled in tattered blankets charging back and forth beneath the freeway, traffic be damned, always mysteriously in a hurry, only to be pinballed back across the road. A woman in a spaghetti-strap tank top on the corner of Sunset and Gower singing to passersby. "You have one eyebrow — you look like a damn fool! Your dress is too short — you are a damn slut!"

Most people are nice on the streets. More, I think, than in the other world. Even people with severe mental health problems who rant and rave and scream don't want to hurt you. Mostly, I think they just want to be seen. All people do, but it's harder for some than it is for others.

I keep walking, not realizing that I am sinking into the world I'm seeing, pinballing across LA just like the men beneath the freeway, singing mean songs to myself about all the rich people who pass. *Assholes, jerks, monsters.* Not realizing that I am only seeing this new world because I am a part of it. I am a player in their game.

It's my body that finally stops me. A long-running cold burns into a fever. I walk too much and I don't eat enough and my body can't fix itself.

My dad died of bronchitis. It's in my blood to cough myself to death.

I am shivering in sixty-degree weather. I am struggling to put one foot in front of the other. It's like my body isn't mine anymore; it's just a deadweight that's tied to me, and it just wants to lie down. I need to lie down.

I am afraid of exposure, afraid of being caught out alone. I need a fortress to protect me. But I can't afford a wall of stone or wood or plaster or whatever it is that makes a house. All I can afford is a wall of people.

I pass the tent city underneath the 101. Michael is there sweeping the sidewalk, a tattered blanket hung over his shoulders, and he says, "You again."

And I say, "I need to lie down, please. Is

there anywhere I can just lie down?"

He chews it over for a second, eyes wide. "Martin's been gone awhile. His tent's empty — but I don't know when he's coming back. He might crawl in on top of you." This sounds horrible but I can't keep walking. My body aches. My brain is shutting down. I imagine Martin crawling in over my corpse and I think, *In this nightmare, at least I'm dead.*

And I nod and say, "Where is it?"

The tent is in a crevice in the freeway tunnel, on top of a pebbled floor the city installed to keep people from sleeping there. It smells of piss until I start to sweat; then it smells of me and that's worse: thick, cloying, hard to breathe through. I imagine myself dying a hundred times, burning in a fire I am powerless to put out.

Time shifts. The light outside the tent flares in and out. Voices assemble and disassemble. Cars rush overhead like racing thoughts, plowing through me.

Then I wake up in the middle of the night. The fever has dissipated, taking its magic visions with it. Leaving only cold reality.

I am in a tent spattered with blood and shit under a freeway. Beyond the thin material, people are talking about Jesus.

I wake up homeless.

DEMI

I find an organization that gives tents to people suffering from homelessness. They give one to me. I stay in the tent city under the 101. I still walk, but not as much. Mostly, I stay in my tent and pretend I am not there. My tent is like a shield. It's just a tarp between me and reality but it's enough. I come out only at night, when fewer people see me and the camp is relatively quiet.

In spite of this, I absorb people. I feel shrouded in community.

One little group gathers by the southbound exit for meetings with religious undertones. They draw symbols on the ground with spray paint and talk about conspiracy theories: 9-11, the coronavirus, lizard people.

Some people take drugs but usually in secret, so they don't have to share. People have hopes and dreams and families. People believe in their own talents. People are upset about their daughters' behavior. People give knowing, smug advice. People are gluten free, vegan or plant based. They refuse fast-food handouts and list the preservatives in treats from 7-Eleven. They argue about the president. They teach one another things.

Everyone talks about astrology. This is LA, after all.

I watch, always keeping myself slightly apart, away from everybody. Sometimes I feel ashamed about it, but other times I think it's the only way I will ever recover from this, the only way to keep me from suffering from homelessness for the rest of my life. To think of myself as separate, observing. Not superior but separate. This is what I tell myself.

I am struggling with homelessness but it is temporary. I have a cold that won't go away, a fever that drifts in and out of consciousness. No matter how many times I wash my hands, they are always sticky, but I am not going to be like this forever.

One night I am the only one awake after dark. This is my favorite time, when the entire camp looks like an oasis in the desert, surreal. When I can be alone and flex the world, make it into something manageable, even beautiful.

I gaze down the street, toward Hollywood, and watch the traffic lights change, watch the people pass at a distance, so few and far between.

I see a woman stumble. She is wearing a big black coat and painful-looking black heels. She is headed in my direction. I am tempted to hide in my tent, not wanting to be seen, but I remind myself that I am invisible to her. And I'm fascinated.

You rarely see rich people up close — I mean, *really* rich: two-thousand-dollar-T-shirt, thirty-thousand-dollar-bag rich. They shuttle in expensive cars to places we can't afford where they pay to be surrounded only by one another.

Apart from that woman in the silver gown who broke our toilet, I don't know that I have ever seen a rich person up close. Until now.

I can tell this woman is rich even a block away. Her coat gleams like it is made of ebony. The bottoms of her black shoes are bright red. Her skin glows like something alien. Her body is sculpted, tight and organized.

She pats herself down wearily, halfheartedly searching for something she has looked for before. Then she sighs, this big, demonstrative sigh, like she lives to be seen. Then

100

she stamps toward me.

She passes under the bright lights beneath the freeway. They throw her black coat into relief. It's long, swollen in bunches like a ski jacket. The collar is fur. Her heels are leather. Her tights don't have a single tear. I watch her, thinking she won't see me, thinking she *can't* see me, when her eyes dart down, when they meet mine.

She swoops in, so fully in control of herself and her presence that I feel myself cowering like a light has shined inside my shell, revealing I was always small, hidden.

"Excuse me? Can I borrow your phone?" Is she kidding?

"I — I dead." I haven't talked in so long, I've forgotten how. "I mean, my phone is dead." It's like a bad reading of a basic line. I sound so strange to myself. I haven't used my phone in weeks. But I know where it is, in my backpack, with everything I own.

"Ugh, I need an Uber. I live, like, a mile from here. Can I ask you a question?" She wobbles suddenly, standing over me with her legs set a little too wide, and I realize she is drunk. Everything about her is so expensive — the peach-tinted gold in her hair, the liner around her eyes, the cashmere turtleneck — that it's hard to see beyond that. "Do you know anyone who sells her-

101

oin?" She breaks into a scattered, victorious laugh, like she has tricked herself. "Or Oxy," she adds when I don't respond. "Damn, I'd take fenty. I would call my dealer, but the phone is an issue. I have cash, though. Some fucker stole my phone. Or I dropped it in the toilet." She sighs, like it's too heavy to remember.

"I don't do drugs," I say, unable to keep the judgment from my voice. My dad's "friends" used to come to our apartment to take drugs, like our home was a sketchy prop in their drug experience. I hate drugs.

"Oh, my God! Look at you judging me! Too funny!" Her voice is so loud, it echoes under the freeway, where we are sleeping, when this is our town.

"Hey!" We both look behind me to where Michael's head has popped out of his tent. His chest is bare. His hair is a tangle of white-boy dreads. "Hey, come over here." Michael is handsome, but not in a safe way. His nose is slightly crooked. His lips are always chapped. He has thick lashes but they dip down perilously, the black tears of Cleopatra.

The woman looks at me like she expects my input. I am close enough to what she is — the right age, more organized than Michael, less wild — that she has decided I am her ally in her adventure. She steps forward, but not too close.

"I can sell you a bead," Michael says. "But it's my last one." There is no way in hell it's his last one, but the jealous part of me hopes he takes her for everything she's worth. "Scarcity and all that."

Her coat brushes my arm as she takes another step. It feels like plucked feathers.

"How much?" she says. "Be reasonable." I shift because her coat is on my lap. I'm furniture to her.

"Fifty?" Michael says, like that is the highest number he can think of.

"I don't have change; I'll give you sixty." She is okay being unreasonable as long as she's in control. She pulls a wad of cash out of her pocket and separates three twenty-dollar bills. Her coat brushes me again as she reaches toward him, from too far away. She hands him the cash; he hands her the heroin, wrapped in a tiny swallowable bead.

She stands up straight, smiles, but it slips; her face pales. She wobbles again. "I think I'm gonna throw up," she says. "Heroin always does that to me. Even just thinking about it." I remember this part. My dad's friends used to vomit and vomit — but blissfully — into the sink or the trash can or the broken toilet.

Then she throws up, right there on the edge of the sidewalk. It splatters on my shoes and my jeans. It smells sweetly of expensive cocktails and champagne bubbles. She brushes her coat but there is not even a speck of vomit on her, like she is protected. She doesn't apologize. Her vomit is a gift. She has blessed us.

It makes me think of that night and that woman, the one who broke our toilet, how she vomited right in our closet and just left it there, not thinking about who would clean it up. Not caring.

"Hey!" Michael snaps. I think he is going to yell at her, and I'm a little thrilled. "You want me to walk you home?" he says instead, unzipping his door, preparing to step out.

"No, I'm good." She wobbles again. Her eyes are red. Her drunk is catching up with her. "This'll help." She slips it in her pocket.

Michael steps out of his tent, all six feet three of him. People like their poor small and nonthreatening, easy to ignore. Michael is none of those things. Fear washes her face, stiffens her spine.

"You shouldn't walk alone," he says. "It's dangerous." Like he is not the thing she's afraid of. He wants to go with her. Probably thinks she will invite him in for a drink, share the heroin he sold her. They will spend the night smoking cigarettes and talking about fate, like good junkies do. Why not? In Michael's mind, he's worth just as much as she is. "Let me —"

"I'll go." I stand up, put myself between them. I feel guilt immediately, like I'm protecting her from him, like he is the bad thing in this scenario. But the truth is, I want to see her house. I have never seen a rich person's house up close.

"Aww, thanks. You're so sweet." She immediately loops her arm in mine, presses her body close, leans on me like we're girlfriends after a long night out. And I'm embarrassed to say it, but it feels good. It makes me feel valuable all the way down to my toes.

DEMI

We start up the street, toward the houses in the hills. She swings wide at my side, drunker than I thought. "The booze is hitting me now — woo!" she says as we pause at the light on Franklin. And I wonder if it's drugs, too, if she's taken something already: Vicodin, Adderall, Oxy? "Woo!" she says again when the walk sign comes on and we start to cross.

The streets are deserted. We are the only two crossing onto the narrow one-way streets that crisscross the hills.

I never walk in the hills. It's too dangerous, the roads too narrow, the people too incautious, the path too circuitous to define a destination.

She rides up and down on a wave, sometimes silent and swaying, sometimes oddly lucid, sometimes desperately demanding I stop so she can hover in place and gag, wait to throw up.

"You're so skinny," she says. "Jealous."

And then, "Are you really homeless? That's so funny."

She laughs at nothing. "Weird."

"I can help you," she decides at one point. "Do you want a job? You can work for my company. Alphaspire. It's a tech conglomerate. Ha-ha."

On the next street she doesn't remember who I am. "Where are you taking me?" And we have to stop and wait for her to remember who she is and where we are going.

And all the time I'm thinking, *How can she have this life and not want to live it? How can she be so rich and want to be out of her mind?*

"I used to be like you," she says when she remembers herself. "I mean, I was middle class but now I'm rich — ha-ha!"

I was never middle class, but middle-class people always like to believe they're poor.

We reach the upper levels of the hills. The houses here are so big, it's frightening. Castles off long, circuitous drives with gates under arches like hollowed-out caves. The kind of houses that are so big, you can't believe that anyone could ever live in them. And they look empty. They have a haunted aura. When the underpasses in this city are crammed with souls and longing, these

107

great big houses are like totems to the ghosts of wealth.

One house is etched along the sky above us. To even call it a house feels absurd. It's a network of towers and turrets and Los Angeles ridiculousness, a leftover set from David O. Selznick. She sees me noticing and says, "That's my landlord. She has more money than God — no, Satan. Satan would be the rich one, right? She has this garden — I'm not kidding — she has a garden designed after the nine circles of hell. I saw it in *Architectural Digest.*"

A light comes on in a far window, as if her landlord can hear us. I will never see a garden like that, not even in a magazine.

It takes us ages to wrap around it, but finally we reach an intricately carved wooden gate. It looks like it was taken from a church, wrenched from God's hinges and stuffed inside a wall of concrete.

"This is it!" She squeezes my elbow. "Hey, do you want to have a drink with me? Do you want a drink?"

I haven't had a drink in a long time. It's such an expendable expense. And even though I'm on edge, even though I feel wary of her, like she might switch and swing on me suddenly, I think, *When will I have this chance again?* I remember a time when I had a job and a place to live, how I used to say to myself, *You need to go out more! You need to do more!* But instead I stayed in. I tried to save money, but it spent itself anyway. Now I am never invited anywhere.

"Hey, we can talk about the job, huh? Maybe I can help you." I am half sure it's drunken bullshit, but it's the best offer I've had all year. Maybe all my life.

I take a step toward the gate, then feel a chill. I have never been inside a house like this and I imagine myself crossing the threshold, looking out over the city like it's something I can see all at once. And my chest aches, and I can't breathe. I'm scared.

"Come on." She throws her arm around my shoulder. "Let's have a drink."

I lick my lips. "Okay."

She unlocks the gate and shepherds me into a courtyard. An enormous fountain gurgles at the center. It's lit from below, so it glows with an extraterrestrial tint. The house beyond it is this modern glass concoction. It looks less like a house than a work of art. You can see inside, all the tight lines of furniture, like a game of Tetris, perfectly stacked.

"Wow," I say.

She frowns. "Not this one. It's down below. This is where Graham Herschel lives," she says like I know who that is. "I haven't met him yet but he's so fucking hot. He's, like, this scion. I heard his wife is totally bonkers, though."

She leads me along the side of the house, then down a steep, crooked stairwell until we reach another house, surrounded by a long, dark porch encased in trees, underneath.

"It's kind of a weird place," she says. "But I couldn't pass up the chance to live at the Herschels'. They're, like, the cream of the cream or whatever. We're talking *billions*." She fumbles with her keys, hoveringly lucid, unlocks the dead bolt. The door creaks open. "Take off your shoes." She sniffs and then steps inside, slips off her heels.

The light is murky when I step inside. She flips the switch and it stays murky. The bulbs emanate a weak yellowy color, soupy, strange. The living room is filled with eccentric objects. Everything is half a work of art, shockingly functionless: a marble statue of a woman that looks like an animal, two tall column bookshelves on either side carved with intricate shapes like scales or dead leaves.

The rug is modern spatters of red and blue and black, so it looks like blood — but not fake blood, not the blood you see in

110

movies, but the real, thick dark blood, the blood no one ever talks about.

"It would look nice if there was any fucking light in here." She heads to the kitchen, opens the fridge. "There's beer, red wine, gin." The light from the fridge is white bright in the doomed house. "Make what you want. I'm going to the bathroom."

It's only when she doesn't come out right away that I realize she is probably doing heroin in there. The bathroom is in the center of the guesthouse, between the living room and the bedroom. I hear her puttering around inside. I pour myself a glass of wine, but I am so hungry, I gulp it down, and then I feel sick, like I can't even enjoy normal things anymore.

I go to the living room, walk along the perimeter, from the windows to the walls.

The place is so strange. One side is suctioned to the steep hill and the other side is open, with rows of small windows looking out into the slanted yard, where mismatched trees wind high, high above it. Between their trunks you can see little glimmers of the other houses on the hill across the canyon: white, sleek, modern, walls of windows, but this place is sunken; this place is clawing; this place is burying itself in the hillside.

I pour myself another glass of wine. I

know I am just drinking because I am hungry. I think of all the food in the refrigerator, how she probably wouldn't even notice if something went missing, but she didn't offer me anything, so I can't take it, can't even open the door to look at her food, and I think how much I hold myself back, how polite I am, how it has contributed to my downfall. As I walk around her guesthouse, I think, *God, if I didn't care so much what people think, even now, even when they have proved, again and again, that they don't care about me . . .*

What if she won't help you? What if you do something wrong and she won't help you? When I know better, know enough to know that won't be the reason she doesn't help me.

I put the empty glass down. My head feels expanded and dizzy, like a balloon tug-tugging away from me.

I hear my dad's voice in my head, *Fuck her. Take what you want. Take everything. Fuck 'em all.*

I force myself to open the fridge. I blink in the brightness of the blue-white light. Everything is packaged exquisitely, like little food gifts. There are premade salmon salads, boxed sushi, sliced prosciutto ham, buttons of cheese with sprigs of rosemary. It's almost too pretty to eat. I could just take one thing, just one sleek little box. She would never know. She probably wouldn't even care.

I shut the door so hard, the bottles inside rattle.

I want to leave. I want to get out of here. I don't want to see it anymore. How the other half lives. Even just this fridge will haunt me, flash into my mind late at night when I'm shivering on my stacked cardboard.

Her sandwiches have nicer homes than me.

My eyes drift to the glass windows, where the view of LA peeks from between the trees. Where shadows undulate. I have this vision of the house collapsing, the roof caving in, the floor sliding swiftly down the mountain, snapped into pieces by the thick tree trunks.

"Hey?" I want to tell her good-bye but I don't know her name. I walk across the living room to the bathroom door. I knock. "Hey? I'm just gonna go." I expect complaints, protest. I expect her to tell me she's almost done. *Just wait!*

I hear nothing.

DEMI

I can't hear her breathing, I think, but that's illogical. I know that's illogical. I wouldn't hear her breathing through a door.

The trouble with living a hard life is that you start to see the world differently. Your mind and your instincts and your outlook are forever altered by negative experiences. You expect bad things to happen. When you're crossing the street, you imagine every car veering to hit you. You plan escape routes in tight alleyways. You think, *What would you do if that man — that one, right there — suddenly punched you?* Would you duck? Would you block? Would you hit back? What weapons are at your disposal? What are your emergency exits, safety nets?

Oddly, this leaves you *less* prepared to deal with bad things when they do happen. You have become accustomed to not trusting your instincts. You are so used to telling yourself that it is all in your head that you

114

can't tell when it's not.

She's probably passed out, with her head on the tiles, like many people before her. You are messed up, paranoid. You need to relax.

I knock again. "I'm sorry. Can you just tell me you're okay?" I wait with my arms crossed. Nothing.

She's definitely asleep. I should just leave. I have this heavy feeling just under my jaw.

I try the door. I knock, then slap, then pound. "Hey, hey! Just tell me you're all right."

I walk into the living room, order myself to calm down. *She's not dying. No one is dying. You're having a panic attack. You've had too much to drink. You're starving and you had a drink and you shouldn't have. And this is all spinning. This is all just anxiety spinning in your mind.*

I stalk to the bathroom door. I knock again. *Just go. Just leave. She's asleep. It's fine.*

I force myself to walk to the front door. I slip my shoes on. Her heels lie beside my sneakers, toppled. I reach to open the door but my muscles are seizing up.

What if it's real? What if it's real this time?

I close my hand around the knob. I unfasten the dead bolt. It's quiet in the house, so fucking quiet. I open the door.

The stairs are steep. The wine makes me dizzy. As I ascend, I feel hooked by an anchor to that dark, weird house. I want to go back. I have to go back.

I reach the wooden gate. It's locked. I rattle too hard in a panic.

I hear a door burst open behind me. I feel a rush of relief — *She's here! She's alive! You were wrong. You imagined everything.*

But when I turn, I see another woman, who could be the ghost of the woman below. She is more than beautiful; her beauty is electrified by a quality of sadness. She is like the icon in a Gothic tale, the one that stands between the turrets with her gown ripping in the wind.

"Are you locked out?" Her voice is like a child creeping up on you. "Oh. You're locked in."

Demi

I step away from the gate. I search for exits but there are none. The gate is locked. There is a high wall all around us. I could go back to the guesthouse or take my chances on the hill. I could run. Or I could hold my ground. *I'm a guest,* I remind myself, even though I feel like a trespasser.

The fountain gurgles so loud, I can hardly hear my heart pound.

"Sorry," I say. "I was just making sure it was locked."

"I'm Lyla. We live upstairs, my husband, Graham, and I. But you probably know that."

She acts like we know each other, but we don't. She acts like we're the same, but we're not. She thinks I am the woman downstairs.

She is staring me down with her arch eyes and I feel my spirit lifting, my bubble bursting. I am *someone* to her. We are on equal footing. We are standing on the same ground. She thinks I am someone else.

She stretches out her hand. I am hesitant to take it, but my hand moves forward of its own accord, as if it is willing to make a deal with any devil. I feel a zing all the way to my elbow the moment we connect.

"Sorry I woke you up." I hover uncertainly. I am locked inside the gate with no key. She thinks I am the woman downstairs, and when she finds out she was wrong, I will be gone, and the woman will be awake, and everyone will be exactly where they belong.

But part of me doesn't want that. Part of me thinks, *This is your chance.* Part of me hums, *You could be someone else. Stop thinking like you. Stop suffering like you. You could be rich and cease to exist.* Maybe it's because this is the first person to look me in the eye in weeks, months. Maybe it's because she is the most beautiful person I have ever seen up close and her eyes are trained on me. Maybe I'm a little drunk. But I feel magical, illusory, like my self is a thing I could discard like old clothes, put on someone new.

My mouth starts in the shape of this new person. *We should go someplace, indoors and warm, lock the bad world out.* But it readjusts, too stuck in its old ways to say anything but "I'd better get back down." Maybe the woman downstairs will be awake. Maybe she will let me out and I can go back where I came from.

"It was so nice to finally meet you." Her smile will haunt me, with the food in the fridge, the castle cut in shadows above. "We'll have to meet again sometime."

Please, God. Design a world, take everyone out, leave only us two players. So we have to meet. Again and again and again. "Sure —"

"Tomorrow." She smiles like she wants to swallow me whole.

That's when the dreamy feeling turns, when reality sets its teeth. The longer we speak, the more she will remember me. And the woman downstairs is. And the woman downstairs might be. "I don't think I can do tomorrow."

She takes one step closer, keeps me in her crosshairs. "I think you can."

A stunned laugh pops from my lips. I look down the stairs, lose my balance and see a vision, like reality is an egg that cracks open with wine.

I see myself walk back into the guesthouse. The woman downstairs is gone. I am the woman downstairs. I take food presents from my fridge and I eat them all. I dress in the woman's clothes, pull books from her shelves, sit on her sofa and gaze out her window. Everything and the view are mine.

I want it bad enough to call it a premonition. I am changing. I am changed already.

Her life is mine.

When I reach the front patio, I pause to scan the hill below. I could slide down the hillside, carefully, from tree to tree, to the valley below where the fence is weak, hemmed with other people's yards and balconies. I could escape that way and never come back. The trees mutter their agreement. But something stops me.

I look at the door — wooden, innocuous — but facing me. Unlocked, so dangerously unlocked. I let the doorknob settle in my hand. I open the door. I slip back into the guesthouse. A beguiling silence stretches over everything, holds the statues and the rugs and the crooked bookshelves still.

I cross quickly to the bathroom and knock on the door, then shiver when I hear footsteps overhead, the woman upstairs crossing over me.

I lower my voice and speak into the bathroom door. "Hello?"

She is probably passed out. *Wait until the woman upstairs has gone to bed, too. Give her half an hour to fall asleep. Then leave. One day she will realize you are not the woman downstairs. It won't matter. You will be far, far away from here.*

I imagine going back to my tent with all these new things to haunt me: the packed refrigerator, the spooky woman upstairs, and, worst, the silence on the other side of the bathroom door.

What if I stayed? Just to make sure. I can tell the woman in the bathroom I was worried about her; I didn't want to leave her. If she asks me to leave tomorrow, what difference does it make? And maybe she won't. Maybe she will wake up with fresh eyes and a swollen heart and think, *I can help you, and I will. I really will.* It would be so easy for her.

A heavy stupor passes over me, as if my body was only waiting, so patiently, for me to give it the all clear. To say, *It's safe to relax now. It's safe to rest and sleep and dream.*

I will wake up in the morning, and she will be alive.

I walk past the bathroom and into her bedroom. I can't find the light switch, but the hallway light bleeds illumination. Her bedroom is a hothouse of luxury. Six or seven creamy blankets wrestle on an egg-shaped bed: some cashmere, some antique lace, some faux fur. There are palm fronds and a gilt makeup table with rows of old-fashioned perfume bottles, dozens of creams and potions for problems I never knew existed. I catch my reflection in the mirror, the spatter of bumps that line my chin. I imagine rubbing her creams there, how my face would beam with a clean, wealthy light that hums, *I'm rich. I can afford to glow.*

I let my fingers run along the tops of the bottles so they clink playfully together. If my dad were here, he would pocket the most expensive one. And I would complain, say he shouldn't have done it, and use every last drop, and keep the bottle.

The floor over my head creaks.

I move toward the corner of the bedroom. A wicker swing is suspended from the ceiling, latticed like a birdcage. It sways when I brush it with my fingers. It's filled with pink frosted pillows. I turn away from it, slowly lower myself inside. It squeaks so loud, I almost jump out, but then it settles.

I sit back, and the room closes warm around me. The darkness folds like wings over me. My eyes drift shut. And every so often I hear the creak of myself suspended.

DEMI

I awake in a panic. I dreamed that I had to pee, and no one would let me use their bathroom. I went from door to door, banging, in residential neighborhoods, asking, pleading, and they all said, *There's someone in there! There's someone in there!* Until I broke down screaming, *There can't be someone in every bathroom!*

I have the most mundane bad dreams.

But I do have to pee. I struggle to pry myself out of the swing. I expect to feel sore, but my body feels miraculously refreshed, like it's trying to tell me something. *We'll take this over the tent, thanks very much.*

I walk to the bathroom. I try the door. It's still locked. And the night crashes over me. I twist the knob again so hard, I wrench my wrist.

The woman upstairs crosses the floor, the ceiling.

I knock, but I try not to knock too loud.

Are you crazy? Scream. Get her to call the police.

I hear a door shut upstairs so heavy, it must be the front door. I wait, give her enough time to walk up the steps, unlock and relock the gate. Then I bang on the bathroom door until my knuckles go numb. I yell, "Hey! Hey! Wake up."

I am shivering now from the cold inside this dark house but also from something else.

If I run now, I can still catch the woman upstairs. Maybe she can help me. I race to the front door, then pull up short. *Help me.* The words are sown on the backs of my lips.

If the woman in the bathroom is dead — I'm not saying she is but *if* — and I am here with her . . .

I take a deep breath. Try to focus on the facts:

If she took the drugs Michael gave her.

If she is dead.

And I am here with her.

And who am I? A woman on the street who followed her home.

And she took drugs.

Why am I here?

I don't think the truth — that I wanted to help her home, that I wanted to see her house, just to see how the other half lived

— will fly far.

Who am I? To the police, I am her dealer. I am a woman on the street who sold her the drugs that killed her.

At the very least, I am the woman on the street who left her to die.

Last night, I stopped knocking on the door. I climbed into her swing. I let myself fall asleep. Did I know she was dead? Did I trick myself? Did my mind and my body collaborate against me to let her die so I could sleep one night in a nice house?

You're a bad, bad person. But that can't be true. I didn't know. I still don't know. The reasonable explanation is . . . The reasonable explanation was . . .

She's asleep. She was drunk and she's passed out asleep.

I don't want to look. And if I don't look, if I never know for sure, she can live forever in my mind.

I start toward the door. Then I stop.

Maybe she isn't dead. I need her to be alive. To save her. To save me.

And I can't leave now.

The woman upstairs saw me. She knows my face, could describe me. If the woman in the bathroom is dead, it's manslaughter. If I walk away, they will think I'm guilty.

You should have just checked. You should

have trusted your tragedy-warped instincts.

I inhale sharply. I think I can smell her. *You need to know. You need to find out for sure.*

I pull my sleeves up over my hands and scan the guesthouse — is there a key? A credit card I can use to jimmy the door? Could I break the lock?

My heart is revving up, burning a hole in my chest. My eyes land on that statue of a woman becoming an animal.

I stalk toward it. I lift it, grunting with the effort. It's heavier than I thought.

What if she's gone? What if I break down the door and the room is empty? What if it's a trick? Maybe she's my fairy god-mother. Maybe this is all a dream.

We were testing you. We needed to find someone pure of heart.

I lug the statue, step by step, toward the bathroom door. I must pitch it, at an angle, toward the lock. I must be careful. If she is leaning against the door, it could hit her. If she is too close, it could maim her.

"Hey!" I try one more time. "I'm break-ing down the door."

I grunt as I lift the statue over my head.

I never would have thought that I could do a thing like this, bust down a door. But the statue leaves my hands. And the door splits like tinder, not where I wanted it to, but right down the middle. And through the crack I can see the curve of her black-tight-covered feet.

My fingers snake through the break, unfasten the lock. I open the door before I have time to remind myself that I don't want to see another dead body.

The door moans across the white tiled floor, splintering in its wake.

Lyla

Even though I insisted we meet up, I don't see Demi the next day or the next. She doesn't go out as much as she used to. She is settling in. I see her coming up and down the stairs and want to catch her, but I am never quick enough. She waits until the exact moment I'm not looking, then slips past like a fog.

I listen all week, learning her. It's like I have a special part of my brain tuned in. I hear her in the kitchen. I hear the squeal of her teakettle. I hear her music and her movies. I try to figure out what they are.

"Three Women," Graham says abruptly one night. He is in his chair scrolling. The music disappears if you don't listen hard enough. "Robert Altman." Every so often Graham says something that reminds me he had a girlfriend before me. "He's a good director," he adds as justification.

The neighborhood is louder at night than

I remember, or maybe I just didn't notice it before. Bean is always barking — suddenly, ferociously — then lapsing into haunting silence. Cars roar past us above and below. Disembodied laughter floats from a party across the canyon.

One afternoon, I go for my walk along the reservoir and slow when I reach our street, encouraging the universe to provide a meeting. I notice the big white van again parked just kitty-corner to my gate. Margo hasn't moved it after all. I imagine a team of analysts crowded inside behind a wall of screens, watching our every move. Maybe this is part of the game. Maybe she is watching me.

My pulse throbs inside my neck. I hurry to the gate, pull out my key to unlock it, but it's already open. I step inside, try to push it closed behind me, but it squeals on its hinges and ricochets away, snapping back open.

I step down into the courtyard. The gate is busted. The wood is cracked and the hinges are broken. It won't swing shut. It just snaps back against the wall.

I peer into the yard. My front door is closed. So is Demi's. But someone could be inside the yard with me. I imagine them hiding in the trees, buried under the porch.

Should I call the police? What if this is a setup? What if someone is watching me?

I look at the van poised along the crumbling LA curb, with its wheels tilted haphazardly toward me. The license plate is from Maine, all the way from Maine. What is it doing here? It's too conspicuous to be accidental. It's all part of the plan. What plan?

I walk toward it. A blue quilt hangs over the front window, like the drop cloths painters use, hiding what's inside. A shadow plays along it, only I can't tell if it's coming from inside or if it's my own reflection. My back bristles.

A dog barks and I turn to find Margo five feet away from me. "Do you see anything in there?"

I step back. "Just my shadow."

"What happened to the gate?"

I look behind me to where the gate is snapped open. "I don't know," I say, moving toward it.

"What an interesting development," she says like it's happened on television.

She flicks Bean's lead back and forth. The fountain gurgles. I look at Margo's face for signs of orchestration. It's been pulled in so many directions, it's impossible to derive an intent. Bean growls at the van. Margo jerks the lead. "No!"

My voice drops. "Is this part of the game?"

"You know we don't interfere. It's all down to you. Or her."

"So you think it was her?"

Margo shrugs. "It would take some nerve to break into your own house."

Demi has a key, but the other night I found her trapped inside the gate. Maybe she lost it, but wouldn't she just ask for another? Wouldn't that be preferable to blowing the gate off its hinges? I frown. "Who is this woman you chose?"

Margo's lips pucker. I wonder again if this is part of her plan, to pit me against an absolute psycho, to make sure I lose, to get rid of me once and for all. Wouldn't that be clever, to make it look like it was my fault? Maybe Demi isn't the subject of the game. Maybe I am. Maybe Margo planted Demi here, like a bomb set to detonate my marriage. I know she blames me for what happened with the last tenant. How far would she go to punish me?

The answer is always: further than I'd have thought.

"Well." She smirks and reveals her dimples. Her eyes sparkle like Graham's do when I catch him off guard. "Perhaps you should consider this a kick up the ass. Stop stalling. We're starting to get bored."

"I have a plan," I lie. I will make one.

"How quaint. Do keep us informed of any new developments." She steps off the curb, drags Bean sideways until she rights herself, then trots along beside her with a big doggy grin.

I cross through the broken gate and approach the stairs leading down to the guesthouse. The stairwell curves and drops precipitously.

I wrinkle my nose. "Hello?"

I place a foot on the top step, grip the railing, take a deep breath. I haven't been down here in ages, not since Elvira left. We used to have dinner together on the porch, share a bottle of wine. *Never Moët,* she used to promise, grinning wickedly. A heavy feeling clogs my throat as I descend.

Just below the house, the hillside drops. It's so steep that they have secured it with trees, created a forest fortress, to stop the earth from eroding. It doesn't affect us up above because we can see over the treetops. But the guesthouse is surrounded by a thicket of trees that holds the dark in. So the air has a fat, moldy taste. So it always smells of mulch. So mildew and fungus coat the pipes, line the wooden support beams beneath the porch, gather invisible in the hot bathroom. Every six months, we ask the tenant to pour root killer down the toilet.

I reach the patio. I stand beneath the awning of Demi's front door. The shades are drawn. I can't tell for sure, but it seems like the lights are out. She was loud this morning, banging around like she knows she's in a trap.

I pull back the screen and knock lightly on the front door. Quiet hovers in the air. I step back. The trees hang shadows over the back porch, across all the windows where the curtains are drawn. Every curtain drawn, every shutter pulled down at two in the afternoon. She's hiding something, but what?

LYLA

Graham is thrilled about the gate. He came home after seven and spent ten minutes trying to fix it himself, in his superfine suit, with a hammer from the toolshed. "Did you do this?"

"Of course not. Why would I destroy our front gate?"

"To throw her off-balance. To scare her." A scrim of sweat brightens his skin. He peels off his jacket, tosses it onto the patio furniture. "That's always a good idea. People in a panic will do foolish things."

"I didn't do it."

He frowns, as if disappointed, then brightens. "Did she?"

"She isn't home," I say, glancing at the street. She could come home at any moment, find us here discussing ways to scare her.

"Of course," Graham says, forcing the gate shut and holding it that way, puffing

134

slightly as he speaks, "she won't admit it." He releases the gate and it snaps back so fast, he leaps out of the way. He wipes his forehead, kicks the wood so it crackles. "It's like a fucking booby trap." He shakes his head and walks away. If something doesn't offer immediate gratification, he moves on quickly. "Did the security system go off? Did anyone try to come inside the house?"

"No. Not that I know of." I follow him in, carrying the hammer and his discarded jacket.

"Why would someone break the gate, then not come in?" He takes off his tie, loosens his collar. "It must have been her." His eyes brighten.

"I don't think she *could* do this." I try to imagine Demi, the pale teenage-sized woman I met on the stairs, attacking the gate, forcing it so hard that the whole system snapped. "She's thinner than I am." I always think of people's weight in relation to my own.

"She was struggling with the lock the other night," he says. "Maybe she just lost it." The dinner our housekeeper made is on the table. He pops off the plate cover and shovels it in without sitting down, starved by his exertions with the gate. "Maybe she's nuts. Maybe we've got a crazy woman living down there."

"Do you think Margo is setting me up?"

He bristles like I have crossed a line. "Of course not. I would know about it. Margo tells me everything." He's right, but it annoys me, thinking about their *special* relationship.

I hang his coat on a hook by the door, drop the hammer there, too. The housekeeper will put it all away. "There's a strange van outside," I say.

"I saw that. Disgusting. If you're going to drive a serial killer van, at least invest in some bleach." He chokes a little, coughs into his fist, then pours himself a glass of Moët.

"And Bean is barking all the time. Have you noticed that? I wonder if there's somebody in there."

"What, living in a van? Don't be absurd." One of Graham's deepest blind spots is poverty. Not just poverty — he doesn't believe in the middle class either. *What's the difference? Point is, they don't have any money.*

"People do live in vans," I argue. "In Venice."

"Where do they shit?" he asks like that ends the argument. "This neighborhood is going downhill." He takes his seat at the

136

head of the table. "Where's the dressing? We need to move higher."

I bring the dressing he likes in from the kitchen, then take my seat kitty-corner to him. I recite, "She moves in and the gate gets broken. The dog won't stop barking. This strange van appears. It's all a little weird, don't you think?"

"She couldn't have broken the gate." He scoops salad into his mouth and keeps talking. "She's tiny." Like I didn't make the same point two minutes ago.

"How do you know she's tiny? Have you seen her?" My voice is suddenly threadbare, thinned.

"I caught her coming in." His voice stays even, but he has a lofty look, a halo that circles his crown. He gets this way with the tenants: dreamier, more beautiful. It's almost animal, the way it comes on, sharpens over time. He looks the way a peacock does right before it kills — I mean, fucks — like something crafted by the hand of God.

My chair squeaks. "What was she like?"

"Small." He shrugs. "But she has a sort of toughness to her. You can tell she's poor."

"I thought she was quite pretty. Like an ingenue."

He grunts. "Don't fall in love with this one, too." Like he doesn't do the same thing: obsess, search for himself inside of a stranger, search for a version of himself he can live with and then find — surprise! He is still the same monster after all.

"How can I fall in love? I've hardly even seen her." I gaze at my untouched plate. "I think she's avoiding me." The more I think about it, the more it does seem like a setup. It's hard to believe that Margo would share the rules of the game with an outsider but maybe she did. Maybe she is trying to throw me off-balance. Maybe she is trying to scare *me.*

He moves his salad across the plate, concentrating. "What's your plan?"

"I'm still getting to know her —"

"They're all the same." He coughs into his fist. "They want what we have, and they can't get it."

"I want to impress you," I say. "Do something really spectacular."

"Well. You're taking *forever.*"

It's been only a couple of weeks. I don't want to rush it. They don't. Once Margo took six months to cuck a separated banker. Even Graham takes his time, setting up elaborate scenarios with lost bunnies and wild horses. He draws them in, then pushes them away, bringing their longing to an artful crescendo. Of course, when it's my turn,

138

it's suddenly not fast enough.

But it's not just that. I can see it in Graham's face, even with no stars out. His temples are tight. His jaw has a light pulse. What happened last time plays on his features, threatening to deepen his shallow.

It was frightening. It caught us all by surprise. It changed the game.

LYLA

That night I can't sleep. Graham smells his strongest at night, all that exposed skin and the single malt whisky he drinks pushing out through his pores, forcing his scent into the air, where it hovers like a mind-bending fog over our rumpled white bed.

When I shut my eyes, I see Elvira, her dark hair in the fountain spiraling so it was almost indistinguishable from the tendrils of blood.

Some nights, when I'm especially tired or especially drunk, I have dreams about her. In my dreams she's always played by Nicole Kidman, and she's the one targeting me. I'm at my parents' house before they disowned me. I'm sitting in the corner in time-out when she knocks. I'm at school taking a test and she shows up, note in hand, to get me out. I'm working at a hot dog stand and she's next in line and she says, "I want you. Let's go!" I always wake up at the point where I get in her car, so we never escape. We never go anywhere. She just keeps showing up with the promise that we can leave now forever.

But tonight, I can only see her dead. The way her face was turned up out of the water, like she could still breathe. How she looked like a doll of herself, something you could buy, and break, and discard.

I think of Demi in the courtyard rattling the gate like she knew, like Elvira's ghost told her: *Escape. Escape this place where death blooms like a body at the center of a fountain.*

Graham's eyelids throb as his sleep deepens. If he could see what I see — but maybe he can. I called him as soon as I found her body. He was away on one of his golf trips. "Don't call the police," he said. "Wait until I get there."

When he got there, three hours later, he just stared at the body. He had a new expression — not a frown or a smile but one that revealed his dimples. The first thing he said was "It's so interesting, isn't it? When people surprise you. I'm never surprised anymore." And then he called Margo and she called her police.

I am sure she paid to keep it quiet. "It's the scandal," Margo explained to the police unnecessarily. "We're worried about how her family will take it." Elvira didn't have a family — Margo was always careful with that — just a sister in some bumfuck town. A sister who managed to track down our house number.

I picked up the phone when she called one afternoon. She kept repeating, "I just want to know why. I just want to know why." I hung up and called Margo. Elvira's sister never called again. Margo probably paid her, like she does everyone, to disappear. Like she once tried to pay me.

On my wedding day, she called me into her dressing room and asked me, "What's your number?" Simple. Straightforward. Just like that.

"You're kidding," I said. "We're getting married in an hour." I was already in a state. My parents had yet to show up. My dad was supposed to walk me down the aisle. My mom was supposed to help with my dress. They weren't there. Their phones were both switched off.

Margo sat before a long mirror so I could see her once in reflection and once in real life. Her makeup table was littered with high-end products. She wore a white dress and a veil cut so stately that no one would ever confuse her for the bride. "I was sure he would leave you at the altar. I would have put money on it, but now I'll put money on you."

"I don't want your money." My phone vibrated in my robe pocket. I glanced at the number, but it was just Mitsi, my maid of honor, probably wondering where I was.

"They're not coming."

My throat caught. "Who?"

"Your parents." She ran her hand over the products on the table, not looking, not touching, like a psychic feeling out a sign. "You'll never see them again if you marry Graham." Her hands closed around a tub of La Mer.

My first reaction was disbelief. I was new to Margo, new to Graham. I didn't understand how easy things were for them. How easy it was to make something happen. How easy it was to make something appear or to make something vanish. "What did you say to them?"

"The same thing I said to you: What. Is. Your. Number?"

Back then I was so holy with my own intelligence. I believed in myself. I had a wedding, four thousand guests, a dress made of lace made by monks. I had Graham. So I said, "I don't have a number."

She pursed her lips. I thought I detected a

genuine sadness in the leftover corners of her redone face. "I don't think you understand. We're bad people. We do bad things. You weren't meant for this life. You weren't meant to be this rich." She took two scoops of La Mer, slathered it on her face. Then she rubbed. It took her ages to rub it all in.

I stood tall, a Dickensian hero. I thought she would be moved. I thought she would be impressed. "I love him."

Her face was cold and heavy, the ghost in the shell. "Then you don't see him. Graham is unlovable."

I tipped my chin. "You're wrong."

She shook her head. "You're too young to understand, so you'll have to trust me: My son and I are the same. We're destroyers. We destroy people. All at once or incrementally, he will destroy you and everything you love. It's in our blood." She reached for me and I jumped at her touch, not realizing we were so close. She squeezed my hand so hard, I felt my bones. "Take the money. No one will ever offer you something of more value."

I thought she was trying to trick me. Graham had warned me his mother liked to play games. She was ruthless in getting what she wanted. She would say anything, do anything, *pay* anything.

144

I didn't understand then. I don't know if I understand now. But sometimes I wonder. Maybe she was telling the truth. Maybe honesty was a tactic, the last card she had to play. I think of Graham's expression as he watched Elvira float.

But I never could have seen it then, never could have understood. It's the things you want that kill you. The things you want but never get. Back then I still believed I could have everything, have anything. Maybe my parents wouldn't come to my wedding, but they would come around eventually. I would earn Margo's respect. I would earn Graham's love. They and the world would relent.

I was young, and I was dumb, and I was sure I would get everything I ever wanted.

"I don't want the money," I told her. "I want the life."

"Stupid girl, you'll lose them both." She turned her back on me, faced her own reflection in the mirror. I could still see her, but as far as she was concerned, I had disappeared.

I knew I shouldn't tell Graham what she had said but I did, on the third night of our honeymoon, when he still couldn't get it up to sleep with me. I told him the whole story, my valiant parts, Margo's wicked insistence.

Once I had finished, he said flatly, "Margo knows everything." Then he walked out onto our deck and jumped into the ocean. He didn't come up for so long, I thought he might have drowned.

When he finally surfaced, he looked hypnotized. He padded into our luxury hut dripping wet. "I need to call her," he said.

"I don't care." I jumped up and embraced him, let him soak me. "Don't you see? It doesn't matter. I love you anyway."

He pushed me off. "How can you love me anyway?"

He called Margo, and he shut the door on me. He spoke to her for over an hour. I would have given anything to know what she said to him, what he said to her, what they decided. When he came to bed, I thought something would change. But he slipped in beside me; he put his arms around me. He held me like a husband does. We never spoke of it again.

I tried to put it out of my mind, but every so often it bubbled to the surface, throwing me off-balance, catching me off guard. I told myself it was a trick, a lie Margo made up to scare me, until the night Elvira died. I saw the look on Graham's face: not a smile, not a smirk, but his dimples were showing. And I wondered for the first time if it wasn't a lie; if it was a mercy. *He will destroy you and everything you love. It's in our blood.*

There my mind stops before it goes too far. It doubles back on itself. It promises me I'm fine. He married me. He must have had a reason. He must know, deep down, I'm good enough. He must love me, in some way.

He won't destroy me, not by accident, not by design. I'm smart. I can keep up with him. I can't give up. I need to stop thinking about it. All of it. It won't get me anywhere. Elvira is dead. I need to stop dreaming about her. I need to focus on the game. It's my turn. Once it's over, things will go back to normal. Tragedy will take its place at a distance. I need to be the destroyer. I need to destroy Demi's life fast so we can all move on.

I know I can win. I have it in me. I can prove to Margo and Graham that I belong with them. I'm out of practice, but I'm a goddamn killer. That's how I got Graham. That's how I got the house. That's how I got everything that everyone wants.

I have a plan.

I'm going to do the most heartless thing a woman can do to another woman.

I'm going to make her my best friend.

LYLA

I am awake before Graham the next morning. I make him coffee, cut his grapefruit.

"I'm going to do it today," I tell him. "I have a plan."

Graham just nods sleepily. He is not a morning person. His eyes are dull. His skin is plump with sleep.

I wait until he leaves, until a sociable hour; then I get dressed. I select my grayest outfit, my most expensive understated shoes. A bottle of Moët for a housewarming present.

I step out the front door. A man is standing in our courtyard.

There is a homelessness epidemic in Los Angeles. They rent vans out in Venice for people to live in. Charities and churches offer swaths of lawn for people to camp. Downtown there are tent cities with shopping cart traffic.

It's easy not to see it up here in the hills, in a city where no one walks. It's easy to drive from one place to another and barely even glimpse it. To avoid it. Even so, there are times when I pass over a body on my walk to the reservoir, times when my car brakes suddenly as someone barges across the street, always bleeding from somewhere: a nose, an ankle, bloody fingers. Times when you notice a pile of trash and realize people have been discarded there, too.

This man is tall, over six feet. He stoops but it only makes him seem taller. He has dark dreaded hair and a hooked, crooked nose. He has a fancy woman's jacket but no shirt. His chest is speckled with mud or blood. I look at him. He gazes back at me, over his shoulder with a grim expression, like we are locked in some endless loop, prisoners in twin purgatories.

I have this funny impulse to invite him inside. He could be my Rasputin. I could be his Alexandra.

"What — ," I start.

He coils, ready to run. My muscles clench. But instead of racing onto the street, he dives down the stairs toward the guesthouse. I follow him. My bra tightens. My heart appears in my chest, beating. I leap down the stairs. I hear Demi scream. She is standing in front of her door, face ashen.

The man freezes on the stairwell, halfway

between her place and mine. He looks up at me, then down toward her, trying to decide who is the weaker link. He makes his choice, barreling down the steps so she falls flat against her front door.

He whooshes past, and as he does, she swings her fist and smacks him between the shoulder blades.

"Bitch!" he grunts in surprise as he crashes down the hillside.

"Don't come back!" she roars as he dodges through the dense trees. A murder of crows explodes from the branches. At the bottom of the yard, he scales the lower fence and is gone.

Demi watches the yard, hand still clenched in a fist. Her feet are twisted into alligator pumps. When she is satisfied he won't come back, she turns to me. Her eyes are wild with alarm.

I'm so shocked, I laugh. "You hit him." I rush down the stairs.

Her eyes slide in and out of focus. "He was trespassing." Her fist loosens.

I reach her patio. "He was huge." I'm awed. "Weren't you scared?"

She tugs at her coat collar like a hoodlum in a fifties film. "I'm not scared of anything." When her eyes find mine, I believe it. Who is this woman living under our feet?

I hesitate on the patio, trying to re-form my plans. I wanted to befriend her. I need to get to know her. "Do you want to come upstairs?" I offer my most radioactive smile. "Get to know each other?"

I open the front door and walk to the kitchen. She stands just inside. She looks at the windows. Not all at once but piece by piece, mapping them.

"It's so dark downstairs —"

"I like it." Her voice is rough, abrupt.

I glance at our windows. It's like a display case up here. "Do you want tea? Or coffee?" Who are you? What do you like? What is your weakness?

"No, thank you."

"Water?"

"I can only stay a second."

Even I don't work that fast. Making someone like you is the ultimate magic trick, a total sleight of hand. Now you SEE the good! Now you DON'T see the bad!

I scrape my mind for something about me that might sound normal in conversation. I went for a walk yesterday, today and tomorrow. I have a husband. I live in a house. I can't find anything halfway normal. I am not a human being. I don't have a soul.

"So. You work in tech?"

151

"Yes."

"How is that?"

She shrugs. "A job is a job."

"What do you like to do for fun?"

"Nothing." It's like she can read my mind, see my intentions.

"You do nothing for fun?"

"I should really go."

"Wine?"

"I don't drink." Alcohol would make this easier, but maybe there's something there.

"Me either," I say. "I mean, hardly. Alcoholic parents," I lie. She flinches. "You, too?"

"My parents are dead."

"I wish mine were," I say before I remember that is not something you say to someone with dead parents. "They've basically disowned me." I wait for her to ask why so I can tell her I'd rather not talk about it.

"I'd better go."

How rude. I hate when people don't want to know everything about me, especially things I can't tell them.

"No. Please, stay." Margo would be better at this. She would make Demi want to stay. Graham would make her beg.

"I can't."

Her expression is set. This might be harder than I thought. She seems determined. Graham was right: She has a toughness about her, an adversarial quality. Her muscles are tight. She stands away from me, but always with her eyes on me, always expecting the worst. She doesn't seem to trust me. At the least, she doesn't like me. It annoys me.

What I hate about people, what I really hate, is that they can make up their own minds about you. If I want a jacket, I can buy it. The jacket doesn't have to want me back. But a person does.

"You seem very cagey," I say, which doesn't put her at ease.

"I have work — I have a really important work call. Sorry."

I rush to the door but she's already leaving. Usually they want to stay. Usually they are grateful to be invited, gushing over the house and all the things in it.

I reach her and her eyes go wide. It's like she's afraid of me. Like she knows what the game is. What if I am being set up? What if she and Margo are in this together?

"Did Margo put you up to this?"

Her lips part. "I don't know who that is."

The very idea shocks me and I stumble. "This is her house, and yours — you're living in her house."

"Oh, that Margo. I got her mixed up." She's lying. Of course, she is. No one forgets

Margo. "I'd better go."

"Another time," I insist. She crosses the courtyard without answering.

LYLA

I tell Graham about the man in the courtyard. He is thrilled. He leads me to the sofa, where we sit together drinking Moët as the sun sets, and he asks me to describe him, recite the moment over and over.

"How tall?" "Were you scared?" "Then what?"

He is shocked that Demi punched the man. "How very cunning! I like a person who can think on their feet."

"We need to fix the gate," I point out, nauseous with Moët.

"Do you think he broke it?"

"I don't know. He was tall. When are we going to fix it?"

"It's being fixed. It's from a monastery in Sicily or something. They can't just repair it overnight. They have to pray over every piece." I can't tell if he is joking. He sips his Moët delicately, gazing out over the trees to the place in the fence where the man disappeared. "I wish I had been here. I would have . . ." He drifts off, riveted. It's his dream to protect his property.

"We should at least put up a temporary gate," I say, but he won't. He likes it. He would probably like to never fix the gate at all.

After he finishes his Moët, he goes out to patrol the neighborhood. He brings a gun, even though I tell him he shouldn't.

"I'm not going to shoot someone!" he protests when I try to explain that's what guns are for.

Graham has an enormous safe in our closet that is filled with guns. He went through a brief hunting phase and then a shooting range phase before he switched to golf. Now he doesn't use his guns for anything but he still has a wild array of them. Anything that's legal, he has. And several things that strictly aren't.

He comes back late and joins me in bed, where he lists all his suspicions like a boy detective: "That van outside hasn't moved."

I cuddle closer, drawn into the game. "It never does."

Graham sets the gun on the bedside table, pointed toward the window. "Maybe there's a dead body in there!"

"Do you think so?"

His lips tighten. He gets a blank look in his eyes, like he's shuffling thoughts in the back of his mind. "Know what else is funny? Demi always has her curtains closed."

"Does she?" My back braces. She was so odd today. First the way she struck a stranger, then the way she answered my questions, hurried out the door. It was as if she was afraid of getting too close. She knows something. What does she know?

Graham worries his lips. "It's already so dark down there. Why would you close the curtains?"

"She said she likes the dark." I tell Graham everything she said, how she claimed not to even know who Margo is. This seems to fascinate him.

"Hmm." He reaches a careless hand out and spins the gun.

"Is that loaded?"

"The safety's on," he says, and then he quickly switches it on like I'm not watching.

"You shouldn't have that out." I roll over, away from him. "Really, Graham, I think you should put that back in the safe."

"There was a robbery next door."

My spine tingles. "What?"

"Last week. I wasn't going to tell you because I didn't want you to worry, but you should probably know. I should probably

157

take you down to the range, teach you to shoot." He seems sort of holy with this proposition, rapt. I remember when we first met, how he would make me watch Westerns and Tarantino films and make annoying clever comments: "That gun would be out of bullets" or "Heads don't explode like that."

He is wide-eyed and dreamy. I move closer, feel the heat coming off him. "What did they take?"

"Everything," he says, beautifully transfixed. "They took everything."

The next morning, Graham is up early. The housekeeper makes breakfast and Graham makes me tell her the story, then corrects my every sentence.

"She was terrified," he concludes like my fear belongs to him, too.

He has a spring in his step. The sky is bright with the possibility of chaos. He leaves me with a gun.

"You have to turn the safety off, see? Right here. Make sure you do that first. Then" — Graham aims the gun at the window — "point and shoot. Simple." He drops the gun on the table in the foyer.

"You left the safety off," I say, flicking it

on. "I really don't think we need a gun out here."

"They all have guns." Graham cautions, looping his finger in a circle around us.

"But —"

"A man trespassed on our property. He threatened your tenant. Someone broke the gate. He's clearly casing the neighborhood, or else he's squatting somewhere." He peers through the slats in the shutter. "I'm not asking you to shoot anyone. I just want you to be safe." He seems elated at the prospect of us having a gun out, at his giving me a gun, like he is the husband he always dreamed of being. He steps toward me, brushes the hair from my forehead and kisses my temple, an actor walking through stage directions. "I need to protect you, darling."

I savor the moment until he pulls away; then protest bubbles up my throat. "I don't know how to shoot a gun."

He frowns. "I just explained it to you. Anyway, it's not for shooting. It's just to have. Because they have it. Here." He takes the remote from the coffee table and turns on the TV, flipping to the news. "Watch. Look. They all have guns."

A woman is standing in front of the 101 freeway, talking about a fire at a tent city with a single fatality. I frown, pick the remote back up and switch it off.

"I hate the news. It's so negative."

Graham scoffs. "Oh, God, don't be one of those people!" But he wants me to be one of those people. He would hate it if I got political. If I became a feminist or a vegan or a social justice warrior, he would nag me into being nothing again.

He picks up his briefcase. "I bet Demi has a gun," he says suddenly. When he talks about Demi, his eyes go slightly blank, like he is accessing a remote part of his brain. "A woman living alone like that, she probably has a whole bunch of them." I follow him to the door. "You should be careful. It sounds like she's not afraid to take a swing."

"Neither am I."

He kisses my forehead again. I wish he would kiss my mouth. "I hope you don't give up so easily today."

"I didn't give up easily. She knows something." I check that the housekeeper is out of earshot, lower my voice just in case. "It's like she couldn't get away from me fast enough. And she wouldn't reveal *anything* about herself. She claimed she didn't even know who Margo was," I remind him.

"I'm not sure what you're getting at."

"Maybe you should ask your mother."

"Margo wants you to succeed." He adjusts his tie in the mirror. "If she didn't, you'd know about it."

"When will you be home?"

"Late," he says like he only decided right then. He's bored already. I'm boring him.

"But —"

"I have a lot of work to catch up on." I don't understand how he is at work all day and still manages to be in a perpetual state of being behind. "See you later."

I watch him cross the courtyard, walk through our missing gate.

I jump when I hear a door bang downstairs, followed by the pounding of the shower. Usually Demi is at work by now. I wonder if she has the day off. I won't give up so easily today. I won't give up at all. I don't know what all of this means — the broken gate, the man in the courtyard, the van on the street — but I can't help but think it has something to do with the game, with my turn, with *her.*

I need to finish this today. Just get it over with.

"Do you want me to clean around the gun?" I turn and see my housekeeper standing next to the table in the foyer, where the gun sits on a silver tray like the last party favor. Her expression is haughty, disbelieving. She's obviously never worked for a rich family before.

"I suppose you'd better," I snap. I check my reflection in the foyer mirror, then take one last glance at the gun as I walk out the door.

I want the game to be over. I don't have time to get to know her. If Demi won't reveal her weakness, I'll have to use one of mine.

Lyla

In addition to every gun known to man, we also have every tool. The toolshed, which is tucked along the side of the house, next to the courtyard, is filled with everything you could possibly need. Six shovels with pointed tips and perforated edges, seven saws, one chain. Most of these things have never been used. One or two are sprinkled with mud that looks like blood.

I have a wide selection of tools, of moves, to finish the game. I choose a set of steel wire cutters, the kind that can break the links of a chain-link fence.

As I cross back into the courtyard, I find the housekeeper standing next to the fountain. She is frozen like a statue, gazing into the water. She catches sight of the cutters as I slip them into my pocket.

"What are you doing?" she asks. Her impertinence is starting to grate. I like my help to be silent as well as invisible.

"What are *you* doing?" I ask back. "I don't pay you to stare at your reflection."

She just stands there and watches me as I cross the courtyard, walk up the steps and onto the street. It's creepy. I would fire her if Graham wasn't obsessed with her cooking.

I take my usual route to the reservoir. When I get there, I find a small break in the fence. I remove the wire cutters from my pocket. I cut the metal links — they snap apart easily — into the shape of a door I can peel back. I make the break bigger, big enough to step through easily.

My weakness. It's always irritated me, the way I can circle the lake, look at it, but never reach it. Trespassing is highly illegal, of course. Dangerous. There's a circular concrete drain that looks like the place they used to drop the bodies of aged-out starlets. There are slippery cliffs and wild animals. Security patrols the perimeter twenty-four hours a day. In a city where people are tucked into every street corner, hidden in every crevice, where people camp on the islands that crop up on the LA River at low tide, this place is protected. Even the rich can't access it.

It's also beautiful: remote, disquieting.

One of the few places in LA that no one can touch. The trees are green and wild. There are herds of roving deer. The water is baptismal blue. Even the air feels cleaner, fat with refreshment.

It's like Margo's gardens, exquisite but fenced in. The beauty is the trap.

When I get back to the house, the courtyard is empty. My muscles are tight, almost cramped, as I look for the man from yesterday, imagine all the places he could stuff his too-big body. I tell myself I'm scared of him, but really, I am scared of me.

I set my shoulders and start down the stairs. I am the predator. She is the prey. It's just a game. I need to win. I walk softly, not wanting Demi to hear me coming.

When I reach the patio, there is a weird smell, sickly, like an artisan candle titled Sweat and Blood. I tell myself I am imagining it. I shake it off. I knock loudly on the door.

I feel her freeze, feel her like she is living inside me, renting space there.

I knock harder.

I hear footsteps approach. I have her right where I want her. She is walking right into my trap. The door opens a crack.

"Hi."

"Hi."

"Hi." Suddenly she pushes through it. She shuts it fast behind her, hiding what's inside. She is standing on the patio in front of me, so close I take a quick step back.

She is dressed in sharp black heels, a bounteous black coat. Her skin glows. She crosses her arms. "Is there something wrong?"

"Not at all." I step out toward the edge of the patio. The air is so close down here, it packs in my throat. The weird trees twitch overhead. The hillside is coated with vines with heart-shaped leaves. "I just wanted to check in after yesterday. That man —"

"I'm fine. Thanks." She is dismissing me but I don't mind it. In fact, I enjoy the discomfort it causes, my not leaving, invading her space. I turn on my toes, face her.

"You've been home a lot this week," I point out. Has she been fired? Was her whole job a ruse? Is anything real? Is everything a game?

"I'm working remotely now," she explains. "So, you know, I'll just be in here on my own a lot, working. It's better if I'm not disturbed."

"Oh."

"Yeah."

I approach the stairwell like I'm going to

166

leave, but I'm not. I have no plans to leave and I wonder if she can sense that, if that is why her eyes are so wide. "I wanted to ask you: I go for a walk every day around the reservoir. I thought you might like to come." It's not a question. That's intentional. "I thought it might be nice for you to have a friend in the neighborhood." I stretch my lips in a smile. It hurts a little.

She tugs her ponytail. "That's sweet of you," she says but her words are prickly. She twists her neck and gazes back at the house. "But I can't right now." She reaches for the doorknob.

"I'll come back later." A lunge.

"You don't need to." A parry.

"I'm sorry." I'm not. "The thing about living here . . ." Does she ever blink? "Margo is very particular about her tenants. We like them to be friends. Family, even." I can practically see the hairs on her neck rise but she holds her own, holds her breath. "This is Margo's house after all. So is mine. We're all living in her *home.* It's important that we all know one another so we feel comfortable." I am making her uncomfortable. "Do you understand?"

"I think . . . I get it." Good. "If you just give me a second to change, I'll meet you upstairs."

She waits for me to start up the stairs before she opens the door. I imagine a wall of televisions playing security camera footage focused on my every move. A small armory. An earpiece that connects her directly to Margo. *She has an attack; we have a riposte!*

I'm paranoid, but anything is possible — that's the thing. When you have the means, *anything* is possible. I reach the courtyard and perch on the edge of the fountain, muscles poised, mouth twitching, ready for her.

LYLA

Demi finally ascends in a black athleisure suit, loose on her tiny frame, pierced in places by bones. She is thinner than I thought. She tugs at her clothes as if embarrassed, but she must work hard for that body. Maybe she works harder on pretending to be embarrassed.

"Ready," she says unnecessarily. I follow her through the opening onto the street.

I study the bristles in her body, the hook of her shoulders, the tension in her hips, the odd way she shuffles on the edge of her feet, toes curled in. She is so tense, so afraid. She must know something, or else she senses it. She is scared of a thing that might be me.

We pass the white van and her eyes are held by it so long that I say, "I don't know where that came from. It just turned up one day."

Demi stiffens as she nods. Her hands are

fisted in her pockets.

I try to walk beside her but she stays slightly ahead, watching me out of the corner of her eye. On guard. We reach the place where the road splits, drops easily down onto the main road or steepens perilously up into the hills.

"Let's go up. I want to show you something."

She swallows hard but follows me. I don't give her a choice.

The streets in the hills are not made for walking. They are not made for driving either. They are designed to keep people out. The roads are steep, curved and narrow. There are no sidewalks. There are blind turns, cracks in the roads and in the walls that hem them. There are cars parked at perilous points with their bumpers shaved, their back ends busted, their mirrors snapped back.

Demi's back is rigid. Her fingers stay buried in her pockets. Her head swivels left and right. I picture a fast car barreling down the road, unable to stop in time, plowing her body into one of the stone walls that screen the better homes, popping, smashing her bones to powder in places so she becomes a mangled version of herself: half a face, no hands, a crooked spine, a missing shoe, shuffling down the same path. I would win then. I would win and I wouldn't even have to lift a finger. I wish there was a God who worked like that. Effort makes victory bittersweet. I want to win by not even trying.

An engine roars from above or below. Her head snaps up. She scrambles, first to the left and then to the right. We balance at the edge of a cliff as an SUV steams past.

It vanishes through a hairpin turn and she shivers, steps back onto the road. "Why do you walk here?" Her voice has a fearful snap. "Do you want to get killed?"

"I've never been hit," I say like it's obvious. "I've never even come close."

"No." She shivers again. "Of course not."

The hill is steep and we walk fast. Our breath puffs in tandem. Soon we are looking out over Los Angeles: the mirrored hills across the valley, the bulging blackish eye of the observatory, the messy stacks downtown. I stop to look at the view but Demi only glances at it, then looks quickly away, like she betrayed herself.

"Left here." I indicate. The walk is easier now. We catch our breath but don't speak. We are locked in this heavy silence, so this whole exercise feels like torture. I scrape my mind for something to say. "You make more

171

money than Graham." I don't know why I say that.

She laughs like she has just landed back here beside me. "How much does Graham make?" Her throaty voice is teasing, playful.

Even if this conversation is inappropriate, even though Graham would be angry, I feel a dark thrill in telling her, in what seems an exceptional betrayal, "Three thirty."

"A year?" she blurts then. "Sorry. Duh. My brain." She brushes her head.

"He has family money, too, from Margo. Margo has more money than God. Or the devil."

"Do you like her?"

"Are you kidding? I don't like anyone who has more money than me."

She bursts out laughing. I feel dizzy with it, that childhood feeling: *Someone laughed at my joke! Someone likes me!* It reminds me of Elvira. She used to have the most wicked sense of humor. We would laugh and laugh for hours out on her porch. Laughter made us feel like we owned the world. Laughter made us feel like we won. Until Graham came down from above. And she stopped laughing.

We are walking side by side now, moving from the left to the right side of the street, whatever side seems safer. A vista opens up

172

to the west, across Beverly Hills and Santa Monica, all the way to the jewel blue ocean. To our right, the reservoir looms.

She stops in her tracks. She is so jumpy, it's making me uneasy.

"Have you been here before?" I ask.

"Once."

"Most people don't know about it. It's really beautiful! I'm convinced it's the most beautiful place in LA — correction, the *only* beautiful place."

She laughs again but it's thinner, fades faster. "I should probably —"

"No," I say. "Just let me show you *one thing.* It'll take five minutes. Ten." Five to ten.

She acquiesces. We continue walking until we reach the trailhead. The lake appears, a tranquil sea in the cradle of the hills surrounded by a tall chain-link fence.

She scowls at it. "How very LA to keep such a beautiful place behind a fence so no one can use it," she observes. "This city is like a game and the locations are all levels. And no matter how high you get, there's always a place you can't access." Her words echo my own thoughts. It's dangerous to relate to anyone, let alone your target. To imagine a world where we could be friends, just friends, like Elvira and I were before

173

the game got in the way.

"That's so funny; I think of things as games, too."

She shrugs. "Life is a game."

I go along with it. "What's the prize?"

". . . Playing." Her tone is dark but she smiles after, like she regrets or relishes it. "Just getting to play."

I'm not sure if I agree with her, but I think I understand what she means. You get what you want and the game is not over. It's never enough. You just get to keep playing.

I think of our game and I shiver. It won't end with this one. Deep down, I know that, but I have to believe it will. I have to convince myself that I can end it. Today. Now.

"I think I like you," I say, and I mean it in that moment. But I have a game to win, and the quicker I can get it done, the sooner my turn can be over. "And now I have a surprise." I tap my nose, smile.

She stops in her tracks. "What is it?"

"Access."

LYLA

We walk along the asphalt road that follows the perimeter of the lake. We pass no fewer than three signs warning against trespassing, with a number to call at the bottom. Beyond the fence, reeds twitch; tall trees curve, malformed by nature, twisted by their will to survive. We don't see a single person. We are the last two people left in LA.

"There's no one here," Demi says.

"It's the best kind of place." Elvira and I used to walk around here alone, undisturbed. In some version of the world, we are still walking. I stop at the place where the fence now curves up like a skirt. "Here we are."

She shakes her head, nervous eyes still scanning the periphery. "Where?"

"If we lift the fence" — I bend down to demonstrate — "we can walk down to the lake."

Demi remains frozen. "I don't want to."

I release the fence. It jangles harshly back into place. "But I thought you said —"

"I should really go back." What is her problem?

"It's totally safe." I wipe my temple with my wrist. "There's nobody around. You said it was beautiful. You said it was inaccessible. Don't you want to go there? Just to prove you can?"

She sets her jaw. "We'll get caught."

I smirk like a fiend. "I never get caught." I turn back to the fence. "You first. You're smaller." I wrench the fence up high enough for a person to crawl through. She hesitates, looks left, then right. "Hurry!" I order. "It's heavy."

She looks both ways again.

"Stop being so paranoid."

"Fine." Her voice grounds down. "Hold it up."

I use my hip to lift the fence as high as I can so she can crawl through safely. I needn't have worried. She can make herself tiny. She slips through the crack like a forgotten secret.

She stands on the other side facing me. Behind her, the water twitches. The sun casts shadows. I drop the fence. "Shit."

"What?"

I can practically see her heart beating in

her chest. "I have to change my tampon. I'll be right back."

"But!"

"Just stay there; I'll be *right* back!"

As soon as I am out of sight, I block my number and make the call. "Hello? Security. Yes, I saw a woman cut through the fence and walk down into the reservoir. I know this sounds crazy, but I think she had a gun!"

I walk as quickly and quietly as I can to the trailhead. I am cresting the last turn when I hear the rumble of tires. A security truck rolls toward me, seemingly in no hurry to arrest Demi.

Instead of passing me by, the truck comes to a stop. I drop my chin and keep walking.

"Young lady!"

My back tightens in a line. "What do you want?" I snap. I want to tell the security guard he should be hurrying before Demi gets away, but I don't want him to know I'm the one who called. I don't want to be used as a witness. I don't want to be implicated at all.

His car door dings as he steps out. What the hell is he doing?

He hitches his belt. "We're investigating a distress call."

"I'm not distressed. I'm fine. Thank you."
I move quickly away from him. He steps in
front of me, blocking my path. He is all belt,
a sour expression. I am his bad day.

"I'd just like to see what's in your pocket
there, if that's all right."

Shit.

The metal cutters are still in my coat
pocket.

DEMI

Murderer.

No one ever prepares you to deal with death. Death is a secret you keep until you die. It is the only thing that unites us all and yet we never, ever talk about it.

No one tells you how to get rid of a body.

In movies, they drag them across the floor, leaving behind a wide trail of blood. They shut them in trunks. They drive out to deserts, toss suitcases into rivers, call out teams of villains with attractive distorted features to do their dirty work. They leave evidence that no one finds, because there is a team to clear the set between locations. And the corpses are gorgeous, bruises and scars carefully applied by a team of artists to match an overall aesthetic: the magnificent, the haunting dead.

Demi looks alive. She looks asleep, even if her eyes are open in a thin white seam. It's only when I touch her skin that I feel that

179

unnatural chill. It feels like a mistake, like something I did. *You're the cold one. You're making her cold.*

I move my hand, searching for warmth: at the base of her neck, on the crown of her head, on her wrist beneath her jacket. I jump, having accidentally brushed her exposed stomach, a place I would never touch if she was alive. A place she wouldn't want me to touch.

She's dead. She's dead, you idiot. Don't act like you didn't guess it.

I try to use my imagination but I don't have one anymore. You have to have hope to have an imagination and I don't have that; the last of it just dropped down through the floorboards.

All I have are the facts.

If I call the police, I will be blamed for something. It's what police do, my dad always taught me. They wait for you to stick your head out, to show them where you are, and then they say, *You'll do,* and they throw you in with the rest of the people who couldn't keep quiet.

Never call the police. Dad bored that into my brain. Besides, the police can't save her. They *can* hurt me.

And I can't leave. Leaving would only make things worse. They would track me down. I don't know this woman, but I know enough to know she's rich, and rich women don't die without someone being held accountable.

It's not just that.

It's the sandwiches in her fridge in their little plastic houses, the shoes in her closet curled on spike heels, the dappled light on the blood-colored rug in the designer living room.

I could go back out on the streets. I could run. I could probably get away, move to another state, another city. But there is food in the fridge. And no one knows Demi is dead. The woman upstairs thinks I am Demi.

I could stay for one day, just one day in this life — who would stop me? Who would blame me? I'm not taking anything that belongs to anyone else. She left her life behind. Who could blame me for picking it up?

All I want is one day. One.

I move her body out of the bathroom so I can pee. I drag her across the floor and leave her by the front door. I brush her hair out of her face, adjust her coat, because I am not such a monster as to leave her disheveled.

I flash back on my father in the supermarket, the scam he used to run, hiding steaks and salmon under newspaper in his basket. Every time I complained. Not once did I stop him. Was I responsible for not stopping him? Was I responsible for not stopping her?

I'm sorry. I mouth the words to her body. I try to ignore the joy. Her life is mine for one day.

I pee on a real toilet: a spotless flushing toilet. I feel like a human being instantly, despite everything. Despite the body in the living room. I am *somebody* now.

My eyes drift to the shower, to the shampoo and conditioner in liter-sized gold bottles, the sparkly bodywash, the rain forest showerhead.

I approach carefully, hold my breath. I turn on the shower.

I stay under the water for ages. I use everything, even her razor, ignore the drifting accusations: evidence, DNA.

I stand naked in front of the full-length mirror in her bedroom. I have never been so clean in my life. I never knew you could be so clean. I never knew shampoos and soaps could smell or feel like this. After I towel off, I clean my face with micellar water, brighten it with lactic acid, soften it with aloe, spritz it with atomized Evian.

I hate to admit it, but I always thought rich people glowed because they were better, and that is how they ended up rich. They were cleaner, brighter. I never realized you could buy things to make you glow.

You just partway killed someone and you look fucking amazing.

The low-level cold I have been running for the past month has left my sinuses. Money has cured me in twenty minutes flat. All I needed was a shower. All I had to do was step over a body.

My filthy clothes are piled on the floor. I can't bear to put them back on. She has a washing machine. I could wash them. I will just have to put on her clothes in the meantime.

Or I could take her clothes.

I start with the idea that I will take the worst things she owns, the things she would miss the least, but then I remember she won't be there to miss them. No one will know. Wouldn't she want me to have them? I think of her last night, sneeringly offering to help me, her bullshit drunk promises: *You can work for my company. Ha-ha.*

I select the nicest things I can find: the warmest jacket, the thickest pants, the sturdiest boots. Her feet are a little smaller than mine, which have spread, flattened

183

from years on my feet, but I can force a fit. I set the boots by the door for when I leave.

My stomach growls. I find her fridge. You wouldn't think you would be able to eat with a dead body less than fifty feet away from you.

You wouldn't think you would be able to do a lot of things until you do.

DEMI

There is a crumpled handful of cash in a tray by the door. I need to buy supplies. I use her fingerprint to unlock her iPad and search for a local market. Luckily there is one just down the road. I wait for upstairs to go quiet before taking the cash and her house keys and heading out.

The glass house looks vacant as I pass but I startle when I catch the outline of a woman sitting on a chair completely still. It's the woman from last night, the Gothic totem. I shiver all the way to my toes and hurry to unlock the gate.

Once I am safely down the street, I breathe more freely. It's so dark in that apartment, so claustrophobic, that I forgot the sun was out. It beams down on me now, lucid, hot, a fever dream.

I snake along the twisted roads toward the market. I pass a glamorous woman walking her dog. Her hair is jet-black. Her clothes are snow-white. Her dog is bright red. She's like an artist's rendering of a human being: *God did okay, but let's try a fresh take!*

My eyes glaze automatically. I duck to rush by. She looks right at me, smiles, says, "Hello."

I am so shocked; I can't even think of a response.

I keep walking. It happens again and again. People look me in the eye. People smile at me. It's actually unsettling.

I want to smile back, but my face stays frozen. I can't force myself to say hello back. I can only frown and feel this hot discomfort.

When I reach the market, I walk up and down the aisles, observing all the packaging, relishing the feeling of being in a store with money in my pocket. I have forty dollars. I could buy anything.

In the end, I buy what I need.

"Wow!" The checker says. "Zip ties! Trash bags! Bleach!" I am going to jail. "Where's the body?" He smiles at me. He is making a joke.

"Ha!" I cough. I quickly toss *People* magazine on the counter, just in case.

I shouldn't have bothered. He is happily packing the items away for me. Of course, he doesn't think I killed someone. He can't even conceive of it. Can't conceive of a situation that could lead to that conclusion.

He bags everything up and hands it over. "Have a nice day! Love the coat!" It is a gorgeous coat.

Once I leave the store, I sit on the stone benches at the center of the square, waiting for my legs to stop shaking. I end up staying for over an hour, not just people-watching but people-watching people watching me.

Because people see me. They acknowledge me. They used to look over my head, through me, around me. Now they are looking for me. Their eyes are sharpened on my expensive coat, my protein-laced hair. They want something from me, instead of fearing I might take something from them.

I still can't smile. I feel like a fraud. But all the way home I wonder, *Could I smile? Could I get used to this? Could I smile back if I was smiled at long enough?*

I am walking up Demi's street when I spot a man standing outside a garage. I know immediately that he is Graham Herschel, even though I had never heard of him before last night. He is the type of person you know on sight, like he has always existed in the back of your mind, in your wildest dreams.

He is gazing toward the castle on the hill. He's the most gorgeous man I have ever seen up close. He looks like a billboard come to life. He has an image quality, like he could be anything you want him to be, on the other side. The sunlight smears his profile. His suit is cut in caressing lines. My ears are hot. I feel this drowning sensation.

I want to cry. I think I'm going to cry, break down right there in the street, start pleading: *All I ever wanted was to be as pure, as blameless, as you are. That's all I ever wanted. But the closer I get, the farther I am. The fight for YOUR life is littered with death, like I caused it, like I am the common denominator to all the tragedy in my life. Like it was all my fault.*

He is the kind of beautiful that makes you feel like a sinner.

He turns suddenly, smiles slowly. His smile is a present he is unwrapping. "You must be Demi. I'm Graham." He puts his hand out. "I live upstairs."

I feel this sudden, panicked urge to confess. *Of course I'm not Demi! I can't even smile when people smile at me!*

He slips his hand in mine. His skin feels like money.

They're so beautiful; he and Lyla both are the toys you keep on the high shelf. *Don't*

touch them! You might break them! And I am
the toy you let your toddler play with. The
one you bring to the beach. The one you
draw on and cut up and leave at the park
and think, *Good. Now I don't have to bother
throwing it away.*

"God," he says. His voice has a rugged
deep. My heart almost collapses. "You're
gorgeous." And I see a schism, another life
in his smile. I live downstairs. He lives
upstairs. We have barbecues, drinks in the
courtyard; we sit by the fountain and drink
wine. He tells me I'm gorgeous. Lyla does,
too. I become a billboard, an image with
nothing behind it.

"Thank you."

"Welcome to the neighborhood." He
presses a button, makes the garage beep.

DEMI

Demi's body is still by the door. It hasn't moved, hasn't jumped back to life. She isn't waiting for me in the kitchen, pouring me a glass of wine, grinning. *Gotcha!*

Did I kill her? The sun is setting again already, or else it's always setting in this apartment, shadows dropping into the trees, sucking out the light.

Did I want her dead?

I think of the exhaustion that came over me like a stupor, how it settled in my bones. When I should have been panicking, when I should have called the police, I went to sleep.

Did my body betray me? Did it draw me to that swing to sleep? Was it hatching a plan, letting it blossom in the back of my mind all along?

You must be Demi.

I can be her. She can be me. We can switch places. I can die so she can live.

I am smart enough to know there is an expiration date on this plan, but I am also, unfortunately, smart enough to know that this may be the best of a bunch of bad options.

Option one: I go back on the streets, with a new coat and no prospects, no future. I leave LA and hope I don't get caught.

Option two: I go to jail, where there is shelter, where I will be fed.

Option three: I borrow her life just for a little while. It's not every day a perfect stranger leaves you a fortune.

But there are so many variables. What about her friends? Won't people come looking for her? But she's just moved in; her neighbors don't even know her. They both thought I was her.

Last night she said she had a job in tech. And I have a degree from a technical college that I'm pretty sure is not technically a college. Still.

I find her laptop in the dresser next to my bed. She doesn't have a lock screen. She does have a history. I find the company she works for, Alphaspire. I use her fingerprint to unlock her e-mail. Then I change all her passwords.

I put on Fleetwood Mac to give my resolution atmosphere. I light candles but leave the lights out.

I take stock of everything she has.

It's amazing what one person can own. She has hundreds of pairs of shoes lined on the white shelves, some still in plastic, tissue stuffed. One closet is dedicated to camping equipment: a sleeping bag, a tent, all tagged and brand-new. Another closet contains thin rows of drawers that pull out to reveal patterned jewelry, some carefully separated, some twisted into an unholy mass: chains as thick as teething rings, strands of pearls, scattered diamond tennis bracelets. It's a mess worth more than my life.

Six watches. Seven bottles of perfume. Two hundred and eighty-three books. Two computers, one laptop, one tablet, one Kindle. Fourteen bottles of wine. Seventy-two rolls of toilet paper.

I have never loved math this much. I will have to be careful selling some things — the idea of selling anything makes me nervous — but there is a lot of money to be made inside these walls.

The woman upstairs crosses the floor over my head. I will have to be extra careful. But everything I need is here. Everything is laid out for me, like the wish granted by a twisted fairy godmother.

There is just one major stumbling block:

the body. I glance at it laid out next to the door. Is it taking on a grayish cast? Is it starting to look more dead?

When I was twelve or thirteen, our next-door neighbor died. They found the body in summer, but he had been dead since January. The police came to speak to us to try to find his next of kin, but we didn't know him, and he didn't know us. They advised us to stay somewhere else that night while they removed the body. Someplace else wasn't a possibility. My dad got drunk; he smoked cigarettes. He turned up his music, Led Zeppelin, the perfect dead-body music. And we tried not to hear, we tried not to see, we tried not to know as they opened the door.

But the smell came in so hard, our insides shriveled. There's nothing that smells like a dead body. There is nothing that sticks to the back of your mouth, coats your nostrils, burns your windpipe. And it stayed for days. It stayed, really, forever in the hallway. So even years later I would be feeling my way along the wall when the overhead lights went out and I would choke on a sudden gust of death smoke still oozing from the seam of things.

Nonetheless, there is some hope in this memory. If a dead body can survive six months without getting caught, how long can I live? Does anyone ever really know their neighbors? Does anyone care? We all want privacy, our own cocoon. We pay for it.

I think of Lyla, her Gothic appeal. Maybe I should ask her to help me. I can knock on her door, smile and say politely, *Could you please help me carry a few trash bags out to my trunk? Sorry about the smell! Just some junk I don't need!*

I almost laugh, feel it bubble wickedly up my throat, but it dries abruptly when the knock from my imagination barks on my own door.

I switch off the music. My eyes go right to the body, her profile in repose, waiting for a spell to bring her back to death.

I don't move. I keep my mouth shut. I should have left the music on, shouldn't have alerted the person outside to my presence. It's too late now.

And it is late. It's after dark. Why would the neighbor be knocking now unless they knew something was wrong? Unless they knew.

Does the body smell? Did someone contact them? Did someone call the police? *We saw this girl in the village and she wasn't smiling, Officer. We knew something must be*

VERY wrong.

They knock again so loud, I think the whole neighborhood will hear. A dog starts barking, louder and louder, as if it is getting closer, as if it is tracking me down.

I have to answer. I have to do something.

"Hey!" A gruff voice calls. A shadow runs along the window. "Hey, it's me! I know you're in there!"

It's worse than I imagined.

DEMI

I hook the body with my hands and drag it into the corner. Her wallet falls from her pocket. I kick it under the sofa. I pile pillows to distort the body, cover everything with a blanket from the back of the sofa.

He knocks again so loud, I'm afraid the woman upstairs will hear.

"One second!" I call. I rush to the door, then glance back at the body to make sure it's fully covered. I think I see whispers of the strands of her hairs on the floor, then realize it's just the fringe on the blanket.

"Open the door."

I fumble with the lock, swallowing hard terror. I don't know what I'm doing, what I'm thinking. The dog is still barking wildly in the canyon, my telltale heart.

Michael is standing on the patio. I don't think I've ever seen him stand straight. He is always stooped, as if trapped in a world too small for him. At his full height, he is shockingly tall.

He is swaddled in his tattered blanket. He moves with the swagger of someone at the end of their rope. He opens the screen, steps into the apartment. His eyes move quickly, frowning at the weird art, the statues and the carved bookshelves.

"Is she here?" His voice drops as if she wouldn't have heard him pounding on the door. His eyes flicker toward the bedroom.

"No," I breathe. I lock the door behind him.

He smiles and his limbs loosen, right at home. He follows the hum of the refrigerator. He flicks on the kitchen light and opens the fridge. "Beer!" He takes one out, cracks it open. He offers it to me first.

I shiver, repelled. Maybe a little jealous of how easy it is for him to take. "No, thank you."

"Where is she?" He takes a long gulp.

"How did you find me?" I counterquestion.

"I followed you the other night." He sips speculatively. His eyes follow the ceiling. "I was gonna wait for you but I ended up in this garden. This place is like a maze. Have you seen the castle on the hill?"

I stop my eyes from darting to where her body lies. It's lucky that it's dark. It's lucky that it's crowded and strange and haunted, the type of place a body fits right in.

"She's away. She had to go away for a while, but she wanted someone to keep an eye on the place."

"A while," he repeats. His smile disappears fast but I see it. Never kid a kidder. He knows something is wrong, but he could never guess what.

Suddenly, he crosses the room, walks right toward Demi as if guided by God. He stops just short of her body and he looks at the books on the shelves.

"The Kid Was a Killer," he reads, removing the red-and-yellow paperback from the bookcase and slipping it in his back pocket. "I bet you she doesn't even reads these, bet you she has them because of the way they look." He talks like Robert De Niro in *Taxi Driver,* but it's an act I think he cultivates. In LA, the best actors are acting for their lives.

"I bet," I repeat, trying to think of how I can get rid of him fast.

"Hmm." He takes another long pull of his beer; then he swivels, lands hard on the couch. "Makes sense, you house-sitting." He stretches his arms along the back of the couch. "Who doesn't invite a homeless woman they just met to house-sit?"

198

"I'm not a homeless woman," I snap. "And she wanted to help me. She said I was smart." The screech of the gate ricochets down from above.

"They know you're here?"

"Of course they do."

"What a lucky break." He pounds his chest until he burps. "When's she coming back again?"

"Soon."

He nods, finishes the drink and sets the can carefully on a coaster. Then he stands. "Lot of nice things in here. Valuable, I bet."

"You can't take anything. She's coming back."

He nods again. "Still. She couldn't notice everything. Things go missing all the time. Maybe just something small? What do you think?"

"No." I set my chin.

"Jewelry. A little ring or something. Something she wouldn't notice."

I swallow again. I feel stiff all through me. I feel stupid. This was all my fault. I shouldn't have gone to the market. I shouldn't have left the house. I should have locked the doors and hid.

I go to the jewelry closet; I slide out one thin drawer.

Michael lights up and strides over. He

smells of urine and my nose twitches like I am twenty-four hours and a whole world away from him.

"This one. And she probably won't miss this either. Or this." He fills his pockets with diamonds and pearls. He can't help himself.

"Michael, we don't want to get caught."

"Sure," he says, sliding one last ring into his pocket. "When she comes back." His eyes have this beautiful lilt to them, lashes darkening on the ends. In another life, he could have been anything: a drowsy playboy, a Greek archer, a serial killer in a broken-down truck waiting for his next victim to come along and save him.

Like every poor man I know, like my father, he has this air of having chosen this life — more, of having stolen it. But I guess that, like my father, there are nights when it hits him — all at once because he stores it away — that none of his dreams have ever really come true.

"You should leave," I say. "I'm not supposed to have anyone over."

He doesn't look concerned. "I want a shower."

"What?"

"I want a shower. You got one." I feel a wave of guilt. It will be the death of me.

"Okay. But we have to hurry." I lead him

quickly to the bathroom, eager to get him away from the body at least. I forget about the door until it stops me in my tracks.

It yaws like an abandoned horror movie set.

He goes still, clicking the scene into place. "What happened here?"

"I don't know," I decide, looking at the axed door. "It was like that when I got here."

He clucks his tongue, then passes through the busted door and shuts it behind him. I can hear every move he makes as he takes off his clothes, as he climbs into the shower. The steam oozes through the break in the door, filling the house with a balmy hothouse scent.

My ears go hot. My mind is sealed in panic but most of all I just feel guilt, guilt at the disgust I have for him, the anger that he is here taking what is meant for me.

When he comes out of the shower, he still looks dirty, but now he glows with it. His clothes seem stiffer; his jeans hang off his slicked hips.

"I want a coat," he says. "A big warm coat."

I find him the biggest and the warmest, anything to get rid of him. Still he hovers in the house, cracks open a beer, gazes out over the falling yard, admiring the view in near total darkness.

"This is a nice setup." He turns to grin at me, cosseted in her big black coat. "I'll have to come back. Say hi."

"I wish you wouldn't."

His face crumples, like he's really wounded. "Hey, that's not very nice. You know, in a way, you owe all this to me."

I mouth the word *Sorry* but I can't say it. I move to the door, open it for him. There is a moment when I think he will ask — no, *demand* — to stay. He looks out the window, transfixed by his inability to see anything. Then a dog barks, and he flinches.

"It's creepy down here." The can makes a cracking sound as he squishes it.

To my relief, he starts toward the open door. I'm safe. Then he darts suddenly, inexplicably, toward her body like my life is a farce run on irony, and he reaches toward it, grabs at it. I squeal as he seems to wrestle with it. "I'm taking a blanket," he explains, and he jerks it hard and the pillows leap up and her face is exposed, wrenched sideways by the upset but still beautifully lit in angelic repose. "Oh, my God."

I shut the door.

DEMI

He sits on the couch. He has switched to red wine, body-finding booze.

"What were you planning to do with her?" he asks again. This is the one point he is sticking on, as if to emphasize how lucky I am that he showed up.

"I bought zip ties. Trash bags. Bleach."

"A saw?" He watches me blanch. "I gave her straight H." He throws back wine from the bottle. "It must have been something else she was taking."

I don't say anything, but I do wonder why he followed us, why he waited all day, hoping to run into me, as if he expected something like this to happen.

He scoots forward, heels scraping the floor. "You know what we should do? We should put her in the camp. I bet they wouldn't even —" He bumps the wine bottle, catches it before it falls. "I bet you they wouldn't even look into it if they found her there."

"They'd still ID her. They'd find out she's some rich woman. Then they'd care."

He slips a crinkled rectangle of aluminum foil out of his pocket, sticks a short plastic straw in his mouth and chases heroin with a lighter, then sits back with bright eyes like he's been enlightened. "We take off her fingers. Take out her teeth. I had a friend once burned to death by a heater in his tent. We could set her on fire."

"That's horrible."

He scowls. "I'm trying to help you."

I say nothing. I know he's right. I need him; that's the worst part.

He nods, as if my silence is agreement; then he runs another line of heroin and coughs. "You got ID on you?"

"Hers?"

"No, yours. We put her in your tent. Leave your bag outside with all your shit in it, personal stuff, whatever you got. They got a license, cops don't need to ID the body." He claps his hands together. "Open, shut."

"But what if they do ID it? Once the body leaves here, we lose control."

He leans back on the couch. "Do you know how many homeless people die in this city? Ha." His shoulders jerk on the laugh. "You think they ID every body? They don't even count. They don't want anyone to guess how many people *actually* live on the street."

My resolve wobbles. This isn't what I wanted. I didn't want Michael. I wanted her life for mine. I wanted control. "Maybe we should just leave. Leave the body. Leave the apartment. Take a few things with us."

He smirks. "I won't stop you."

"You're staying?"

He shrugs. "When a tornado drops a house on you, you live in it."

"What if we get caught?"

"The police don't have time to look into everything, especially in this town. People govern themselves; most of them are just too dumb to realize it." He taps his temple with his finger. He reminds me of my dad, the things I loved and hated about him, the things I envied.

"What about the people upstairs?"

"They're rich, right? They won't even notice. Rich people live in a different world." I want to live in that world. I want to live in a world where I can step over a body, not look need in the eye, where I can be free of want, free of *me*.

He gets to his feet.

"What are you doing?"

"We're doing this. We're doing it now."

205

I move to stop him; then I stop moving. He's right. If I'm going to do this, I need to do this now. And I need his help.

Her keys are by the door, where she dropped them when she came in. She has a BMW with an automatic unlock button. I can walk up to the street and find her car. I can park down below the yard. We can load up her body, take her to the camp, take her anywhere.

Maybe I can trust Michael. He has looked out for me. He directed me to a tent the night I was too sick to keep walking. In a way, he has kept an eye on me all along.

He saw me even when I was invisible. It's unfortunate that this is the best I can get.

"Okay," I agree.

He smiles from one end of his mouth to the other.

He walks to her body, kneels down over her. He peels back her sleeve, weaves his fingers around her wrist. "You idiot," he says, and I think he is talking to her. "She's not dead."

And then he slides his huge hands up her face and cracks her neck.

DEMI

I am screaming inside, screaming so loud I
can't hear anything. And it's like I'm dreaming. Then it's like I'm too awake. Then I'm
dreaming again. And I have a choice: wake
up or keep dreaming.

"What do you mean, she's not dead?" I
rush to the body. It feels warm. Warm all of
a sudden and she tricked me, she lied to
me, she made me believe she was dead.
"She's alive?"

He sits back on his haunches, stretches
toward the bottle of wine. "She was probably in a coma or something. Brain-dead."
Had she really been alive this whole time?
Did I know? How could I not?

I touch her and she's cold again and I
don't know what to think. Maybe it was the
blanket that made her seem warm. I didn't
even check her pulse when I found her on
the floor. I just dragged her away so I could
pee in private. "What did you do?"

"You saw me do it."

"What did you do?"

"You saw me do it." He sips his wine. "This could make you."

"Did you just . . . kill her?"

He shrugs "I helped you. You asked for my help and I helped you."

I stand up, move away from her. My body is shaking, wildly shaking, but that's not the worst part. The worst part is that I know it will stop eventually. All bad things do. It will stop. And this will just be yet another bad thing that happened to me. Add it to the list.

I shake my head. "This is my fault."

"This is your blessing." He takes his foil from his pocket, gently unfolds it. "That's the problem with you, y'know? You're poor-minded. You look at things and see the worst."

"You killed her."

He slips his straw between his lips. "Be optimistic."

I gag.

He lifts the foil. "Everything happens for a reason." He flicks his lighter on and chases a thick black line. "Be the reason."

The truth is, nothing has changed. Whether or not she was dead before, she is dead now.

208

My options are the same. My need of Michael is the same. I can't bring her back to life if she is dead again.

Instead, I find a hammer at the back of the cupboard beneath the kitchen sink. Michael agrees to knock out her teeth if I will cut off her hands.

"And her feet, just in case," he adds.

At first it is sickening, wrenching and disturbing. But slowly it becomes just a task, just something you do, like anything: right.

"You're fucking it up," I say. "You can't leave pieces. You have to take the whole tooth."

"I'm taking *most* of it. Do you know how deep roots go? I should just detach her jaw."

"No."

And later: "They keep breaking! I want to keep one for a necklace, but they keep breaking."

"You're not keeping one for a necklace."

After we are finished — or at least at "good enough" — we bag everything; then we shower.

It's well after midnight when I help him carry the body into the yard, where we split up. I go above to find the car while he slides the body down the hill, through the trees and undergrowth. I find the car by clicking her proximity key until the headlights flash.

As I activate the ignition and gaze at the dark road, a surge of panic rushes through me. I want to drive. I want to keep driving. I want to leave all this behind. A car like this could drive me to another world.

But I force myself to focus, to see this as a series of obstacles. Release the parking brake. Achievement unlocked.

Therapists say to take it one day at a time; it's the same with dumping a body. If you separate it into pieces, it's totally manageable. You can achieve anything. You can achieve the unthinkable.

Step one.

I move slowly down the hill, through the twisted streets. I get lost a couple times before I find the valley below the glass house, where the yard ends at an uneven fence. Michael's head pokes over the top.

"I'm gonna have to throw her over." His eyes flash in the dark and he ducks down.

Step two.

Her hand appears first, reaching as if asking me to help pull her over. She is stiff and loose at the same time, weighed down with death. And I try to manage all the pieces of her as they move in ways you wouldn't expect, in ways no living thing does.

"You're scratching her up," he says. I try to respond, but my voice is muffled by her coat, her black ski coat, the one that brushed against me on the street.

I lose my balance. She falls on top of me. She reeks of mulch and leaves with just a hint of expensive perfume. My heart races. For a second, for a minute, it's like she is embracing me and then it's like she is trying to kill me.

I can't move. I deserve to die.

Michael's heavy boots land on my side of the fence. "What are you doing?" He helps me out from under her.

"This doesn't feel real." I shake my head.

"No real thing does." He lights a cigarette, then drags her toward the open trunk.

Step three.

DEMI

Michael sits in the front seat. He inhales so deeply from the foil that he frizzles the heroin. The burned smell makes me gag.

We drive in silence toward the camp.

"Someone is going to be awake," I say. Michael sits back, starting to nod out. "Someone is going to see us."

"No one sees us." His eyelids are heavy. His lower lip hangs, a drop of spit at its center. "We don't even see ourselves." His head falls back, bounces lightly on the seat, and it is clear I am going to do this the same way I do everything, have done everything ever: alone.

I park the car at the dead end below the freeway off-ramp. I grip the steering wheel and order myself to be calm.

The camp stretches under the freeway, streams loosely across the sidewalk. You forgot to put your things away; now someone lives in them. I could go back to my tent. I could change my clothes; I could slip back in and no one would ever notice.

And there's the rub: No one would notice. I think of the people smiling on the street in the village. I think of Graham. *God. You're gorgeous.* Like he was seeing himself in my eyes.

It's pathetic. It's probably evil. But I want to be seen. I want to be somebody. I want to be rich. I want to be the reason.

I shut off the engine.

It feels like I haven't been here in years. It's been one day. And I remind myself, in another day, in another day and another day, I will hardly even remember this night.

The guesthouse is a magic box, a place that will transport me to another life. And I won't remember what it feels like to sleep on cardboard, won't know the smell of blood and urine, won't taste fear on my tongue first thing every morning or lie back dreaming of sleep. I will be someone else. All I have to do is set my old self on fire.

The car door dings as I open it.

Michael smacks his lips. "Don't forget the heater." He means the heater in his tent, the one I'm supposed to use to burn the body.

Demi must weigh over a hundred pounds, but it's suddenly easy to drag her. Adrenaline is coursing through me. I have to stop myself from going too fast, from drawing attention. And I think of my dad, how he'd walk into grocery stores and walk out with food, how he'd piss in the street with a cop watching or pinch cocaine at a park, and I think, *They won't see you unless you want them to see you. I am the architect of reality. I am the reason.*

Cars drive past, a pedestrian staggers by, but lucky for me, everyone averts their eyes at a tent city, afraid of being asked for something they *can* afford to lose. It works because I am invisible. We are all invisible on this side of the line.

But from the camp, on the curb, a single set of eyes watches me. A man nods. He reminds me of myself because he says nothing. We all say nothing. It's a pact. We all say nothing on this side of the line.

My tent is waiting for me, calling me home, door still unzipped, and I duck down and drag the body under the open flap. I leave my backpack outside, set away so it doesn't catch fire. My tent is set in a crevice away from the others, so it will burn safely, alone.

I find the heater in Michael's loftier tent. I don't know how to turn it on, let alone how to make it catch fire, but I find a bottle of vodka and I take it back to my tent and pour it over everything. Then I hesitate, heart racing, trying to pound its way free of my chest.

I look at her face one last time, because I think I should. I force myself to do it. *Mourn her,* I think. But I don't know her and I never will. So instead, I thank her.

I step outside. The cold air brushes my cheeks.

I light her on fire.

DEMI

I drive through the hills, getting lost on purpose. Michael is asleep in the front seat, unburdened, while I climb up and up into the hills, adrenaline pumping, every shadow a cop chasing me, every light a chance to be seen.

I end up outside a park cradled in the hills, looking out over the Westside, all the way to the ocean. Below me, a reservoir gleams.

I never knew there was a lake here. All my life and I never went this high. I watch it for a while through the chain-link fence. Then I exit the car with a bag of hands and feet and teeth.

I am drenched in sweat as I walk along the asphalt road that circles the lake. I feel like I have never felt, and there is something awesome in that. I can feel my old self dying, like the fire I set was inside me, but I am still carrying my body. And then, blinking through the trees with the sun, is another existence, the person I am becoming: Demi on a morning walk in the chilling air.

I scale the fence. It's easy. Everything is easy now.

I startle when I nearly run into seven deer. They all look at me, ears spread wide. I tell myself it's a good omen, even though I stopped telling myself those kinds of stories.

I walk until I reach the water; then I weigh the bag down with rocks. I wade out into the lake, alone in the middle of this monstrous city. There are bigger rocks beneath my feet and I dive down and lift them. I bury her parts underneath.

When I crest the surface, I gasp for breath. The lake glitters all around me, beautiful, laughing. It's laughing at me for being the last ugly thing in a beautiful world.

I swim to the shore. I watch the sun flush through the valley, bringing it to light. I see blood spattered in the dirt and don't know if it's hers or mine. I use her shoe to cover it.

The sun rises. I try to say a prayer but all I can manage is *You made this world. What did you expect?*

When I get back to the car, Michael is gone. I have to remind myself that he didn't vanish. He *will* come back. But the moment I think it, the thought disappears. I am free. Free of myself. Free of anything that ever held me back.

I drive back to the glass house. I do not miss a turn, the location already hardwired in my brain. I park on the street. As I am getting out of the car, I see Graham standing next to his Rolls, waiting for me.

"Demetria." He smiles, waves, then hitches his leg and climbs into his car.

And I don't even want to tell him, *No, she's burning in a break in the wall beneath the 101.* I want to ask him about the stock market, suggest we all go skiing in Aspen. I want to tell him I am just like him now. Except I earned it. I earned it the same way every rich person does: by stepping over a body.

Back at the apartment, I get down to business. I open her e-mail account and research her voice. I try to discover who she is, who I am in her, the hand in her sock. Then I find her lead at work and I send a sloppy e-mail:

This is so embarrassing but admitting you have a problem is the first step, so here goes. . . . I am drug addict. I regularly use

218

heroin, OxyContin, even fentanyl. I have used them at work. Last night I had an overdose and slipped into a coma. The people with me thought I was dead. It's only by the grace of God (Godette???) that I survived. I need to take some time out at a long-term rehab facility. I need to take a deep look at myself and figure out what went wrong, how I ended up here. . . . I hope you can support me.

I expect immediate approval; instead a barrage of e-mails comes through:

We need to TALK.

PICK UP THE PHONE

Her phone is gone. She lost it that night.

You can't do this again.

We are well aware of your issues but WE NEED YOU AT WORK.

Everyone's got problems.

I'm kind of shocked. If I'd admitted to using heroin at any of my small-time jobs, I would have been fired without compensation. I might have even been arrested.

Demi's lead doesn't care that she almost (except actually) died.

I am so incensed that I want to message her, *Hi. This is really (technically) a criminal impersonating Demi, who IS dead. PS You're an asshole.* But I really didn't steal Demi's life so I could learn a lesson about poor little rich girls.

And then I feel a different species of anger. My dad did drugs. His friends did. And they were called the scum of the earth. Demi is called back to work. There is no such thing as a rich junkie.

My finger twitches, searching for another tack.

I'm sorry. I have to prioritize my mental health.

Her response is fast: Selfish bitch. I'm turning this over to HR. Which is a little ironic.

Ten minutes later, I am hit with an e-mail from legal.

We understand that you have had a traumatic experience but we do need to see something from a doctor, as per your contract. There is a process on these things unfortunately.

And here my web design degree comes in handy because I build a person, a doctor with a website, and I message them, saying, *overdose, risk of organ failure,* trying to stick as close to the truth as I can.

Demi doesn't seem to be in touch with her parents, so I decide it's best not to say anything, but to keep monitoring the situation.

One friend from New York has messaged her on Facebook, so I write her a long, rambling message about how I'm going into rehab and won't be in contact.

Self-care! Be my best self! Gotta do me!

All phrases that have never come out of my mouth, the phrases privileged people use when they want to steal our sympathy, too.

I hit SEND and sit back. And I'm done. That's it. That's all it took.

A night that lasted a million years, one dead body, one lost soul.

The next two days are as close to perfect as any I can imagine. I keep the curtains drawn on all sides but leave the back windows open. I wear warm clothes and take long showers and savor designer food.

One night, a crazy wind picks up and howls deep through the canyon. I watch it from behind the double doors, sipping whisky, and I hope the wind keeps blowing. I hope the whole world blows away and all that remains is me and my house. I forget it's not mine — I forget it's not real — for as long as I can.

DEMI

I am cooking eggs the next morning when I hear the quick patter of steps falling toward me, a fast pounding on the door.

Reality rushes in, in stereo sound. It's the police. Of course it is. Did I really think I would get away with this? And the worst part is, it wasn't even worth it, not yet. Two days of having dinner wasn't worth a lifetime in jail.

They can't come in, I remind myself. *They need a warrant.*

But I know that doesn't work in practice. Once my dad was arrested for shouting at someone in the street. The police showed up at our door. We made the mistake of answering and they burst in, wrestled my dad to the floor. I kept repeating, "You don't have a warrant! You don't have a warrant!" But what did that matter? It was my word against theirs; they could do what they wanted.

But this time, I won't answer the door. I will disappear if I need to. I will shut my eyes until I'm gone.

"Hey! Open up!"

My stomach drops. I completely forgot about Michael.

"I'm coming," I tell him. I wrestle with the lock, not wanting to let him in.

He bursts into the living room, carrying masses of shopping bags that clink with booze. "Before you start," he says, "she went out."

He removes a bottle of Guinness and drops the rest of the bags in the middle of the floor.

"I brought supplies," he says as if I have been needing two dozen bottles of ale, three packs of sour worms and a box of Emergen-C.

"How did you get through the gate?" I ask.

"S'broken." His eyes catch mine and then he bites the cap off the bottle, spits it out on the floor.

He doesn't take the couch or any of the three chairs. Instead he sits on the floor, next to the door.

"What did you do?"

"I didn't do anything." He spreads his fingers across his chest. "I told you: It was broken. I wouldn't do something like that — I'm not like that!" The other night, he broke a woman's neck.

"You can't go through the front door. Someone might see you."

"What about you?"

"What about me?"

"You're not the tenant. What if they see you?"

I don't know how much I should tell him. I think the less the better, but I also know our wires could get crossed. "They think I'm her."

His eyebrows jump. "You're kidding?"

I shake my head.

"That's perfect! I can be your boyfriend, your brother. It's *your* house. You've got rights! You can do whatever you want!"

"The last thing we want is to draw attention."

He taps his fingertips along the bottle. "We agreed, split everything fifty-fifty." I don't remember that. "All of her assets. This is her most valuable asset." Suddenly he's a lawyer, and his eyes flash. "It's as much mine as yours." I guess that's true, because it's neither his nor mine.

He bows his head to search his pockets and reveals a hook of a scar buried in his dark hair.

I picture his hands sliding up her pale cheeks. The cracking sound that must have been her neck — so quiet, too quiet — as he put her to sleep.

Maybe she was already dead, I remind myself to make myself feel better. *Maybe he wanted me to believe he killed her so I would be afraid of him, so I would think I owed him.* My gut tells me he killed her. But when has my gut ever been right? I can't afford to be certain. It costs too much.

"There's a man upstairs, you know."

He snorts. I think of Graham in his tailored suits, breathing sunshine, like he has never had a bad day. Maybe he could smile Michael into submission. "Fuck him! If he's got a problem, I'll kill him." This seems an oversized solution, but I am beginning to see that is the magic of Michael. He contains multitudes.

He pulls three beads of drugs out of his pocket.

"You can't do that." It's like my childhood has followed me here.

"I want to listen to music," he says, untying the tiny knot of one bead, setting the others on the floor where he can see them. "Led Zeppelin." Dead-body music.

"Michael, please." This was supposed to be my chance, and it feels like I'm losing it to my past, like I'm cursed, can never escape. And it's not fucking fair. I'm so close.

His eyes catch mine, shiny in their whites. "We'll keep it down. Wouldn't want to disturb anybody."

I march to the computer. I put Led Zeppelin on Spotify.

"I'm going in the other room," I say. He takes a needle sealed in plastic and a box of Narcan out of his pockets and sets them neatly on the floor.

The house is open-plan, so there is no door between the living room and the bedroom, just a long hall. I can't escape him. I tell myself that even this is better than living on the streets. I tell myself not to be greedy. I tell myself this is enough.

When has that ever been true?

I ignore Michael as much as I can, which, it turns out, is not a lot.

He gets high and watches Pixar movies on Demi's desktop, cradled in the corner of the house. He keeps them on low volume, nodding out so he has to watch them over and over, trying to catch all the parts he missed. *Finding Dory, Toy Story 4, Cars 3.* They play in a near constant loop — breaking only for the occasional art house film to prove he is a man of taste.

He goes in and out of the apartment as he pleases. His belongings slowly filter in, too. His tent folded up beside him, his sleeping bag, even the cardboard he used to sleep on.

His most prized possessions are his "paintings." They are not actually paintings but collages, which is enough to convince him he's an artist. They are filled with cutout penises and breasts with clever words like "FUCK" and "PUSSY" written between them — in case the images alone are too obscure. Whenever he goes out, he always checks with me, oddly coy. "Hey, will you keep an eye on my paintings?" It's almost endearing, how important these hideous creations are to him.

He pawns Demi's things. We split the money. I buy food and things we need for the house. He buys heroin. He insists it's what Demi would have wanted. I can't fault him. She would absolutely want him to kill himself.

I am shocked that we haven't been caught. So shocked that I begin to feel divorced from the event, like I never even did it.

When I'm lonely, we talk. Michael is just like anyone. His mind is a network of contradictions and booby traps and strange perversions; his are just more obvious.

Like most poor men I know, he is convinced he is gaming the system. He brags about how he doesn't have to work, how he stole his brother's identity and now gets food stamps for two people, how he's walked out on multiple hospital bills.

He tells me how tough he is, how many fights he's been in; he walks me through all the strange trials of his existence, all the times he survived when he shouldn't have. That is the thing he is most proud of, his survival, as he shoots himself up and dares himself to die.

The more he tries to convince me his life is his choice, the less I believe it.

I want to be alone. It doesn't seem fair that he is invading my dream.

Every time he leaves, I hope he never comes back. Every time my eyes shut, I see him disappear.

DEMI

I am careful about our trash. I don't want the woman upstairs to see me carrying empty bottles and crushed cans, bloody paper towels and used needles, so I wait until she goes out.

She goes out only once a day, for almost two hours exactly. I keep my ears pricked for when this happens. I keep the house clean, while Michael quietly fills it up with junkie debris. I collect it, pack it away with care so the bottles don't knock together when I walk.

I wait for her to leave; then I encourage Michael to go. "Now's the best time. Before she comes back."

That afternoon, he pushes back, whining and delaying, but I know he will leave, needs to leave, because he has run out of drugs.

"I'll go later," he says.

"She'll be back later."

"So what? Have you seen her? She just

sits there like a doll."

"Her husband will be back later."

He scoffs but I know he's afraid of him. He passed him on the street once. He said he reminded him of "Christian Bale in that movie." *American Psycho.*

Now he takes another shower, coats himself in rose-scented bodywash, then puts on her long black coat. "I'm coming back," he says at the door.

"I know." The pressure ticks in my mind.

I clean the house slowly. I enjoy cleaning. It's a luxury I have never been able to afford.

Once I am finished, I slip on a pair of alligator pumps and I take the trash out. I pass through the hole in the wall. The gate is gone. They still haven't replaced it, which is strange. Michael claimed he didn't break it, but he lies about what he had for breakfast, so I take that with a grain of salt.

I think of Demi stalking the streets in stilettos with her neck snapped. Ghosts have never scared me before. In fact, I always thought it would be nice to be a ghost because you don't have to worry about health insurance. But there is something about having things to lose that makes me afraid in a different way. I used to be numb, accepting everything that came, but now I feel almost *more* vulnerable.

I walk the bag far down the street so the trash won't be connected to me. Walking back up the street, I notice a big white van parked across from the duplex. The windows are blacked out with makeshift curtains. There is a spray of dried dark liquid down one side. I wonder who it belongs to. I imagine the FBI coiled inside behind a wall of buttons and screens, watching me. Or a family of human mice piled up inside, trying to survive.

For a second, my imagination takes on a supernatural aspect. I see a big writhing octopus, the monster of my guilt, crammed inside, waiting to get out. And when I walk down the stairs, its tentacles will shoot out and chase me, blast through any obstacle.

The van doesn't fit in this nice neighborhood. I walk away from it fast, like it's chasing after me, like I brought it here.

Paranoid, I think. *You're being paranoid.*

My eyes dart to the courtyard as I pass. Light gathers in pools everywhere, like some sweet oasis. I wish I could collect it, take it down with me, set a bundle of light in the middle of the room and let it glow, illuminate everything.

I steady my hand on the railing as I continue down the stairs.

232

Suddenly, I hear something pounding, racing toward me. Denial pops like a balloon in my ears. Panic explodes and I know: They're here. They've come to get me, like I knew they would.

I leap, kneecap cracking, down the stairs and toward the woods, but it's too late. A body falls against me. I crash into the door, grasping for purchase, almost knocked off my feet. Then I smell Demi's rose-scented bodywash. *It's her! She never died! She wants her life back!*

I wheel to face her and I see Lyla watching from the top of the stairs. Then Michael pushes past me, soaked in Demi's perfume. My hand reaches out on instinct, makes a fist, punches him right between the shoulder blades.

"Bitch!" he snaps.

"Don't come back!" I snap back.

He dives down the hill, all the way to the fence. I picture Demi's body lurching over the fence. I shut my eyes until the image floats away.

When I open them Lyla is still there, dressed in clothes that seem to pull away from her, afraid to touch.

"You hit him." She looks right at me and my stomach twists. I feel sick.

Be normal, I instruct myself. *Be a human*

being. But it's too late for that. I've become something else. Or else a human being was never what I thought it was. . . . "He was trespassing."

"He was huge. Weren't you scared?"

I am more scared of her. I remember the real Demi's warning, that Lyla was "totally bonkers." She does seem a little *off.* She is like a painting where the artist got everything right except the feeling you get when you look at it.

"I'm not scared of anything," I lie.

"Do you want to come upstairs? Get to know each other?"

My instinct is to say, *No, I would not like to come upstairs. I would not like to get to know you, if there is a* you *beyond the seamless, crinkle-free exterior.*

But when I glance into the yard, I see Michael peering over the sloppy side of the fence, waiting. And I think, *What if? What if I could get more, climb higher than this? What if I didn't stop? What if I kept going?* I am so close, I can taste it. This might be my only chance.

I force my eyes away from Michael. I set my sights on her: a Hitchcock blonde, rose lipped, anatomically correct. Perfect.

I tell her, "That would be wonderful," in my richest voice.

Demi

I stand on the threshold as she opens the door and the whole house appears, all at once, like some well-harvested dream, like a house in a reality show, like someone motioned from inside the screen and said, *Come in, it's real! It only looks pretend!*

A woman is cleaning in the far corner. She looks at us, then looks away.

The light settles in pools as my eyes trace the windows, locked together by nearly seamless seals.

"It's so dark downstairs —"

"I like it," I say like she might snatch it away.

She looks at the windows and nerves grip my spine. If she looks down, she will see Michael waiting on the other side of the fence, maybe climbing back inside, maybe walking up the path, maybe opening the door. What will she think? What will she do? Seeing him will finally make her see — *really see* — me. She'll know I'm not Demi. She'll know exactly who I am.

"Do you want tea? Or coffee?" She slips into the room and my nerves go into overdrive. I am having a panic attack, as always, for no reason. But I think, *She wants to kill me.* I believe, *She wants me dead.* She is looking at me with a hunter's eyes, down a scope, as I shrivel.

"No, thank you." My twisted instincts tell me to run. Go back downstairs, close the curtains, keep the lights out. Hang on as long as I can. It's dangerous here. I can sense it. I can see it, but my eyes also want to swallow it whole. They traverse the lines of her house, eating everything. The wedding portrait on the wall, her grinning with surprise and maybe a little fear as Graham tightens his grip around her waist, smiles tirelessly, a slight sheen to his temples, a sharpness to his lips. He's packaged her off, his freshly purchased queen, and my chest aches like I wish somebody would buy me, too.

"Water?"

"I can only stay a second."

Silence falls like a gavel. All the light is tightening and I don't belong here. I should leave. A pair of his shoes is discarded in the hallway, like Graham stepped out of them midwalk. It's beautiful but frozen. It's like time has stopped up here, and if you told me she had paid for that, too, I'd believe it.

I feel like a fraud. I feel insecure. I think of the person I was days ago, dragging a body under a freeway, sawing off hands and feet. And yet here I am in a fancy living room with a fancy person, thinking, *Oooh, I wonder if she hates me! I wonder if she can sense I'm worthless!*

"So. You work in tech?"

"Yes."

"How is that?"

I shrug. "A job is a job."

"What do you like to do for fun?"

"Nothing."

"You do nothing for fun?"

I shift and peer out the windows, trying to find Michael below. "I should really go."

"Wine?"

"I don't drink." I do, but I have to keep my wits about me with her.

"Me either. I mean, hardly. Alcoholic parents. You, too?"

"My parents are dead." *Be positive.*

"I wish mine were." *What the fuck?* "They've basically disowned me." She waits for me to ask her about it but I don't want to know. It's creepy that her parents think of her as something they owned.

The trees feather and fan, dancing for the audience below. I see Michael, perfectly framed, climbing over the fence. *Shit.* "I'd better go."

"No. Please, stay."

"I can't." I can hear Michael rattling leaves as he climbs up the mountain.

"You seem very cagey."

"I have work — I have a really important work call. Sorry."

She moves as if to stop me. I freeze on the threshold, petrified. Why am I so scared? Is it because of what I did? Or is she really looking at me through crosshairs? "Did Margo put you up to this?"

My throat is dry, but my mind is confused. "I don't know who that is."

"This is her house, and yours — you're living in her house."

Stupid. That's why this is dangerous. That's why I can't come back here. By wanting more, I am only guaranteeing that I will lose everything. "Oh, that Margo. I got her mixed up. I'd better go."

"Another time." Why does she insist?

I leave. I pass through the courtyard and hurry down the stairs. I see Michael waiting down below, but in my head I see something else:

I see Lyla and me upstairs, like I have left

another me behind. We are sitting down together, laughing at some little thing — the same thing — huddling closer when it gets dark until we switch the lights on, shove the shadows back.

Demi

"You hit me," Michael says, too loud for my liking.

Quiet, I mouth.

I unlock the door, shepherd him inside.

"Take it easy," he says, suddenly unhurried. He hunkers back into his corner, makes himself comfortable.

"What were you thinking, running through the gate like that?"

"A red dog was chasing me."

"If you run, dogs chase you. Stop running." I shake out my frustration. "You can't let her see you. She's going to get suspicious."

He shrugs, runs a line of heroin. "I guess you'll have to go out and score, then," he grunts. "Pawn things. Keep this house together." He is really overstating his importance.

I shake my head. "It's like you want to be seen."

He runs another line and speaks through smoke. "She can't see me." He coughs. My eyes go up automatically. I hear her cross the floor. "You know what a rich person's blind spot is? Poverty. She doesn't have any idea what we do, how we think. Doesn't have any idea at all." He smokes some more. "We can use that."

Upstairs, I was afraid of being seen for what I really am, afraid of not belonging, but Michael is right: She couldn't see me if she wanted to, couldn't conceive of the machinations, the lies and the crimes that got me here.

I can hang on down here as long as I can, a rat picking up scraps, while Michael takes everything, while my chance evaporates. This has been my life so far. I clung to my wild dad, and when he died, I moved from place to place, a living, breathing apology. I felt bad for who I was, for all the things I wasn't responsible for and I lost, again and again and again.

I don't believe that the disadvantaged can "pull themselves up by their bootstraps"; they're born without boots. But I'm not poor anymore. I have been (re)born to privilege. And I can't let Michael or my past or my own poor-minded self keep me down.

So the next morning when Lyla insists I

241

go for a walk with her, when she denies my refusals, I capitulate. I give in. I accept.

I need to think rich. I need to think *Me.*

I am blessed.

She is the blessing.

We follow a narrow, winding road up the side of the hill. It's not the kind of path I would ever choose. The pavement is uneven, split open at the seams. Hairpin turns all but guarantee that any car will hit you; no brake could seize in time. It sends my instincts into overdrive.

She doesn't notice the danger. It doesn't exist for her. We pass cars with cracked mirrors, punctures and scrapes that run from bumper to bumper, and she just chatters away about nothing.

As we walk, the pressure of recognition slowly builds. She is taking me to the lake. Does she know what happened? Does she sense it?

The path around the lake is deserted, and it's not really a path. It's a wide asphalt road rimmed with pipes so wide you could crawl inside; you could *sleep* inside if it weren't for the thatched bars at every opening.

An asphalt road encircles the reservoir, but it's separated from the water by a fifteen-foot-high chain-link fence.

The reservoir itself is a pristine, untouched lake in the middle of a city touched by everything, touched by too much, but it is upended by a soulless dam. There is an enormous concrete ring in one end where the water drains, sucked down endlessly, that looks like the kind of place you would dump a body.

We walk along the trail together. I want to enjoy myself but can't, which could probably be the title of my memoir. Lyla stops, smiles eerily.

"Here we are."

"Where?" I see my escape routes, but I see my defense, too. *She's smaller than you are. She has a lot of hair. She is too Zen to move very fast.*

"If we lift the fence up" — she bends down to show me — "we can walk down to the lake."

"I don't want to." My heart is pounding. I know it doesn't make sense. I am panicking unnecessarily, but I need to. I need to panic sometimes and my brain says, *Why not now?*

I have flashes of forcing the bag under the rocks and it's filled with body parts, when it didn't seem that way, not in the moment. *You're not a murderer; you're a survivor. There's a difference.*

"But I thought you said —"

"I should really go back." I need to leave. I am having a panic attack.

"It's totally safe," she says. "There's nobody around. You said it was beautiful. You said it was inaccessible. Don't you want to go there? Just to prove you can?"

"We'll get caught." I don't mean for this.

"I never get caught." I believe it. "You first. You're smaller." The fence squeals as she wrenches it up. "Hurry! It's heavy," she snaps, and I'm breaking a sweat. But she doesn't know, couldn't possibly know; this is just a coincidence. A terrible collision, like the kind that happened that night when two lives happened to overlap, almost as if they were living in the same world. "Stop being so paranoid."

It's all right.

"Fine. Hold it up." The metal creaks as she holds it and I pass through. This is not what I imagined at all. I thought we would go shopping. I thought we would have drinks. If I wanted to break and enter, I would have stayed on the streets.

I face her on the other side of the fence. It feels so much like a trap that I know it can't be.

"Shit."

"What?" My heart is pounding.

"I have to change my tampon. I'll be right back."

"But!"

"Stay there; I'll be *right* back!"

This is a setup, my paranoia roars. *You were right. You're always right. Everyone is out to get you.*

I feel exposed standing next to the fence where anyone walking along the path could see me. There is no formal trail on this side, but the weeds are flattened in a line and I follow that into the brush. I am gazing out over the nervous water when I gasp, cover my heart with my hand.

Six deer are standing on the shore, with one lone buck watching over them, antlers lifted like benevolent hands. And behind them, a black trash bag laps gently against the shore, clamoring with teeth and hands and feet.

I am blessed. God really does look out for people with money.

LYLA

The security guard passes me over to the police. They Breathalyze me. The security guard seems disappointed when it comes up clean. He won't look anyone in the eye and he keeps muttering phrases like "criminal damage," "attempted bribery" and "I'm supposed to be on my lunch."

The officers look too ordinary to be cops. They have no necks. Their hair smells oily. They seem distracted and confused by their own roles.

"Should we book her?" one says.

"She broke the law," the security guard points out.

The other officer looks at me. I think they're uncertain about booking a rich white woman, like *they* might get punished for it. "I guess." He shrugs.

I try to convince them to let me off too late. Now that they have decided to "book me," they are righteous with it.

"But you just asked him if you should even book me!" I say. "It's obviously not a big deal!"

The officer seems not to remember. "Put your hands behind your back."

"You're going to cuff me?"

"You're resisting arrest." He is getting more into it now, like I am just making it more fun.

"I'm not resisting arrest. I'm just not thrilled about it." I huff and put my hands behind my back. He cuffs me and escorts me to the back of his cop car. I pull against the restraints. I might as well get some good handcuff bruises.

"You guys having a good day so far?" I ask the officers. "Busy?"

The driver's eyes flick back at me in the rearview mirror. His partner grunts. "Ma'am, this is serious."

I laugh once. "Sorry," I say. "Serious."

I am so distracted by the booking process — *Mug shot! Fingerprints! Blood test!* — that I forget about my phone call. I remember on the way to my cell and stop in my tracks.

"I forgot my phone call! I get a phone call!"

A female guard shoves me forward. "Keep moving." It's like something out of a movie.

She takes me down a narrow hallway to a

small, windowless cell. I thought I would be with other inmates in the drunk tank or something like that. It seems unfair that I have to be alone.

"I get a phone call," I tell the guard again as she locks me in. "You're breaking the law."

She just grins at me. I guess it takes a special person to be a prison guard. At least she enjoys her job.

I pace around the cell, looking for things to do. They really limit your options in jail. There is a slim mattress rolled up on a cot, a crumby blanket and a deflated pillow, like the ones they give out on airplanes. There is a small silver toilet in the corner of my cell. A barred door looks out onto the hall, but I can't see or hear any other prisoners.

The guard drops by once to deliver two identical ham sandwiches. I never knew food could taste like a punishment.

Other than the ham sandwich drop, I'm alone all day. If I'm going to be in jail, I would at least like to have an *experience.* I have never been arrested before. Like most things, it's a total letdown. I would give it one star. *Don't believe the hype! Jail is super boring! Try prison.*

I roll out the mattress and sit on the bed. I stare at the wall instead of my window.

I wonder what happened to Demi. She probably just waited a while and then went back, slipped through the hole I made in the fence. She probably thinks I just ditched her, which is only going to make her more wary of me.

I am more worried about what Graham and Margo will think. It strikes me now that this was an idiotic plan. Even if it had worked and Demi had gone to jail instead of me, all she would have gotten is a slap on the wrist. It would hardly *destroy* her life. It wouldn't make her lose everything.

I need to think bigger if I ever do get out of jail. But first I need to face the music back at home. To be honest, I'd rather stay in jail.

I sit until I think it's nighttime and then I fall asleep. I dream that I am on my own street. I see our outdoor light on the porch calling me home. When I reach the house, all the lights switch on at once. I see Graham at the dinner table. A woman dressed in black crosses in from the kitchen, carrying a serving tray. She bends over him and turns to face me. It's Demi, and she smiles richly at me and purrs, *You live downstairs. Go down.*

The cracks in the street open beneath my

feet, glowing like embers, spreading wide. I fall so fast, it wakes me up.

I'm still in the cell, but it's dark. They have turned out the lights.

I am so bored, I think I will do anything to stop it.

So I detonate myself like a weapon. I cry — heaving, crazy, wild sobs. Graham hates when I do this. *You can't scream like this, Lyla. You can't act like this.*

I think someone will come, but no one does. It's actually kind of freeing, just crying and crying with no one making me stop, asking me what I want, giving in to me.

I consider that maybe I would feel better if I didn't always get what I want.

I am released at three o'clock in the morning. They give me my phone, which has died, and my wedding ring. When I ask the desk where I can charge my phone, they say, "Not here." There is a pay phone outside but I don't have coins or a card.

I feel this uncomfortable itching beneath my skin. I feel activated, like someone has stuffed my skin with dirt.

I am in the middle of nowhere: Van Nuys. All the shops have bars on the windows. Everything is shades of gray. It smells of gasoline. Honestly, jail was better.

I walk toward a main road improbably titled Victory Boulevard. I gaze in both directions. To the east, I recognize our hills: shadowed, doomed. To the west are other hills stretching on and on. I have this sudden, wild thought: What if I didn't go back? What if I went the other way? I gaze west and I feel it, hot on my face like a fire I could walk into. I would burn away, become someone else. Who?

But Margo wouldn't let me go; I know too much. Without Graham to shield me, she would target me. Graham would probably join her. They would make it game. They would make it fun. They would leave me wrecked.

I have made a point of avoiding looking into the tenants after Graham and Margo are done with them. It hasn't been hard. We don't exactly run in the same circles. But one time, by accident, I met one of their victims on the street. They were living on the street.

"You're that girl," they said, finger shaking as they pointed like they couldn't quite place me. "You saw what happened. You know what happened to me."

I offered them five dollars from my purse. They refused it, so I put in an extra twenty. They took that. It chilled me to know that

251

was the price — that would be the price — of pride once Graham and Margo were through with me: twenty-five dollars. Not even enough to buy a jug of milk, probably.

The prospect of going home to Graham, telling him what happened, is humiliating. He'll make me tell Margo. She'll say she was right. I'm not like them. I don't belong. And what if Graham believes it? What if he decides she's right? Game over.

I can't deny that things have not been going well with Graham for a while. Maybe from the beginning. But like other couples have children or jobs or hobbies to distract them from their imperfect pairing, Graham has the game. I let him play. I tolerated it. I didn't interfere. Until Elvira. That is when the tide well and truly turned. That was why they decided it needed to be my turn. Graham needs me to prove that I'm on his side, needs me to prove that we are the same after all.

But what if we aren't the same? What if that isn't the reason I fell for him? What if, like every woman ever, I wanted him, *needed* him, to change? And he can't. He won't.

Why was I ever even friends with Elvira at all? I knew I was interfering, knew it wouldn't last. Yet I kept on going to her, out

252

even take off his clothes. His lips are on mine. His hand slips between my legs. He pushes me against the wall, first softly, then roughly. My brain rattles, like I am waking up, coming home only to find that I have landed in a strange new territory.

"I can't believe you went to jail," he growls. "That's so fucking *hot.*"

"I love you." He kisses me on the jawbone. We are in bed together at noon, like it's a Sunday and we're hungover, a million years ago.

Graham isn't going to work. He is hanging all over me like he just invented me, twirling my hair around his finger, kissing my cheeks, tracing my collarbone, sucking my neck. He is wearing the cashmere sweatpants I got him for Christmas, a soft T-shirt with an overstretched neck. We are like an ordinary couple finally. I want to enjoy it but I am distracted. I can hear Demi downstairs, taking one of her endless showers. Graham wants to know every detail.

"My little criminal mastermind." He kisses my fingernails.

I start with the metal cutters.

"Wait." He pulls away "You were trying to set up Demi?"

I prop myself up on a pile of pillows.

"Well, I wasn't trying to get *me* arrested."

"And you ended up in jail?"

"It was a stupid mistake." I observe my fingernails. The paint on my left index finger is chipped.

"And a stupid plan. Trespassing? The worst they would do is slap her with a fine." Like he knows everything. Except he's right this time.

"I know that now. I've never *been* arrested. How was I supposed to know? I did say she might have a gun."

"Did you give her one?"

I shake my head. He looks disgusted. So much for our idyllic morning. I should have waited to tell him. I should have lied.

He's right. It was a stupid plan. I wanted it to be easy. I wanted it to be over. He is scanning my eyes, as if reading my thoughts. He flounces out of bed in annoyance.

"I've never done this before!" I add in undertone, still loud enough for him to hear, "I don't want to." I pull my knees up, try to look small. "Can't you just do it?"

"Of course I can," he says, taking off his shirt. "That's not what this is about. It's about you proving yourself." He drops his pants. He is scolding me in his underwear, and it's a credit to how handsome he is that he looks sexy instead of ridiculous. "You went against the family. How can I trust you? How can I ever trust you again?"

"You can trust me." My voice is reedy. I thought maybe this directive was coming from Margo, but hearing Graham now, it's clear it came from him. He doesn't trust me. If I don't get his trust back, I will lose him, his money and probably *my* life.

He marches to his closet. "By the way, we're having dinner with Margo tonight."

"Tonight?" My heart flutters. "Can't we do it another time? I didn't sleep very well in jail, if you can believe it."

He disappears into the closet. "We need to meet. Discuss the situation." Reappears with a dark blue suit draped over his arm.

"What situation?"

"The *you* situation."

"You're not going to tell her." I know he is going to tell her. He knows Margo hates me, but he doesn't see why that should affect *their* relationship. He doesn't see why anything that upsets anyone else should be any concern of his.

"I called her when you disappeared."

"Why would you do that?" He hates when I use that tone. He ignores me, slips on his shirt, buttons it all the way to his throat. I adjust my tone. "What did she say?"

He slips into his trousers. "Hmm?"

"When you told her I disappeared?"

Buttons and zips. "Wait forty-eight hours."

I know I shouldn't but I do. ". . . What did *she* think happened?"

"I don't know." He slides his arms into his vest. "You used to run away." He is referring to the times early in our marriage when I would storm out over something, use his money to check into a hotel, usually down the street, hoping he would come find me. At first, he did. But when that game got boring, he just left me to *cool off*. "She said to keep an eye on my bank accounts." He acts like he is doing me a favor by telling me the truth.

"Charming." I get hot. What if something had happened? What if I had been kidnapped? Killed? Graham would call Margo. Graham would check his bank accounts. Graham would wait. I can't even complain. It would be like telling him he doesn't love me, and I can't risk him believing it. For our relationship to work, we both have to believe the lies we tell ourselves.

"I had to call her." He puts his jacket on last, the finishing touch. He looks so divine it should be criminal. He should be the one in jail for more reasons than one. He bends down and kisses my neck. "I was so worried about you." He stands, adjusts his collar.

"Demi didn't say a word."

I sit up. "What? You spoke to Demi?"

"I ran into her. In the courtyard. I came home for lunch to surprise you." To check in on me, more likely. I did promise him a plan.

"And she didn't even mention it? She didn't even mention that she was with me?"

"No."

"She lied." She's running a game. Maybe Margo *did* put her here. I am *not* just being paranoid. I am a king and my court is filled with secrets, machinations and whispered plans. "What is she playing at?"

"Not everything is a game," he says, which is a truly exceptional statement from Graham.

It's a statement that can only mean one thing: He's lying, too.

LYLA

Margo's garden is known in all the important circles. It was even featured in *Architectural Digest*. She let me in the family photo, because even I am preferable to a swinging single son. The three of us crowded in together on the lawn with the tower behind us, the Addams family with more money and fewer laughs.

The garden is terraced over nine levels. It's themed. Each level represents a circle of hell. It's a joke, of course, rich people humor, which is always about pushing boundaries. *I can't believe you said that! I can't believe you did that!*

We usually have dinners in Gluttony, but today Margo meets us in Anger. Ha-ha.

The Anger garden is stuffed with roses genetically engineered to be a darker shade of red, black birds-of-paradise and oleander. The flowers clash, but Margo likes the friction created by things that don't go together.

262

She would rather be different than beautiful, dangerous than safe. Many of the plants that grow on her hillside are poisonous. She likes to list them as if it's an accomplishment.

We always drive to Margo's house. Graham thinks walking is barbaric. We pull around her long, circuitous drive and the house gets closer, then farther, then pounces.

One of Margo's staff arrives to park our car. I can see our garage from here. It's ridiculous.

I observe the towers and turrets as we pass alongside the house, the way they seem to puncture holes in the sky, leaving scar-tissue clouds.

"Nervous, darling?" Graham purrs. You would think he enjoys it.

Bean meets us at the top of the garden stairs with a big grin. Then she trots along ahead of us, looking back every so often to make sure we are following.

When we reach the fifth terrace, we find Margo smoking a black clove cigarette behind a white table. Margo's dinners are her masterpieces. They are always themed, but unlike Mitsi's or any other themed parties, Margo's themes seem to emanate from her, like she is the throbbing brain of the party animal. Walking into one of her dinners is like walking into one of her acid trips. You think you're going mad but really you're just going Margo.

Tonight, she is wearing a white dress with silver spikes along the shoulders, a silver headpiece that drips like silver sweat around her ears. She would look ridiculous anywhere else — but in her own garden, she looks divine. Even I can appreciate that.

"Did we catch you midbattle?" Graham says, kissing either cheek.

"Always." She smiles wide at him as he takes his seat beside her. Bean puts her paws on Margo's lap, careful to avoid the sharp bits. Margo squeals at Bean the way other women squeal at babies. I was shocked the first time I heard it. Now it just makes me nervous. "Aren't you the most beautiful girl?" she pleads with Bean. "Aren't you the *best* girl?" She bounces her hands back and forth on her lap. Bean bobs along, chasing them, delighted. "You're so *good.*"

"Nice to see you, too, Margo," I say like she is talking to me.

"Lyla." She smiles at me the way she always does, as if she has just been told a terrible secret about me and is about to spill. Bean drops to the floor, licks her crotch, then perks up like she hears something.

"What is it, darling?" Margo asks. "Do you smell something *bad*?" Bean is frozen, head cocked, ready for anything. Suddenly, she explodes, races to the stairs and bounds out of sight, wildly barking.

"What's gotten into her?" I ask. No one answers. You don't mess with Bean. Her bark gets more and more distant as she descends.

I take the chair Margo has set for me on the other side of the table. It's a dining table I haven't seen before — arctic white with a real silver inlay — and will probably never see again.

Margo ashes her cigarette. One of her staff appears behind her. "Gin martini. And what do you drink, Lyla?"

"Red wine with dinner."

"Oh, yes, she likes that Spanish crap." She smiles like a kid who's made a dirty joke.

"Mom," Graham cautions with a disarming smile. If I can give Graham credit for one thing, it's admitting his mother hates me. It's the one thing he doesn't make me feel is all in my head.

"How's my baby?" She brushes his jawline. "Do you want a cigarette?" Graham smokes only with his mother. In a few days, he will complain about his throat and say, *Why did you let me do that?* But now she slips one in his mouth, then lights it for him. "So handsome." She tweaks his chin.

Margo worships Graham like something she created by will alone. She never talks about his father; you would think Graham were the virgin birth. I once asked Graham about him and he explained that his father ran off with the maid. "Do you ever see him?" I asked. He seemed confused: "Of course not. He's dead." I didn't ask if Margo killed him. I just assumed she had.

They talk about his birthday for a while. Margo is determined to find something he wants. She does a big present every year. One year it was a biplane. The next, a yacht. Graham used each once or twice, mostly to please Margo, but they bored him. Everything bores him. He's too good for this world. Or too bad.

When I told Margo about my plan for the party, she was furious. She said it was a great idea. She said she couldn't believe *I* thought of it. "Maybe you're not as stupid as you look," she added, so I knew she really liked it. She insisted I hold it at her house: "That will be my gift."

"But it's going to be very messy," I explained. At the time I was planning to rent out an army base or something. It might have been expensive to bribe the US government, but I had a feeling it would cost less than I expected.

"Not a problem! I was planning to redecorate anyway." This is not a surprise. Every rich person I know is like Sarah Winchester: The ghosts can't haunt them if they keep on building. "Blow the place apart! It'll be a blast! It will be much more fun for Graham if the damage is real." She knows him well.

I had to accept her offer. She was right. Graham would have been disappointed with a piddling old army base. Margo's house is beautiful, stately, a castle in the clouds. And I'm not too proud to admit, the idea of destroying it thrilled me, too.

"So" — Margo turns to me now, inviting the full force of her regal costume — "you had a little breakdown?"

Black fairy lights flicker over our heads with maddening speed. "I was arrested."

"And you didn't think to call?" She rubs Graham's knee. "Don't you get *one phone call*?" She tosses off a laugh. "Isn't that the thing?"

The waiter arrives with the drinks, thank God. I take a gulp of wine. "I asked for one. Correction officers are not as accommodating as one might think."

Graham chuckles but Margo frowns. "Why is it always *you* who has the problems? Everyone else seems to get along just fine." She spreads her fingers across her chest. "I've never been arrested. And Lord knows, I've broken the law!"

"You must be so proud," I say, which she doesn't like.

"Where are my grandkids?" Margo asks, like they were here earlier. Her eyes bore into me and I want to tell her, *You don't have grandkids and you never will because your son doesn't like fucking me. Not in a box, not with a fox, thank you very much.*

I can't imagine having kids. I have my hands full with her son.

Graham rustles in his seat, drawing our attention. "You had better tell Margo everything. Every dirty detail."

I take a fortifying gulp of wine. Bean has stopped barking like even she wants to hear. "I had this idea to set Demi up. . . ."

Margo opens her mouth to interrupt when three waiters appear. "Octopus," they say, setting the tiny plates in front of us. Two asparagus tips lie over the top in a cross. A white pansy sinks in black ink.

"Thank you," Margo says. "We'd like the next ten minutes to be undisturbed."

"Mom," Graham starts.

"Twenty." They disappear. Margo listens in stone silence as I tell her everything. Graham smokes. I feel myself shrinking, but I keep talking until I get to the end. Our plates remain untouched.

Margo stretches like this was a long, taxing story. "I was afraid this would happen."

"This specifically?" I snap. It annoys me how she pretends to know everything. You would think having money made you psychic the way she talks.

"It is her first time," Graham muses, chain-smoking blithely.

"She's not one of us," Margo dismisses his remark. "She never has been." Her hands drift over my form. "She doesn't have the killer instinct. It's only a matter of time before she tries to *save* someone else." Margo picks up her knife. "She's a liability."

"I'm not," I insist. "I've kept all your secrets. I've never said a word."

Graham clears his throat. My husband the great mediator. "I hate when you two argue," he says, but that's not true. He loves it.

Graham loves conflict. That is probably why he married me. Not because I conned him, like Margo seems to think. Or because I keep his secrets. He married me — he just *had* to — because his mother hated me. His life has been too easy. I watch him stretch back and smoke, the picture of indolence. That is why he gave me a gun and doesn't fix the gate, why he thought it was sexy that I went to jail. He wants to get his hands dirty.

"We're not arguing, darling. We're just chatting," his mother says. "*Girl talk,* isn't it, Lyla?"

"I don't see how what happened to Elvira is my fault," I snap, breaking character.

Margo's metal chair scrapes the stone floor. "You warned her."

I keep my mouth shut. I remind myself that she doesn't know. She is just good at guessing. I don't remind her that she warned me on my wedding day: *No one will ever offer you something of more value.* But the truth is, I did warn Elvira. It was my fault in a way.

The conversation happened by the fountain, ironically enough. I caught Elvira sitting there that night alone, staring at her own reflection. I didn't know exactly what Graham got up to when it was his turn. I knew about the game but I didn't want to know the details. I prided myself on being sophisticated. Some wives look the other way when their husbands have affairs. I look the other way when my husband crushes people's lives. But I didn't want him to crush Elvira. I liked her. She reminded me of myself, the parts that had deadened with time.

She looked up at me, water shadows undulating on her face, and she said, "It's not that deep, is it? It looks so deep sometimes."

I was slightly spooked, so I hurried toward the door. "Do you want a glass of Moët?"

"No." She paused. "I get so sick of it, don't you?"

I laughed. "Of course."

Then she plunged her arm into the water suddenly, all the way up to her elbow, soaking her jacket. She held her arm up, victoriously, marking the waterline. "This is how deep it is."

I was frozen by the door. "You're right. They're bad people," I warned her. It was interesting that I said *they're* and not *we're*. Margo would have found it interesting.

"Who?" she asked, like she found it interesting, too.

"Them. You know, rich people."

She just laughed. "Good people are boring." It was something I would say. She was just like me, really. And now she is dead.

At the time, I laughed, too, and I went

inside. Graham was standing by the door, listening. I was caught. "What was all that about?"

"I was just making conversation —"

"You were interfering. Do you want me to lose?" Like he could ever lose.

"No." I just didn't want her to.

Graham and Margo are both watching me now, awaiting my reaction. An admission of guilt, a plea for mercy, nothing would be enough. They don't know what they want. They already have everything.

Graham stands up. "If you'll excuse me, ladies." I have to remind myself he is going to the bathroom. This is not a tactic. This is not a plan.

Margo and I watch him disappear up the stairs. As soon as he is out of earshot, Margo lights another cigarette. Bean has gone quiet. I'm about to ask where she is when Margo announces, "He's bored," like it's a death sentence. She ashes her cigarette too early. "He's been bored for a while now."

"You're such a dear to care so much," I growl.

Smoke spools from Margo's nose, dragon-like. "You're going to lose."

My nerves coil. "You set me up?"

Margo shakes her head. "She's smarter than you. She plays dirty. Do you know how she got her job at Alphaspire? She left a trail of ruined careers behind her. She destroyed people's lives. You won't best her. She's nasty. I selected her especially for you. You're going to lose."

No one has ever lost before. There is no hard, fast rule for what will happen. But it is obvious. These people don't lose. If I do, I am not one of them. If I am not one of them, I am out. Graham will leave me, and that is just for starters. I know too much. I can't just walk away.

"Does Graham know?" It's the only thing I care about. Is he in on it, too?

"Not yet, but it's for the best. I'm doing him a favor. He'll appreciate it in the long run. Not that long." The sad thing is, I don't think she's wrong. He *is* bored. He's tired of me. I don't want Margo to be right but she is. "It's her or you." Her dimples are showing. She thinks I still have a chance. I do still have a chance.

If anything, this makes it easier. Demi is nasty. She's destroyed people's lives. She's not the nice, nervous girl she seems to be. She's not a victim; she's an adversary.

I can prove myself to Margo, to Graham.

I can keep them entertained. I can shock them.
I will destroy her.

LYLA

I drink too much at dinner, and by the time we get home, my body feels tight. My muscles ache. I want to collapse into bed. Graham reeks of cigarettes. He smoked all the way home. He takes one last puff and pitches the cigarette into the dark. In California. Where the whole state is a tinder-box.

Our entryway is pitch-black.

"The bulb must have gone out," Graham mutters at the gate, looping his hand around my waist to help me, shepherding me down the short steps to the courtyard. My foot lands on something soft. It gives beneath my weight and I startle, try to back away when it caves in with a wet popping sound.

I scream. Graham flicks on his phone light. It washes over the steps and I see Bean lying on our patio. Her eyes are glassy. Her tongue licks the floor. Blood stretches like fingers toward our door.

Graham pulls me back up the steps. "Oh, my God."

"I'm going to throw up." But I don't.

"She's dead." He peers over my shoulder. "Maybe a coyote . . ."

I leave a bloody footprint on the stairs. I slip my shoe off and stand in one shoe.

"Shit." Graham's fingers play along my hip. We scan the dark: the cold stones of our patio, the sharp drop to the apartment below, the weird trees twitching. He kisses me quick on my neck. "Margo will never recover."

"We can't tell her," I say just as fast. She will think it's me. She will think its retaliation for what she confessed to tonight. Even though I was with her. Even though I have an alibi. The dog is on our doorstep. "She'll find a way to blame us." We both know I mean me.

Graham nods, but I don't know if I can trust him to keep a secret from Margo. "Maybe we should call the police," he says. "I don't think an animal would do this." A human is an animal, but I know what he means.

The police seem skeptical at first, but once Graham gets on the phone, they're convinced. Graham switches out the shattered

276

bulb on the outdoor light. He bags it.

"Evidence," he says, proud of his work.

Two officers arrive. They look like father and son, like they were cracked from the same mold: black hair, cropped pants, one neck more crinkled than the other.

They seem happy to take their time, circling the body, taking pictures on their iPhones of the dog, the broken gate. They seem like amateurs dressed as cops, the way every cop does.

The younger one bends down, brushes the fur aside where the blood is the darkest. "It looks like a knife wound —"

"We can't say for sure." They are like this on everything.

"It was probably the same guy who blew through your gate."

"That's just conjecture."

"Looks targeted."

"It coulda been anyone."

Like the best partners, they balance each other out so nothing gets solved.

Graham is walking the baby cop through the intricacies of our discovery, waving his cigarette with boozy enthusiasm. "We were just having dinner with my mother! It's the house with the tower! Up there! I noticed the light was out and then — I was helping my wife through the gate and she stepped right on it! It made a popping sound!" He slaps his hands together. I flinch.

The officer moves to the dog, points his flashlight directly at the wound as a fly crawls free. "And your gate was broken when?"

"About a week ago," I say.

He drops the light. "You should have it fixed."

The other officer peers down into the yard. "Does anyone else live here?"

"Demi." My stomach drops. In my shock, I forgot about her. What if this is her retaliation? But this hurts Margo, not me. Maybe she is setting me up. Maybe I am missing some crucial clue. Maybe this is all part of some master plan.

It doesn't make sense, and that's the scariest thing about it. I keep searching Bean's body for evidence it was me. Even though I know it wasn't. I am so sure I am being set up, so sure I am to blame, so sure this is all about me.

Graham hitches up his pants. "There's the van, too." He points through the open gate, where the van glimmers in the dark. "It just turned up one day. Can you open it? See what's inside?"

"We'd need a warrant," the older officer grunts. "Probable cause."

I shiver something loose. "Why us? Why is all this happening to *us*?"

LYLA

I wish the police would take the body with them, but I know from experience that the police expect the victim to clean up the crime scene. "What should we do with it?"

"I'll take care of it." Graham slaps his bloodstained hands together, and when that doesn't work, he walks over to the fountain to wash them.

I follow him, perching on the edge of the fountain beside him. "Do you think it was Demi?"

He cocks his head. "Motive?"

"Margo told me she was a plant when you went to the bathroom." I debated telling him, but I can't help myself as usual. I am too keen to see his reaction, too hopeful that he will leap to my defense, storm the castle, demand Margo change her plan.

"A plant?"

"Demi is a plant. Margo set this whole thing up to take me down."

"So Demi knows about the game?"

"No. But Margo chose her because she's smart. And nasty apparently. She doesn't think I can beat her."

He grunts softly. "How funny." That's it. I just confessed to him that his mother wants me to lose and all he can say is *How funny?*

"Do you want me to lose?"

"Of course not, darling. I want you to slaughter her."

Someone screams. I wheel around to find the source. Demi drops her shopping bags at the gate. They spill down the stairs: necklaces, bags and dresses. Her face is ashen. Her eyes are wide. Her shock seems genuine, or she is working hard to make it appear that way.

Graham leaps up from the fountain, races toward her. When he reaches her, he wraps his arms around her, the way he does me sometimes. It's odd watching your husband hold another woman. It's like an out-of-body experience. For a second, I am her watching myself.

"It's all right," he says, brushing her hair, rocking her gently back and forth. "It's all right." It's spooky, the way Graham becomes someone else for other people. He never does it for me. I get to see the real him. I don't always think that's a privilege.

He is soft with her. His voice is gentle. His tone is soothing. I just told him that she's a plant. I just spelled out that it is her or me. Why is he touching her? Why is he acting like he's on her side?

Even worse is her reaction. She looks comforted. She looks soothed. She sinks into him incrementally, like Elvira did, always tuned to him. He is so manipulative, it's scary. Even I still believe he's a good person deep down. *Way* deep.

"It's Margo's dog." I cross under the overhead light. "It's dead."

"She can see that," Graham scolds me, parting her hair carefully. It passes as a kind gesture but I know he can't stand a crooked part.

"Well, we're not telling Margo just yet," I say. He shoots me a look like I shouldn't be saying this. He's probably right, but it's too late. "She'll be devastated."

Graham turns to Demi solicitously. "Do you want me to walk you down?"

"I'm fine," she says. "It's just shock."

"We both love animals," Graham says as if they've talked about it before. As if I hate animals.

"Bean was the best dog," I volunteer. "Margo didn't deserve her," I can't help adding, which doesn't score points with

Graham.

Graham collects her scattered purchases: necklaces and bags and dresses. Her alibi. How convenient that she showed up with them right after we appeared. She is out to get me; everything is a part of her plan. The whole world is conspiring against me.

Graham shepherds his wounded bird to the stairs. She clings to the railing like a delicate flower, not a dangerous plant.

Everyone is playing a game all the time. It only matters when you're losing.

Once she is gone, Graham lifts up Bean's body, carries it into the shed. He's gentle with her, too.

I follow him to the shed. "It had to be her. Who else could it be?" There are only Demi, Margo, Graham and me. The rest of the world doesn't exist, is too far away to matter. "It was on our doorstep."

He lays the dog down on the floor. "Bean wasn't killed here. We saw her at the house, remember? She ran off barking. It was an inside job."

"I still think it was her." I can't explain to Graham the way Demi looks at me sometimes, like I am the trap.

"Perhaps we *should* tell Margo." I know he will tell her eventually. It's only a matter of time. He tilts his head at Bean's deflated body, considering.

"No."

He rubs the back of his neck. "What about the van? Should we open it?"

"The cops said we shouldn't," I say before realizing how stupid that will sound to him.

He steps over Bean's body and stands before a wall of expensive tools we never use. He selects a stone mallet, cocks it on his shoulder. I follow him and the mallet into the courtyard.

"What are you doing?" I say, just a little thrilled.

"What does it look like I'm doing?" He bounces up the steps, weapon ready. He comes to an abrupt stop. "It's gone."

"What?" I climb up behind him, peer around him. The van is gone. It was here when we were talking to the police, but now it's gone.

"Maybe there was someone in there," I say. "Maybe they heard us talking."

"This situation is getting out of control," he says, casually flinging the mallet into the shrubbery. "Shall we open a bottle of Moët? All this excitement is making me thirsty."

Lyla

Graham tosses and turns in bed that night, like he is the one thinking torturous thoughts. Something has changed. Margo is out to get me. It's only a matter of time before she does. Graham's bored. He'll stop protecting me. Maybe he has already. The dog and the gate and the van and the arrest. Why does every bad thing happen to me? Why *me*?

What does it all mean? There has to be a connection, something that makes sense. Demi and Margo and Graham and me, and maybe God pulling the strings. Maybe God is punishing me, but that's silly. God never punishes people with money.

Graham rolls over in our bed. I stay perfectly still.

There has to be a way out of this mess, a way to sway Graham back in my favor. The birthday party will help, but will it be enough? Fake murder with fake ammunition. Blasting your friends with gold dust. I think of Elvira's real dead body. That's where the game changed. That's when *everything* changed.

That's the only way to change it back. I know that. Margo spelled it out: It's her or me. And the van and the gate and the dog. It has to be Demi. Nothing like this ever happened until she moved in downstairs. It has to be her fault. She is trying to unbalance me. She is throwing me off.

Demi is willing to kill. And even worse than killing a human, she killed a dog. Or had it killed. It had to be her. She wants what I have.

But even if it wasn't her. Even if it was a coyote, an accident, an act of God: It's her or me. The game has changed. There is only one way to end it now.

I'll invite Demi to the party. I'll make sure she comes. I know her weakness, and it turns out it *was* my weakness all along: Graham. I think of the way she leaned in when he held her. She trusted him, with awestruck eyes, when she won't let me anywhere near her. I will tempt her with Graham, the most delectable of us all. I'll dangle my husband from a string and get her to come. Get her to play.

We'll start the game. I will wait. I'll find

someplace to hide to make sure I don't get killed too early. I'll cheat. I'll hide someplace out-of-bounds: Margo's wing, which I'm sure she'll make off-limits. I'll wait until the game is past the point of fun, when it's dead serious. When everyone is tired and hazy. I'll find a way to separate Demi from the pack, tempt her out to the garden maybe, tell her Graham is looking for her, waiting for her, *wants* her.

I won't use Simunition. I'll load my gun with a real bullet. I can google how to "shoot to kill." There'll be so many guns, so much chaos. No one will see. No one will know. Until the cleanup crew arrives the next morning.

Margo will cover it up. She'll have to. It's her party, her house. But they'll know it was me. They'll know I won. I consider, for a moment, that Margo could try to pin it on me — the murder I commit — but that's not how Margo works. She'll be appeased. Graham will be entertained. They'll congratulate me on a plan well executed, emphasis on "executed."

Could I kill another person? It's a question worth considering. I could if I had to. If it is down to her or me. I'm not killing her; I'm saving myself. I think of Elvira, like Ophelia in the fountain. She killed. She killed the most important person in her life: herself.

All I need to do is tell myself it's not real, convince myself that it's all part of the game. That it's her or me. I can do it. I can win. I know I can. It's just a game, Graham's birthday game.

The guests will arrive.

We'll eat cake, sip champagne. Then I'll give him his present.

LYLA

Step one, make sure Demi comes to the party.

I wake up the next morning stinking with resolve. The mechanical shutters have been programmed to rise at exactly 6:05, and I watch as the house reveals itself in pieces, as the sunrise turns our modern furniture yolk yellow.

Graham flings off his covers. "I couldn't sleep all night," he says, rubbing his eyes, "thinking about that damn dog."

I remember. "It's still in the shed. We can't leave it there."

"I'll take care of it." He swings his legs over his side of the bed. The shutter rises, caressing him with light. "I'd like to mount it on a stake as a warning to whoever fucked with my mother's dog."

"I don't think Margo would like that." I don't think many people would. Graham sometimes seems to think he lives in an ancient world or else he wishes he did.

"She's going to be . . . *distraught,*" he says like that isn't a word for it. Like there isn't a word for it. "You don't know. When Muffin died, she was apoplectic. She had this woman give her shock treatments. Then she paid someone into the millions to make a clone. Turns out, they can't do that." He pauses. "Or they wouldn't."

He shoves himself off the bed and toward the bathroom. I follow him. "That's exactly why we can't tell her."

"I think she's going to figure it out, darling." Graham has the least extensive beauty regime of anyone I know. He wakes up. He pees. He washes his hands. He looks in the mirror. He's perfect.

I sit on the chair next to the bathtub while he pees. "I mean that it was at our house. Maybe we should just leave the body somewhere. Out on the street."

He flushes the toilet and goes to wash his hands. "We shouldn't have called the police. There'll be a record now."

I feel cold. "But that was your idea."

"Hmm . . ." He muses like it might not have been. He regards himself in the mirror, adjusts a single tendril of hair. Graham has so convinced me that he doesn't make mistakes that it's hard to believe this is one.

That it wasn't intentional, a way to set me up.

He starts toward the closet. I chase after him. "Can't we, like, erase it? Take it off the record?"

He flicks through his shirts, debating. They all look the same, which makes it harder to choose. "It's only going to be a problem if Margo calls the police."

"Won't she?"

He shrugs, selects his shirt. "Probably."

"But what can we do?"

He changes out of his pajamas efficiently. "There's really not a lot we can do generally, darling. We just have to let the chips fall how they may." First, he told me not everything is a game; now he is championing some laissez-faire philosophy? What the fuck is happening to my husband?

I watch as he changes into himself: blue three-piece suit, pocket square, calfskin shoes. Everything immaculate. And I realize what the difference is.

He's not being himself anymore. He's being someone else. He's distancing himself from me, hiding something. He's running a game.

Maybe all the recent tragedies weren't caused by Demi; maybe they were caused by Graham. Maybe he is punishing me, try-

291

ing to mess with me, trying to unbalance me. He hasn't fixed the gate. He hardly reacted to the dog. He suggested we call the police. And the way he comforted Demi; it was obvious that wasn't their first interaction. They seemed almost intimate.

Either the whole world is out to get me or my husband is.

I try to focus on the thing I can control: Demi. I have to win the game, put an end to all this chaos, bring our perfect life back. Graham leaves. The housekeeper arrives. I dress in my most gray outfit. Then I call all the girls, arrange a pre-party shopping trip. Then I go downstairs to invite Demi.

There is a funny burned smell that magnifies as I journey down the stairs. It smells kind of druggy but it could also be the trees, the mold, weed. Demi bounces out the door before I even reach the patio, like she heard me coming down, was waiting for me.

"Hi!" Her voice is hard. She kneads her fingers nervously. "Is everything okay? Sorry I freaked out last night. I . . . I really love dogs."

"Everyone loves dogs," I say. I don't want to talk about that. I don't know if it was her. I don't know if it was Graham. I don't know if it was God. All I know is that I need to get her at that party tomorrow night. And to do that, I need to track her, and to track her, I need to buy her a dress. I don't have much time. It's *Ready, aim . . .* "I wanted to invite you to a party, Graham's birthday party. It's tomorrow night."

"I don't think I can go." This doesn't surprise me. Anything I offer, she doesn't want. Anything I ask, she declines. This time I'm ready.

"Graham's asked for you especially." She doesn't say anything, which tells me more than she could say. "He talks about you all the time. Honestly, I think he has a crush."

"He's your husband." Her voice is flat, but I know she likes him. I know she does because he wants her to.

"Oh, no, it's nothing like that. We're practically separated. We just live together."

"He did say —"

I don't want to hear it. I take her hand to shut her up. "Marriages are so complicated. Especially when money is involved. I just want Graham to be happy. He's such a *good* man."

She blushes. "I feel uncomfortable."

"Don't. I'd rather we all just be friends. I feel like . . ." I take a deep breath, reset my bullshit meter. "We were destined to meet, all of us. Don't you sometimes think fate is

293

just guiding your life?"

". . . I think money is," she mumbles.

"Exactly." I smile. "Fate is money."

LYLA

We take my Rolls-Royce down to meet the girls. Graham bought it for my birthday last year when he was particularly happy about how a game turned out. He got a man hooked on fentanyl. The man left his wife and children to live in the guesthouse. He is currently living on the street. Or dead. The car is gray, my signature color. The one I had before was taupe.

We meet the girls at the secret rooftop bar in Sunset Tower. Only monsters shop sober. These girls shop trashed. They spend more time drinking than shopping. When I arrive with Demi, they all flock around her, exclaiming over her shoes, her coat, her bag. So much that I know they don't like any of them. This is a tough crowd. They know Demi is from the guesthouse. That she's a charity case, relatively speaking. They liked Elvira, though. Everyone liked Elvira. But her death has made them only less inclined to liking new tenants.

"So you're in the guesthouse," Peaches quickly points out so everyone can breathe easy, knowing she's worthless.

"Yes," Demi says. Her lips are even tighter than normal, which is saying a lot.

"That's so great the Herschels do that," she says, drifting away, never to be heard from again.

Posey, who likes to prove she's "down with the people," immediately attaches herself to Demi. She grills her about her life and her job and her hopes and her dreams like none of them is good enough.

"You should have been a lawyer," I note after she demands to know how Demi's parents died like the answer could put her in prison.

"I'm just being friendly." Posey flashes an animal smile. No wonder she dated Graham.

Demi shoots me a grateful look. She doesn't drink. She doesn't talk. She just wants this to be over. I could shoot her now; it would be so easy. She's just standing there, curled in on herself like a scared little mouse. Then I remember I would definitely go to jail if I shot someone point-blank on a hotel rooftop. Sometimes it's hard to remember where the game ends and the outside world begins.

"I want to hear more about the party," Mitsi says. She is dressed in some over-designed black-and-white dress that probably costs twice as much as one that would actually flatter her. "Does Graham know what you're planning?"

"No, it's a surprise — and nobody here tell him." As if Graham would ever entertain any of them for more than a minute. Everyone gathers around me as I explain the setup: the guns and the gold-dust Simunition, how Margo has agreed to let us have the run of the house. I am mid-explanation when I glance at Demi. Her face is slate white.

"That's wild! That's just wild!" Peaches says, because she doesn't understand anything I just said. None of them does. They think it's overkill. They think it's too much. But for Graham it might not be enough.

"I'll be going home straight after dinner," Mitsi says. The saint. "I don't want to be around the boys when they get crazy!"

"It sounds a little dangerous," Sienna says.

"It is a little dangerous," I say. "That's what makes it fun."

"You're just trying to impress Graham," Posey snips. She's entirely correct.

"He *is* her husband," Peaches points out.

"I think it's sweet." She makes a face. "I just wish Henri wasn't playing. No offense but Graham is kind of a bad influence on him."

"Graham's a bad influence on everyone," Posey says.

It strikes a chord. I've never been honest about Graham with Posey. Of course I haven't. That would be weird. It's awkward to even acknowledge that you dated the same person as someone else — loved them, pretended they were the only one for you — let alone have an actual conversation about that person with them. But I do wonder if she has some stories that would sound like mine.

I glance at Demi again. She looks uncomfortable. As always.

"You'll have to play," I tell her.

"No, thank you." She swallows, watching the bubbles rise in her untouched champagne. "It's not my kind of thing."

"But you must." She will.

"I don't like violence," she says in this sanctimonious thread of a voice.

I scoff. "I saw you punch a homeless guy." The more she acts like a good girl, the surer I am that she is not. Margo said that she was nasty, that she left a trail of bodies on her rise to the top. This curled-in quiet is all an act. It has to be. A solid act, but still an act.

"You punched a homeless guy?" Peaches snorts. "Isn't it usually the other way around?"

Sienna starts laughing suddenly, hysterically. I think she's had too much to drink.

"I'll play." Demi's voice is so quiet, I don't think the others hear the edge. But I do. She says it again: "I'll play."

"Hooray!" I say, toasting her untouched drink. "You won't regret it! It's going to be so much fun." I temporarily forget it won't end well for her. I'm just glad she capitulated.

"What do I get if I win?"

I sip my champagne, nudge her playfully. "What you always get." I smile, then quote her own words back to her: "To keep playing."

Demi hates my friends more than I do. It's hard not to like her for it. We have all relocated to a private shopping room at a boutique on Rodeo Drive. My friends are still stuck on the homeless thing.

"My mom says they're all, like, millionaires," Peaches says, drunkenly twisting around in front of the full-length mirror in a beige taffeta dress. "That it's just a lifestyle choice."

"That's a lot of fucking millionaires," Demi grunts. She is slumped on the lounger beside me. I chose our outfits ages ago. Demi seemed perfectly happy for me to buy and pay for everything. She didn't raise an eyebrow when I said I'd have it sent to our address.

"I once saw a Rothschild busking on the Third Street Promenade." Peaches scoots in beside Mitsi, wearing the same taffeta dress and looking just as bad in it.

"Oh, my God!" Mitsi clutches her heart. "What were you doing on the Third Street Promenade?"

I nudge Demi's waist. "Let's go have a cigarette."

"I don't smoke."

"Neither do I," I whisper, dragging her up by the elbow.

I take her out to a private terrace at the back looking out over a parking lot. It smells like gasoline.

"Your friends are horrible," she tells me.

"I know."

"Why are you even friends with them?"

"You have to be friends with someone." I look at her and I look at the parking lot and I wish I did smoke. I'm not sure why I brought her out here. It's not going to help me kill her. I guess I just felt bad for her. I guess I just wanted to help her. Not a wise impulse. "We're trying to figure out what happened to the dog. Any ideas?"

"No." Her voice is modulated, not too fast, not too slow. Is it a trick? But Graham is right: She doesn't have a motive. "Maybe it was a coyote. Or a car."

"An act of God," I say.

"Exactly. God's the worst."

I laugh once, fast. "Should we go back?"

"No."

I laugh again, sip my Moët. "What are your friends like?"

"I don't have friends," she says, which is kind of refreshing. "But I'd rather not have friends than have friends like those."

I find myself telling her, "I had a really good friend once. We were like the same person in two different bodies. We used to stay up late, sitting by the fountain, just talking about how horrible everyone else was."

"Why aren't you friends anymore?"

It's like I forgot Elvira was dead, how intensely it washes over me. "I guess we are," I say, because I am not dumb enough to tell her what happened. "We're just not as close. What about you?"

She looks unsure, like she is trying to decide if she can trust me, even with something as basic as this. "I had friends once. I guess I just started to feel like I didn't deserve them. Like I was raining on everyone's parade." She sighs. "I think when your life is so different from everyone else's, you start to feel like you don't belong with anyone."

My smile is genuine. "I know exactly what you mean."

It's really strange, connecting to a person you are going to kill. It's probably not the best strategy to win.

LYLA

That night, Graham has birthday drinks with friends and I have to go to Margo's house to oversee the party preparations. I have hired a crew to strip out all the valuables to protect them from any accidents. I want the party to be as out of control as possible. I want to impress Graham. We can't be worrying about Monets and Fabergés and Biedermeiers.

I drop Demi off outside the house. She seems relieved that it's over. She unbuckles her seat belt, starts to climb out of the car.

"Wait!"

She freezes halfway out of the car, leg dangling over the asphalt. I have this weird feeling, like I am dropping my daughter off at school. Like I should warn her about all the bad things when I am the bad thing that I would warn her about.

"I just wanted to say thanks. Thanks for coming."

Her shoulders are tight. "No problem." And she climbs out of the car.

She vanishes and I grip the steering wheel, feel a twisting in my stomach. I must've had five glasses of Moët, and I am stone-cold sober. What if I am sober for the rest of my life? What if that is what murder means? A kind of manic frenzy that keeps you awake forever. A hyperconsciousness that never ends. Eyes stapled open. Stomach in knots.

I tell myself it's not. I promise myself I'll sleep once it's over.

I put the car back into drive. I climb up the hill to Margo's. I haven't seen or spoken to her since Bean's accident. She must know Bean is missing. She must be distraught.

As I arc into the drive, I see Margo. She is dressed in a bounteous white nightgown that ripples in the breeze. She looks like Lawrence of Arabia wandering in the desert of her terrace. My housekeeper is beside her, arm looped in hers, her guide. What. The. Fuck?

I pull up beneath the terrace and leave my car with her valet, who looks troubled. "I think she's losing it," he says under his breath as he climbs into the car. He doesn't speak to me directly, doesn't look me in the eye, so for a second it feels like he could mean me. Or both of us. Or all of us.

I take a deep breath, straighten my dress and march up the steps to the terrace. The sky over our heads is dark and milky with clouds. The perfect setting for these two wanderers. There are chicken bones scattered all over the ground and what looks like bloodstains on the marble. My housekeeper is lighting sage. She has acquired several new necklaces and a heap of scarves.

I don't know what she is doing here, but if I tell Margo she is my housekeeper, she will probably make me fire her. It's so hard to find good help. Plus, Graham really does like her cooking. Luckily, my housekeeper looks just as shocked to see me as I am to see her, and I think she is just as keen to keep our connection secret.

Margo grips my housekeeper's elbow as she waves the sage over her head. Margo has pressed pause on her skin routine and aged at least ten years. Deep lines squiggle in snakelike patterns across her face. There are dark circles under her eyes.

She loved Bean but it's more than that. I remember what Graham told me about the last dog: clones and shock treatments. It's about more than a dog. It's about control. Margo is used to controlling everything: the light, the mood, the weather. She is so used to getting her way that she can't stand to lose anything.

"Bean is dead."

My stomach drops. "I — What? Why do you say that?"

"Viola told me." She squeezes my housekeeper's hand. I can't remember her name off the top of my head but I don't think it was Viola. It was something too pretty for her.

"I don't know how she could know that," I say through gritted teeth.

"She's a psychic," Margo says. "Don't be fucking obtuse."

I want to ask this next question privately but Margo is clinging to this woman like she will fall without her. "Where did you two meet?"

"She showed up at the house this morning. She said she had a vision of Bean. She described her exactly. Didn't you?" Margo shakes her wrist encouragingly. My housekeeper killed the dog. Then she left it on our doorstep. Some housekeeper!

Now she's using Bean to climb the ranks. It happens all the time when you have money. Your staff gets ideas about moving up. She killed the dog — maybe on purpose, maybe by accident — and where others would see a body, she saw an opportunity. Why be a housekeeper in a glass house when you could be a psychic in a castle? I don't begrudge her it. I like a diverse résumé. But she had better keep cleaning my house.

Margo grips her arm, desperate, then wails, "She said Bean was crying out for me . . . *in hell*!" I don't know what terrible things Bean could have done to deserve that fate.

"I didn't think you believed in hell," I say.

Margo rolls her eyes at me. "She knew things about Bean that no one could know."

I have always found that rich people are ridiculously inclined to believe in fate. I guess because they like to believe that the providence of their wealth is divine, to justify hoarding it. Still, this is a wild pivot for Margo. She looks completely mad. She's going to ruin Graham's party.

I am tempted to expose the reason my housekeeper knows so much, but of course that would implicate me and Graham. I would be punished. I'm pretty sure Graham wouldn't.

I turn to my housekeeper. "And how do we get her out of hell?" Might as well be proactive.

"It's a punishment." Her voice is deeper than I remembered, more portentous. She is really taking to this role. I recognize the star and the moon and the cactus around her neck. She has added a guitar, a branch and a cowboy boot. "Someone in this house has done something terrible, and Bean is being punished for it."

"No!" Margo moans. She's a mess.

"This is Margo's house," I point out. I like the idea of Margo being punished.

"Not here." My housekeeper shakes her head with witchery. She presses her chipped nails against her temple. "I'm seeing a fountain."

What exactly is she playing at? I hired her *after* Elvira died. Maybe she spoke to the previous maid? Or maybe there was evidence we left behind; maybe she found it when she was cleaning and is using it to fuck with us.

"A girl died in the fountain," Margo says before I can shut her up. I am pretty sure she has paired her grief with a very strong cocktail of drugs.

"That's it!" My housekeeper waves her hand decisively through the air. "This whole house is cursed."

I set my jaw. "How can we lift the curse?"

She meets my eyes. "You can't. It's too late for that."

"Elvira," I say. "Her name was Elvira. She was my friend."

"We all loved her dearly," Margo inter-
jects, undermining my sincerity. "It was terrible, what happened . . . but it wasn't
Bean's fault!"

"Everyone will be punished," my housekeeper says. How ridiculous! As if a curse
could ever take them down. Hell has nothing on these people.

Even Margo, sopping mess that she now
appears, could pull herself together in an
instant. Even her grief is a power move. She
can afford to act insane. She can relish it,
indulge it, throw money at it for as long as
she wants.

My housekeeper doesn't understand these
people. I should expose her, but she can
expose me. If Margo finds out I lied about
Bean on top of everything else, she will end
me.

So I smile a genuine smile and tell her,
"Margo's so lucky to have you!" Margo just
grunts, because she doesn't like me to smile
for any reason. "If you'll both excuse me, I
have to check in on the party preparations."
I start toward the house.

"I sent them home," Margo croaks.

I stop in my tracks. "But . . ." I swing to
face her. "You're going to ruin everything! I
want it to be chaos! We can't be worried
about statues and artwork and crap!"

"I don't care about any of it." Margo flicks her jewel-weighted wrist. "I want it all destroyed. I'm leaving this place."

"You can take your things with you," I point out.

"No. You heard Viola." Margo squeezes her hand encouragingly. I scan the blood and chicken bones scattered across the marble. I realize what Margo loves about her: chaos. But chaos under her control. If someone can take Bean from her, then Margo will go one better: She'll take everything from herself. "This house is cursed. I don't want any of it." Margo sniffs. "Maybe a sacrifice will bring my darling Bean back."

"I don't think destroying priceless artwork is going to bring a dog back from the dead."

"Maybe not." Margo pats Viola's hand. "But it won't hurt. We'll call it a wake."

I huff. "It's supposed to be Graham's birthday party. You're going to ruin it with all this *death*." I wave my hands at the blood on the ground.

"Don't worry about your silly party — as if I'll be attending! I'm in mourning." She gestures to her nightgown. "I'm going to stay in my rooms. Bomb the place, for all I care! You have no idea what it's like! You've never lost a dog!"

"Bean was a good dog," I allow.

"The best!" she hisses. This may not be a bad thing after all. Let Margo stay in her room. We can have the run of the house. Graham will like the party better with all the artwork hanging, all the statues up. It will only make it more fun if the damage is real, the destruction irreversible.

"If that's what you want."

She pulls my housekeeper closer. "I want my darling Bean back. That's the only thing I want." She drops her head on my housekeeper's shoulder. "Life is so unfair."

LYLA

I am asleep when the sound of someone attacking the door infiltrates my dreams. They're kicking it, scratching it, clawing at it. My first dream-soaked thought is that it's Elvira, risen from the dead, trying to get back in. Then it's Demi. Then it's Margo. Then I'm awake, and it's Graham.

I throw the covers off, swing my legs over the side of the bed, hurry toward the door. The banging gets louder. The wood moans in protest. My eyes drift to the side table, the gun in the silver tray. I remind myself he's my husband. I don't need a gun.

I unlock the door, open it to find Graham ready to hammer it with his fist. Even in the weak outdoor light, I can see his hands are dark and pulpy. Tomorrow, they'll be bruised.

His suit is torn. He reeks of cigarettes. I'm not surprised the boys got him drunk, even though they promised to take it easy.

The party is tomorrow. He's going to ruin it. Everyone is falling apart. First Margo, now Graham. The fountain glitters behind him, reminding me of what my housekeeper said. What if we really are cursed? But that's silly. It's like I said to Demi: Money is fate. We have money; we have fate.

He blinks at me, then speaks with a fat tongue. "Why is the door locked?"

"Why do you think?" I keep my voice even.

Graham kicks the stoop for no apparent reason. "Don't be a bitch, darling."

"We need to fix the gate." If he thinks I'm a bitch, I might as well get a jab in.

"I'm *never* fixing the gate!" He raises a fist victoriously.

"Why not?"

"Because, darling, somebody broke it." He calls me "darling" in excess when he's drunk. "I'm daring them to come back. Break my house, kill my mother's dog . . . *Ha!* I dare you to come back!" he shouts at the empty street.

"Let's go inside." I slip my fingers around his shoulder. Drunk Graham is annoying, but managing him makes me feel powerful, like I can hold a dangerous thing in my hands, catch a flame and not get burned. His breath is labored. He's probably taken pills, too, or whatever designer drug his friends are currently peddling. "Come on, I want to tell you a funny story."

He is winding down, dropping off from whatever hot plateau he wandered to. He flexes his fingers in and out, admiring their pain. "I don't think anything is funny," he says so hopelessly, I almost laugh.

Once we are inside, he insists on another drink. I open a bottle of Moët to keep him away from the liquor cabinet. He spreads himself on the sofa, kicks his feet up on the armrest, then struggles to light a cigarette with his solid-gold lighter. "Fucking lighter fluid!" he complains.

I'd better pour myself a drink, too.

He has his hand over his face when I bring the drink, so I can't see his expression. I don't see it coming, but then I never do. "You're so boring," he moans. "What did I ever do to deserve such a boring wife?"

"You're drunk." I hand him a drink. He takes it.

He takes a sip and makes a face. "I fucking hate Moët."

"So do I." I sip mine and take a seat on the far sofa, away from him. I should go to bed. I should leave in a huff and check into a hotel. But even now, after everything he's done to me, after everything he's put me through, I'm tied to him. I want him to like me, need him to love me. For his money, for his beauty, for my punishment — I don't know. I'm a bad person, and he is the bad in me.

"When I married you, I thought, 'This is a woman who will never bore me.' But I'm *bored.*" He says it like it's the worst thing in the world.

I wiggle in my seat. "Wait until you see what I have planned for tomorrow. You won't be bored then." I try to make my voice sound firm, powerful, but I am starting to doubt myself. Maybe Moët isn't enough. Maybe blowing apart a mansion isn't enough. Maybe murder isn't enough.

"Whatever." He downs the entire glass, then drops it on the floor so it shatters. "What-*fucking*-ever."

I down my drink and stand up, straighten my pajamas. "I'm going to bed. Your birthday is going to be unforgettable. You'll see." I start toward the bedroom.

"You can't even do a simple thing." I stop. I always do. He slides his hand from his face. "Can you? I ask you to destroy some bitch's life and instead my gate is broken. My mother's dog is dead —"

"None of that has anything to do with Demi."

"Of course it does! Of course it does! Demi's haunting us. She does things without even doing them!"

I hold my ground. "Wait until tomorrow — or wait until you see your present. Then tell me I'm boring. Then tell me you're bored."

He puts his hands over his face again, speaks into his fingers so the words are muffled. "You're not one of us. You have no idea how hard it is when everyone expects you to be like them."

"I am one of you. You'll see tomorrow." I reach the door and check if he is going to follow me. He always does. He needs me as much as I need him. He has to.

"I killed her." For a second I think he means Demi and I feel this wild terror shoot through me. I don't know if it's because I want or don't want it to be true. His hands slip from his face and he looks so young, so beautiful, like this is the source of his beauty. "Elvira." He shakes his head like a child who broke his toy. "I was so bored. I was just *so* bored."

"I found her body."

"Yes, you did so well with that." His voice softens.

Mine gets hard. "You said it was my fault. You said she killed herself and it was my fault."

"Well, duh." He is not his most elegant when he is drunk. "It was Margo's idea. It's really a classic psychological sleight of hand. You make a person believe they're guilty and they never suspect you are." Of course. It's Rich People 101.

"But . . . why did you do it?"

"I told you: I was bored." He sits up, suddenly very grave "This is exactly what I mean, darling. This is exactly the thing. You just don't understand what it's like for me. We're just" — *sigh* — "so very different. It happens all the time — unfortunate!"

"Why didn't you tell me?"

"Margo didn't think we could trust you." He shrugs. "She said we had to get rid of you. I told her to give you a chance to prove yourself," he adds like he deserves a gold star. "But Margo was right. You're not like us. You don't get bored like we do. You don't like playing with people's lives."

"Wait until tomorrow." I repeat myself because this time he's listening. "Wait until you see your present. Then tell me I'm boring. Then tell me you're bored."

He nods, calming, trusting me. I turn toward the bedroom and his voice follows me. "Lyla? We aren't playing for your soul. It's just for fun."

So much of what I feel lives beneath the surface of me. It only occasionally swells and rises, when under extreme duress. When my husband confesses to murder, for example. Or when I have to wait in line. I can feel it now, this toxic rising, reminding me it's always there inside me.

I don't allow myself to even think about Elvira until I am alone in bed, and even then it comes in waves. I feel it washing over me, wrecking me, and then it's gone, and I'm me again. Whoever that is.

DEMI

Dad always taught me that most criminals are caught because they give themselves away. They want to be caught. We all secretly want to be punished for our sins. We think that we are bad people when really we are just people. We hate our baser instincts, but this is anathema to our survival. We punish ourselves. The way to steal is to not believe you are stealing. The way to take is to believe you deserve it. The way to survive is to believe you'll never die. And it works to a point.

This might be that point. I am carrying a bag of water-bloated hands and feet and clicking teeth down the street in the Holly-wood Hills. I try to look innocent, blessed. I try to look rich.

My heart is racing. The heavy bag is cutting marks into my palms. I have no idea what I am going to do with these hands and feet and teeth once I get them home. I don't think about that. If I separate it into pieces, it's totally manageable. I can achieve anything. I can achieve the unthinkable.

This is step one.

I wind back through the twisted streets, trying to remember the path Lyla and I took. I don't know what happened to Lyla, and she is my biggest threat. There's a stench coming from the bag — not dead body exactly, but something wetter: seaweed, octopus, rot.

I hear the roar of an engine, magnified in the narrow space. I move from one side to the other. I pass a woman walking her red dog. The dog leaps up, barks viciously at the bag. The woman smiles and tells her, "Good girl. Precious angel."

I walk faster, steps running together until I am practically flying. I reach our street, turn the corner. Duck past the white van and through the opening. I gush a sigh of relief when I reach the courtyard. Then I see a man crouched over the bushes. His blue suit is stretched tight across his back. I can tell by the quality of the fabric that it's Graham.

I stop in my tracks. Do I turn around? Do I hurry past?

His back rises. I swing the bag toward the stairwell. It flies through the air, then tumbles wetly down the steps.

"Just picking up trash!" I explain, flinching with every sickening drop. My heart is racing so fast that my chest aches. I need help. I need my heart removed.

His voice is soft, creeping up on me. "There's a rabbit."

I have lost my mind. "Sorry. What?"

"Hiding in the bushes." He frowns lightly, like a model in a perfume ad, thinking about all the troubling consequences of smelling so good. He folds his arms. "I think it was someone's pet."

"Oh." The bag has settled halfway down the stairs. I can smell it from here. I'm sure he can, too, but maybe he's too polite to say anything. "Do you want help?" I move away from the stairs to keep him from moving closer.

"I wouldn't mind the company. You just have to be patient. It will come out eventually." He crouches down again. He doesn't have a carrot or anything to tempt it. It will probably see his expensive shoes and leap into his arms.

I walk across the courtyard, sit on the edge of the fountain.

"Have you seen Lyla?"

My heart darts. "I think she went on a walk."

"Oh. I thought I might catch her on my lunch."

"She'll probably be back soon. I would guess."

"Oh. Be careful with her," he says in an undertone; then he darts forward suddenly. There is a weak animal grunt, and when he stands, there is a rabbit in his hands. He holds it tight against his blue suit.

"That doesn't look like a wild rabbit."

"No." He cradles it carefully. "It looks like something you'd pull out of a hat."

"What are you going to do with it?"

"Margo has an animal sanctuary upstairs. Margo is my mother," he explains. "Do you like animals? Would you like to see it?"

"Um . . ." I stretch back toward the stairwell. The bag has landed under the eaves, halfway in a planter. His nose wrinkles. He takes a step toward me. "I would love to see it."

"Excellent." His smile is extra sharp. He holds the rabbit over his heart. It buries its head into the crook of his elbow.

As we cross the courtyard and pass above the stairwell, the smell hits my nostrils hard. There is no way he can't smell it, no way he won't know. But he doesn't pull a face. He just smiles at me without teeth, so dimples appear on either side of his lips.

We pass onto the street. "I'm sorry about the gate," he says. "You would think this was a bad neighborhood."

On the other side of the street, we step through a gate and into his mother's famous gardens. He leads me through all nine circles of hell, pauses at each to explain what they are, what the joke is. He thinks I want to appreciate them. Really, I just want my heart to stop racing.

"Fraud," he says. My chest compresses. The garden is meant to look like flames, with bright red and yellow and orange flowers climbing up the wall. A topiary scorpion is frozen in the fire, caught midsnap.

I point at it. "It's supposed to have the face of an honest man. Geryon, right? It has the face of an honest man but the tail of a scorpion."

He cocks his head. "You read?"

"I have a library card." What I don't tell him is that I have spent actual *years* in the library downtown. It started when I was young. I would go there to hide. Walk through the stacks, build a great pile of books, then hunker down in a cubicle — the one on the top floor next to the staff elevator was best. And I would read one book after another, as if I could read my way into another world, make it stick. I read to save my life. Someone like him, meanwhile, reads so they can misquote books at dinner parties, corner someone and argue them into submission.

"What's your favorite book?" he says brightly.

"Candide."

" 'The best of all possible worlds.' "

"Exactly."

"Funny." The white rabbit is so at ease with him that it falls asleep in his arms.

I keep following him into the garden. I guess that makes me Dante. I guess that makes him Virgil. *Anger. Greed. Gluttony. Lust.* By the time we reach the top, although I can see his glass house down below and the trees and Demi's car, I would swear we were in another world.

It even *smells* different here, although I suppose I can hold the flowers responsible for that. But the air is better. My fear has subsided. I can breathe again.

I wonder if wealth isn't a little like heroin. My dad once explained to me the feeling of being high: *You don't feel good. You don't feel bad. It's the absence of feeling. Good and bad cease to exist.* Dressed in Demi's clothes, at the top of this elaborate garden, standing with a man in a three-piece suit cradling a rabbit, I feel nothing. And it's the best feeling in the world.

I am looking at the view, drinking it all in. He waits politely.

"Why did your mother make this?"

His dimples show, and he strokes the rabbit. "It started as a joke, I guess. My mother is quite outrageous." He looks up. His eyes have the most compelling blankness. "She likes to make people uncomfortable. She's funny like that." He sighs. "She's a great fan of animals. She prefers them to people, but who doesn't? Let me show you."

I imagined the animal sanctuary would be like a kennel, with wire cages and boxes, but it's not. The rabbits hop freely in a rabbit field surrounded by a low rock wall. A circular barn holds miniature horses and goats and alpacas. It's idyllic and pastoral, the way rich people imagine farms to be.

At the rabbit enclosure, Graham struggles to extract the bunny from his arms.

"Do you think the rabbit came from here?" I ask. "It likes you."

"Do you think?" He removes it nail by nail, then deposits it on the lawn inside the fence. "I suppose it could have come from here. My mother is very careful but sometimes the staff's children like to play with the animals." He swings his legs over the

325

rock wall, sits down and watches his rabbit friend hop off. "I used to play here myself as a child. I always loved the animal world. Do you?'

"Yes. I mean, I never had a pet because we couldn't . . ." I stop myself from saying "afford it." I remember Demi was middle-class. I remember Demi. I was so distracted by his wealth that I forgot. The air is different, not just here but around *him.* Money causes amnesia. "We just didn't have any."

He nods like he understands anything I say when he can't. "I used to want every kind of animal — you know, a real Noah's ark." He frowns. "But only rescued animals, ones that didn't have anywhere to go. The ones that needed saving, you know? It's an indulgence of ours. My mother, too." The space between his eyebrows is plucked with worry. "But then I realized, you know, people need saving, too." He looks at me. I mean, really looks like he can see everything inside me, like he is processing my charac-ter, analyzing my weaknesses, open-mouthed, eating me. "That's why we have the guesthouse. To help people like you. This world is so hard to access, you know. We want to give people a leg up. Do what-ever we can to help our tenants succeed."

I have to remind myself that he doesn't

mean it. That it's bullshit, empty words. Like the pamphlets they give out at Helping Hands. It's an image that promises you the world. Like Demi that night: *You can work for my company. Ha-ha.* He doesn't really mean it.

And even if he did, I am not who he thinks I am.

"That's so nice." My jaw throbs, as if remembering pain. I want to be Demi so badly. I want him to save me. It's so easy, standing here at the top of a beautiful garden, beneath a house shaped like a castle, to believe that he is divine, that he is God, reaching out, if only I would let him. Like it's my choice.

I have to remind myself Demi is dead. She is not a person I want to be.

"We selected you." He keeps his eyes trained on the view but he reaches out blindly, grabs my hand. "Because you're special." He squeezes my fingers with his money hands.

I take in the whole view, dare myself to remember it, remember this, forever: the lush gardens, the flowers that sway in the controlled breeze. It's like the books I used to read, except it's real.

I'm here. At a point past feeling.

I never want to leave.

DEMI

He has to go back to work, so he leaves me at the broken gate. He kisses my cheeks, European-style. His smell up close catches me off guard. It's musky, like a firehouse, like something strong and feral. He smiles and his dimples show.

"I'm glad you're here." I watch him walk away from me, how still he seems even in motion. He presses a button. The garage beeps. He disappears inside it. I take a breath.

Then I swivel toward reality. My steps are hurried, tumbling over one another. I reach the top of the staircase, grip the rail. This afternoon has been so surreal that the realization hits me like a kick in the teeth: The bag is gone.

I tell myself, *Maybe Michael.* I try to force myself to walk down the stairs, but my knees are locked, my throat closing with panic. I want to run. I need to leave *now.* While I am still free. While I am still standing. I am getting too close to danger, too close to discovery.

Run.

But then I see the garden, already taking a quality of a dream although I was there minutes ago. The flowers on fire. The bunnies hopping. The sky drifting overhead. I see Graham's lips breathe: *To help people like you.*

I need help.

"Everything okay?" I wheel around and see Lyla's housekeeper standing beside the fountain. Mascara dust clogs the lines beneath her eyes. She is wearing four silver necklaces, all tangled up together. She looks like a psychic. My future is bleak.

"I —" My tongue is swollen. I can't speak. I can't not. I force words out. "I just left some trash — *um!* — at the bottom of the stairs." I am so scared my words are slurring. I need to sit down. I am going to faint for one, two seconds. Then the world slides back into place with the pieces too tight. "Have you —"

"I took it out."

"Oh, God."

"Sorry. I thought — You could smell it upstairs."

The fountain is warbling. The sky is still blue.

"It was an animal. I found outside. Dead. Thank you."

"Sure." I focus on her necklaces: a star, a heart, a moon and a cowboy boot.

"I'm — *Demi,* by the way." I was *thisclose* to giving her my real name.

"Astrid." How do I ask her where she took the trash? She must have put it in the cans on the street. Do I leave it there? Do I go get it? I can't do it now. I'll have to wait until tonight.

"Thank you. Astrid. I really appreciate it."

"No problem." She is looking at me like she pities me, but it can't be because she knows what was inside. That wouldn't inspire pity. That would inspire a phone call. Fear. She must think that I have gross trash, that I am some gross person, leaving things to rot.

"Thank you," I say again and regret it. I don't want to draw attention. *It's too late for that,* I caution myself.

She turns back to the fountain, pierces the surface with her finger.

My knees stay buckled as I journey down the stairs. My mouth is coated in panic. When I step inside the apartment, when I shut the door behind me, my legs shake so badly that I have to sit down. I can barely see the apartment around me. I am having a panic attack, some blast of conscience. I want to cry but no tears come. I want to throw up but my stomach is empty.

It's so unfair that I covered up a murder and might get discovered. While upstairs they have a hell-themed garden more beautiful than any heaven I can ever hope to get to.

The guesthouse has shrunk in my absence. It has a sickly, close feeling: heroin and sweat and strife. I take a shower but even her toiletries have taken an ordinary caste. They smell the same as the last time I used them. There is nothing artful about them, nothing unexpected.

I sit in the living room and try to read a book, but what's the point? Books don't transport you. Money does.

Michael comes home with a bundle of flowers so decadent and disparate that I recognize them immediately. "Where did you get those?"

He plucks a vase from the end table and takes it into the kitchen to fill with water from the tap. At the kitchen counter, he arranges the bouquet, tugging a daisy, spreading a rose's petals. "Found them."

I stand in the doorway. "You went into her garden."

"You did." How does he know that?

"I was invited. I went with Graham. It's his mother's house." He shrugs, slips a square of foil from his pocket and chases a line. "This house reeks of heroin. How did you know I was there?"

"Saw you. I was in the red garden. The one with roses." Lust.

"What were you doing in there? Do you want to get caught?"

"Looking at the flowers," he says through smoke.

The flowers are already starting to die down here. "It's not our garden. You can't just walk around in there."

He snorts. "Yes, I can. You ever seen a place like that? You ever seen anything so beautiful?"

"I don't know," I lie.

He chases another line, then leans against the counter. "They hoard beauty, too, along with their money." He speaks like an oracle, a heroin prophet. "The world is a beautiful place, or it would be, but they take it *all*. All the beauty, and what do we get? Broken sidewalks and spattered blood."

"Write a poem about it." I hate when people are high and right.

"He's good-looking, isn't he?"

"Who?" Like I don't know.

"But you'd better watch yourself," he counsels me, shaking his lighter at me. "Bet you he's bad. Bet you he's worse than we are. Money is immoral. Money is the only thing God doesn't forgive." That's convenient for him.

I rest my shoulder in the doorframe. "He said he wanted to help me." My voice is weak with hope.

"He thinks you're someone else."

I trace the cracks in the molding. "Maybe if I explained to him what happened, how it was an accident."

Michael springs from the counter. "No." He pushes around me through the doorframe, carrying his flowers. He sets them in the corner, then sits on the floor beside them, just staring at them.

I should leave it. I don't know why I want to convince Michael of all people, but all people are gone. "A person like that could . . . he could get us out of this for good." I say "us" but I mean "me." Michael knows it. "He could fix everything — he actually could." That much money, you could do anything. Anything.

"No."

"You said not to be poor-minded," I

persist. "You said to *be the reason.* This is an opportunity."

He shakes his head, shuts his eyes. "Rich people are not opportunities. Poor people are opportunities. *Dead* people are opportunities. You can't trust someone who doesn't need anything. Trust me."

I want to point out that I watched him kill someone, and he wants me to trust him? But I don't want to remind him. I don't want to remind me. He will just tell me again that he did it to save me, but save me for what? This half-life hiding in the guest-house while right over our heads there's a castle and I have the key.

He's right: The people upstairs have all the beauty. I'm tired of sinking in tragedy, of feeling dirty with it. I'm tired of being trapped in this house with only Michael. I want more.

I would rather be in a rich person's hell than a poor person's heaven.

And I am so fucking close.

DEMI

I take another long shower. There is a cotton feeling in my ears. When I get out, Michael is gone again. I grab one of his beers from the fridge. I drink it on the sofa, then another and another. I think about Graham.

You're special. It's a line. I know it's a line. But it's nice to have someone care enough to give you a line. When I am tipsy, I think about his animal sanctuary. It's nicer than all the places I've lived before this. I should ask if there's room for me. I laugh out loud.

Then I hear it: footsteps on the stairs. But these are heavier; they take their time. They are in no hurry. They are inevitable. They are cop footsteps.

I forgot about the bag of hands, feet and teeth.

I was supposed to go and get it. I had a chance, and what did I do? I took another shower. I had another beer. I forgot who I was and what I did to get here. I've been sloppy — with everything — and now I am going to get what I deserve.

A fist raps — *Bang! Bang!* — on the door.

I don't move. I am so used to not answering doors — to cops, to neighbors, to landlords — that it's second nature. *They can't come in if you don't open the door. Don't open the door.*

"Hello?" a teatime voice calls out. "It's Graham from upstairs."

The fear flushes through me again, drops to the floor. I'm safe. I'm protected. I have been lucky so many times lately that it's starting to feel like I deserve it.

"Just a second!" I go to the bathroom to check myself in the full-length mirror. My face is still fear pale. I spritz it with an atomizer. I spray perfume and light a candle, hoping it will mask the scent of heroin when I open the door.

Graham stands behind the screen with his hands in his pockets. The sun glows along his neck and he smiles slightly, like we have met again by chance. "Sorry to bother you. It's just that — God, I don't want to scare you!" His cheeks turn pink, and he ducks his head.

"It's okay." As if he could scare me.

He flinches, rubs his neck, nervous. "Can I come in for a moment?"

"I —" I think of Michael's junk piled in the corner, the stench of heroin that permeates the house. "The porch. Can we talk on the porch? Do you want a beer?"

He smiles, like it's something no one has ever asked him. "I would love a beer."

"I'll meet you outside." I shut the door behind me. He must think I am hiding something, but he probably thinks it's a messy living room, a dent in the wall, a wine stain on the wood. Not a man's life and a woman's death.

I grab two beers from the fridge. I promised myself I wouldn't drink around Lyla and I should maintain the same policy with Graham, but I'm already tipsy and it's different with him. He doesn't look at me like I'm a rat in a trap.

I use a side door to step onto the porch, shut it behind me. "Sorry," I say. "I just haven't finished decorating. It's —"

"It's all right," he says. Everything about me is all right with him. "I don't want to make you uncomfortable." I hand him the beer. He opens it with his teeth, which catches me off guard. "Sorry. Party trick. You know us rich boys. We like to pretend to be down with the people." He winks, but I like him better for it. It makes him seem more real.

"I'm not uncomfortable," I say. I am, but not for the reason he thinks.

He tips his beer delicately into his mouth. He even drinks like a rich person.

"Is everything okay?" I ask.

He purses his lips, gathering himself. "It's Lyla. My wife. She . . . I'm worried about her, you know?"

I don't. "Is she back yet?" I have been so distracted, I completely forgot I left her at the reservoir. But she left me first. Still, my heart bumps like it's my fault. I left her, and now I am sharing a beer with her husband.

He crosses away from me on the porch, gazing out over the yard, past the trees, where you can see two or three stars. "She does this sometimes. Disappears. She . . . Never mind. I don't want to bother you with my problems." He shakes his shoulders wearily, then sits on one of Demi's hand-carved rocking chairs.

I take the chair beside him and lose my balance briefly when the seat sways. "To be honest, it would be nice to have a break from my problems." I don't mean to be judgmental, but I can't imagine his problems are very big. He probably wants a divorce but is afraid of losing a few million. Rich-people problems.

He takes a long drag of his beer, wipes his spotless lips, then says, "I've always tried to help people. But some don't want to be helped. . . ." I know he is talking about Lyla, but it feels like he's talking about me. He told me they put me here to help me. Shouldn't I let them?

But it's not you *they want to help,* I remind myself. *It's Demi.* Michael says I can't trust Graham. He's probably right. I know that, and a month ago I never even would have entertained the idea, but I've been living in this guesthouse for weeks now. I've gotten away with everything. And I'm starting to feel like I deserve it.

I take a fortifying gulp of beer; then I say, "You know, when you said you would help me, what exactly did you mean?"

His dimples show. "That I would help you. With anything. Anything you need: money, work, clemency." He smirks but my heart jerks. He's joking, isn't he? God, he can afford to joke about anything.

He leans forward suddenly, reaches out, brushes my hair back, like men only ever do in movies. He settles back but looks unsettled. "You're different, you know? I can tell. I've never met anyone like you." I believe that. "I would love to give you whatever you need. It would be a pleasure to me."

"What if I don't need anything?"

"I don't mean to be rude but you reek of need." I don't know how I'm supposed to take that as a compliment. "I find it so *compelling.*" He tips back the last of his beer. "I've never needed anything." Then I understand: To him, it is a compliment. It's something he can't have. He stands, brushes off his immaculate suit. "I've held you captive long enough. Sorry. I'll throw this away," he says, lifting the empty bottle. Standing at the end of the porch after dark, he is etched into silhouette. He looks like the white knight they instruct you to dream about, the one who is too good to be true. But what if he is true? What if he was always there but just out of reach? God in money. God in a three-piece suit.

He's good because he can afford it. Not like me, who has to pay for everything in blood. If I were rich, if I were like him, I would be so good. I'd be a human being, not a bag of needs.

"It's okay." I stand, too. "We're supposed to be friends — family, right?" I quote Lyla and he flinches, like he knows my words are hers.

"Of course. We're here to help." He looks so sad, and he glances at the stars again. Poor little rich boy in love with all the things he can't save. "You will let me help you, won't you? If ever you need something."

"Of course."

"Anything." Great.

There's a murderer living with me.

There's a body I set fire to.

There's a bag of hands, feet and teeth.

And I've always wanted a Chanel bag.

DEMI

I wait twenty minutes after Graham leaves to go out, count almost every second. My nerves are clamps. My temples are tight. I need to find that bag of body parts. I need to put it in the BMW. I need to drive out to the desert, in another state maybe, and set it on fire. That is what I need to do.

When twenty minutes pass, I journey up the stairs. The lights are on inside the glass house. I even see Graham sitting on a chair in the far corner where the windows meet, scrolling through his phone. I don't see Lyla. I wonder if she ever came back, but I have bigger problems now.

I creep through the courtyard, through the vanquished gate. I am passing the white van when I hear scratching. I stop in my tracks. It stops with me. Maybe I imagined it. Or maybe someone is inside that van. I keep my eyes on it as I walk toward the trash can alcove.

I open the first bin. A dog barks so close, I drop the lid. The sound echoes through the quiet street.

A car door opens. "What are you doing?"

I spin around and see Astrid, Lyla's housekeeper, standing on the street. The dog is still barking. I can hear it pacing through the bushes, rattling branches.

What do I tell her? She threw the bag away. She's probably already suspicious.

"I was just throwing away some bottles." I have no bottles. She might have seen me come out here empty-handed. She might know I'm lying. I search her for signs of suspicion, but she just looks like her eerie self: worried, astrological. I have to be smart. I have to turn my suspicions on her. "You're out here late."

She presses her lips together. The dog barks viciously from above.

"They don't have you working this late, do they?" That's when I see it: the open door of the van. The van in the street. She's living in the van.

"You need to leave here," she says. Her lips are blue in the half-light.

"Sorry. I didn't mean to wake you up." I put my hands up. "I'll just go back down."

"Leave." She knows. She knows and she is giving me a chance to run.

"Thank you. Thank you so much." I keep my hands up, which probably doesn't help my case. "I'm leaving. I'm leaving soon. I just need a little more time."

"Bean!" a voice shouts down from above, magnified, so close. "Bean! Come here! Stop that barking! What are you barking at?"

Astrid comes toward me. My first instinct is to block her. She grabs my hand. "They said my sister killed herself. She was their tenant, too." It's not Demi she's talking about. It's someone else. I'm safe. "Be careful!" She doesn't know who I am.

"Bean, damn it!"

I run.

My heart is still racing when I get downstairs. I can't go back for the bag, not with Astrid living across the street. It's too late. I will have to hope whatever God there is will help me. Or else, I'll have to help myself.

DEMI

The next morning, I put on a pair of Demi's headphones and open up her laptop. I need to check in. I need to make sure no one is getting suspicious. But there are no new messages, no new e-mails. Who was this woman? Why was her life so easy to take? I click through her in-box, looking over old messages again. I realize they are almost all work related. A few friends slip in here and there, but their messages are shallow. They're effusive, but they lack definition:

I miss you, babe! We need to have drinks soon!

Sorry it's been so long.

We'll have to catch up next time! Love you!

Not one person is worried. Her life is mine for the taking. I put the laptop on the table, then get down on my hands and knees. I reach underneath the sofa until I find her wallet. I don't look enough like her to use her ID, but her cards are all there: black, silver, gold. Begging to be used.

All my life I have apologized for who I am, ashamed, exhausted, overwrought. All my life I have wished for just a glimpse of what it was like on the other side. And now I'm surrounded by it.

I look at the flowers in Michael's corner and I rankle. I walked in that same garden and didn't even touch a single petal. I was careful not to squish the grass. I made sure to wipe my feet. What the fuck is wrong with me?

I set fire to a dead woman's body but I won't use her credit cards? A billionaire wants to save me and I don't think I'm worth it?

I need to stop apologizing.

I need to think rich.

I go to Rodeo Drive, because it's the poor person's conception of where the rich person shops. I go to Chanel first. I've always wanted one of their bags. Demi doesn't have one. I walk into the store and I think, *But she has other bags, dozens and dozens of bags! It's wrong — it's immoral —*

to have more than one bag.

I walk through the center of the store, like I'm afraid of what will happen if I get too close to anything. Alarms will go off, shutters will come down, the world will end. I see Demi's cold face turned up from the floor. I cover it with a blanket.

I approach the cashier. "I wanted to get a bag."

She analyzes me, assessing my value. I think she will see through me, like designer shopgirls are half Divine, but all she sees are Demi's clothes. "Which one?"

"Um." I am scared to look around me. Scared to touch. It's like I've walked into a police station and confessed to a crime: *I want a Chanel bag. Lock me up.*

"I always wanted a black one. Just classic. And a necklace, you know, with all the little charms? Like in the movie . . ." I drift off, can't remember the title, can't remember my own name. Buying designer clothes is like dying a little. *La petite mort,* the little death.

She looks at my clothes again, double-checking I can afford it. Then she shows me bags. She opens and shuts them. She shows me their size, makes comments about the life she imagines I have. I pick the one I want, not the one I can afford. I don't even look at the price. Then she shows me necklaces so heavy, I can feel my own importance. They drape between my breasts, hang heavy over the sweat collected there.

I look amazing. I look like a million bucks. All the bad days disappear from my reflection in the mirror. It's not the same as Demi's clothes. These are *my* clothes, and I have this wild idea that I will replace everything, start over, become a new person, myself in her.

I don't stop at Chanel. I am carrying so many shopping bags that I look like a girl in a movie, the way no one shops in real life. When I get tired, I stop at a restaurant. All my bags gather around my feet like tributes. I drink expensive wine and eat raw fish.

If I could choose a moment to end my life, this would be it. I can't imagine that things will ever get better. It's stupid how wonderful it is. All my life I've been told that true happiness comes from friends and family. It's been drilled into my head: *You have everything worth having if you have love.*

Bullshit.

I loved my dad more than anything and it never felt like this. It hurt. Watching him do things I hated, watching him suffer and get it wrong. This feels like clarity, like the answer to every question. It's like heroin is to Michael, an absence of struggle, every bad thing disappears, maybe every good thing, too, but isn't happiness a kind of pain? In knowing, always knowing, it will end?

I think of Graham's offer. I want his help. I want to live like him. I can't take back the things I've done.

But money forgives everything.

Demi

On my way home that evening, I pass by the tent city in my car. I have money in my pocket. I could stop. I tell myself it's too dangerous. I don't want to be recognized. I dropped tens of thousands of dollars on designer clothes I didn't need and I can't even toss a dollar out the window.

As we climb up the hills, I justify it. It's different for me. I earned this. No one helped me. I helped myself. I was poor. I don't want to be poor again. I wasn't born privileged like Graham and Lyla. It's not fair that I should have to share with anyone. I think of my dad, the way he used to give everything away like it was nothing. But he was wrong. It *was* something, and *I* lost it. I deserve this. It's only fair.

The Uber drops me off in front of the house. I collect my shopping bags. I thank my driver. I walk to the open gate. The smell of death washes over me so strong, it's like something from a dream.

It's all right. You've been through this before. You've walked through fire to get here. You'll keep walking.

I grip my shopping bags, protection. I step into the courtyard. There is blood on the stairs. I follow it to the body. The red dog from the street with its head snapped back, like it reached too far and broke apart.

I scream. I fall back against the railing, fight the cage of my ribs for my breath. I don't know what I am afraid of — everything suddenly overwhelms me: Astrid's warning, Demi's hands, the camp beneath the underpass, the nothingness in Margo's garden.

I feel a body close to mine, a hothouse scent. Strong arms wrap around me. A voice hums in my ear. "It's all right, it's all right." Everything is all right.

My shopping bags are scattered on the ground. I don't remember dropping them. My Chanel necklace winks like it's in on the joke. I can't catch my breath. I see the dog even when I'm not looking. I have this weird, wet feeling that I am somehow responsible. I imagine all the different ways that I could be, contort myself in guilty shapes, like I hope to one day be held accountable.

Graham holds me. Lyla is cold, watches me with arch eyes. She tells me the dog belongs to Margo and not to say anything. Graham scolds her, pets me like one of his animals. The guesthouse is my enclosure.

I shake it off. "I'm fine. It's just shock."

Graham helps me with my bags. He scoops up the necklace, delicately lowers it into the case, tucks it in the bag, arranges the tissue paper.

He offers to help me down the stairs. I insist I'm fine. I don't know why I'm so upset. Demi's body didn't have nearly the same effect on me. I do love animals but I think it's more than that.

It's easier to cry over a dog than a human being.

The scent of heroin is almost comforting when I step back into the guesthouse. I should have stayed inside. I definitely shouldn't have gone shopping. It's like I'm losing touch with reality. This place brings me back to earth.

Michael is in his corner, nodding out. He rouses himself enough to sneer, "What is that?" at my shopping bags.

"Upstairs bought it for me." I set the bags in the bedroom, where he won't see them. Then I come back to the living room, where he has nodded out again. He seems more high than usual, which only makes me surer of what I am about to ask. "Michael?" My voice has a dangerous snap. "Did you kill that dog?"

"What?" He blinks awake. "No! I wouldn't kill an animal."

"I saw you kill a human being."

"I wouldn't kill a dog."

"Then who did? There's only you and me here."

"Probably he killed it. The guy in the suit."

"Why would he kill his mother's dog?"

"Why would I?"

"Because —," I start, and then think, *Astrid.* Last night the dog was barking at her. What if it got loose? What if it revealed her location? "Hey, do you know there's a woman living in the van outside?"

" 'Course. Astrid. She helped me break the gate into the garden. She has this magic tool. *Clomp!* Cuts right through it."

My heart is pounding in my brain. "Do you think she broke the gate upstairs?"

He shrugs. "Probably."

"Why?" I ask out loud but he doesn't answer. I know the answer. She's spying on them. She thinks they killed her sister. But who? All of them? I remember Graham's weird warnings: *Be careful with her. I don't want to scare you. I've always tried to help people. But some don't want to be helped.* Lyla. At the time, I ignored Graham. I assumed he meant she was a Mean Girl. What if he meant she was a Murderer Girl?

"We should leave," Michael says. Michael. He pushed me to stay.

"Why?"

"I don't know." He shivers so hard, his eyes wobble. "Just a feeling I have. A bad feeling."

That night, I toss and turn in my bed. I don't want to leave. It's dangerous to stay. There's no way out except — there is one way.

I could tell Graham everything. I could make him understand it was an accident. I could trust him. He could help me. Only he could. He said he liked to save people. He could save me.

I shouldn't trust him. I never would have thought I could. But all this good fortune has changed me.

Hope is burning a hole in my chest.

I am waiting for him outside the next time I hear footsteps on the stairs. I found a birthday present among Demi's possessions. It's silly but I think he will like it. But when I turn to look, I see gray pumps. It isn't

Graham; it's his wife.

She is dressed in her utilitarian gray like someone sucked the life out of her clothes. She insists I come shopping with her and her friends, in the odd way she has, like I'm her target, like she has to meet a deadline. And Graham's words are in my ear: *I don't want to scare you. Be careful.*

She smiles fiercely at me. "He talks about you all the time. I think he has a crush."

"He's your husband," I remind her.

Her laughter plays an uneven beat. She says they're separated. I feel his hand on my ear.

"I just want Graham to be happy. He's such a *good* man."

She takes me shopping on Rodeo Drive. She's jumpy and drunk. Her friends are all assholes. Sometimes I catch her reflection in the mirror when she's not looking, and think, *Is this the face of a killer?*

But then, I might as well be looking at my own reflection.

DEMI

Lyla drops me off outside. I am just grateful I survived the shopping trip. Michael is right. This is all getting too complicated. I need an exit strategy. I need Graham. And then, like money magic, he appears.

"Hey." He is stepping out of his front door as I step into the courtyard. He smiles at me all the way to his ears. "How was shopping?" He thumbs through his keys, locks his door.

"It was fine. Lyla bought me a dress." She wanted us to wear the same thing: *twincesses!* I didn't protest. I doubt I'll even go to the party. If I tell Graham everything, I doubt I'll ever see her again. "Oh!" I say, remembering. "I got you a present. It's silly." I reach into my Chanel bag, pull out the book from Demi's bookcase. He walks all the way to me and I hand it to him.

"Fear," he reads.

"It's a joke. I have no idea what it's about.

I was trying to think of something you wouldn't have and . . . the only thing a rich person doesn't have is fear."

"That's very clever." His face has warmth, like he's not used to getting gifts. He flips to the title page. " 'For Demi. Hope this scares you!' "

I shudder. How could I not have checked for an inscription? I think of Demi suddenly, dead on the floor.

"I love it." He winks. He shuts the cover, slips the book in his coat pocket. I need to tell him. I should tell him now, but up close, I'm afraid. I'm afraid he won't like me anymore. "Hey, how would you like to come to a party?"

"Lyla invited me already."

"No, not tomorrow. Tonight. Me and some of the boys. Do you want to come?" He looks at me through long, lazy lashes. My cheeks warm.

"Okay."

He grins. "I should warn you, they're terrible people."

"I know. I met their wives." He bursts out laughing. It echoes through the courtyard.

Graham's friends are doing cocaine in a private room on the top floor of a strip club. Rich people never get points for creativity.

There are about eighteen bottles of Dom scattered on the table. They're mixing it with top-shelf whisky. Graham is drinking along with everyone else but he is sitting with me in the far corner, away from the action. He hasn't left my side all night.

His crew bursts into riotous laughter and I lean closer so he can hear.

"You never told me your favorite book."

"Bambi."

"Really?" He nods, eyes glassy and sincere. I sit back a little. "I bet you every last man here would say something by Bret Easton Ellis."

He shakes his head, tugs at his tie, which is like a nervous tic — he loosens it and tightens it once every ten minutes. "I can't stand him. Patrick Bateman's a pussy," which wasn't my exact criticism but I joke back anyway, "Yeah, Bambi was tough."

He tugs the bottle of Dom out of the ice bucket and tops up his glass. I have been around a lot of drinkers but I don't think I have ever seen someone drink so much so fast and stay so even. We've been here for hours and it's only now starting to show in the loop of his movements, in his oversolicitousness, the way he bites his bottom lip. "You sure you don't want a drink, darling?" He shuts one eye as he pours the dark whisky over the top. It weaves like blood through the crisp champagne.

"No, thank you." I am afraid to drink. I have been trying to get my nerve up all evening to tell him who I am and how I got here, but the drunker he gets, the less that seems like a good idea.

"Hitler never drank," he says. It's unclear why he thought that would be relevant. He definitely has more edge under the influence, a tendency to say inappropriate things like he's daring you to scold him. I should wait. I'll tell him tomorrow. Or after his birthday. There's no immediate threat. I can wait. Forever. He downs half his cocktail, then looks hard at me. "You might want a drink for what I'm about to tell you." And something in his tone makes menace in his red-ringed eyes.

He moves closer to me. I want to move away but instead I freeze. My tongue starts to buzz, numbed by fear. He tightens his tie, loosens it. "I was throwing away my mother's dog . . ." For a moment it's like time stops, and I slip into a world between his words. Everything, *everything,* that's happened comes racing to meet me and I see it: those tricky stairs, Demi's dead body, the hands and the teeth, the fire and the evidence bobbing up from underwater. And then my eyes catch on her ring on my finger, and I feel anchored to that at least. ". . . when I found something. In the trash." My bowels loosen. I almost piss myself. Instead, I grip the seat. His eyes drop. He notices it. He notices everything. He can smell fear. "It was a bag and inside it was two hands, two feet, a collection of teeth."

My voice is so soft, I doubt he can hear it. "You said you would help me."

"Darling, it seems like you helped yourself."

Across the room, two new dancers arrive. They line themselves up. They drop their fur coats. Their dresses glitter. Their legs part at the same time. I wish I were them. I wish I were anyone else.

"What did you do with the bag?"

"I haven't decided." He sips his drink. "I wanted to ask you first." What do I say? What do I do? There's no escape. I scan the seedy club but my eyes stick on one woman's undulating back. Graham sidles closer. "Would you like to join me at an alternate location?"

I swallow hard. My voice cracks. "Where?" I'm panicking. Is he going to take me to the police? Is it all over? Is this how it ends? In a seedy private room at a fancy strip club surrounded by champagne and cocaine?

His pretty eyes shine. "Wherever I say. Right?"

I go with him to a hotel next door. I have to. He knows. He didn't tell the police. I don't have a choice.

He said he wanted to help me but of course that was a lie. I was right not to trust him. I was wrong to get close to him. When I could have been running, I was shopping. When I could have been free, I was buying.

We walk into the vaulted lobby. All the staff recognizes him, welcomes him.

"Mr. Herschel! Mr. Herschel!" they exclaim like they've been waiting for him, hoping for him, all this time. He makes small talk, watching me all the while. He is enjoying this. He has me pinned. I look at the Maxfield Parrish reproductions along the wall and wonder what Graham is going to do to me. Whatever he wants.

He gets the presidential suite. Of course he does. We walk through the door and through a circuit of rooms to the master suite. He doesn't turn on any lights. The walls are golden. He is drinking whisky from the bottle now. He takes off his tie, removes his jacket, unbuttons his vest and climbs onto the bed.

"Darling." He looks up at me with bedroom eyes. "Tell me, whose teeth are they?"

I look at the glass doors leading onto the balcony. I could run. I could jump. "They're Demi's," I find myself saying. "They belong to Demi Golding."

This actually shocks him. He coughs. His eyes expand. But he doesn't run. He doesn't even move away from me. In fact, he moves closer. To help me, to trap me, to bask in my need. "I thought you were Demi Golding."

"I'm not."

He purses his lips, looks up at me through hooded eyes. "Who are you?"

"I don't want to tell you."

He grabs my hand so tight, I can feel my own pulse. "Come here." He tugs, then yanks me onto the bed.

I grasp, half-blind with fear, for the whisky bottle. Cheers to my demise.

He crawls closer to me. I can feel him breathing, feel his drugged heart beating, as he watches me with something like . . . appreciation?

"Tell me everything," he begs me. "I want to know everything." It takes me a second and several strong swigs to understand what he is saying. "Please! I want to know every dirty detail. From the beginning."

So I tell him. My whole life, every tragic

detail. He listens with rapt attention, like a little boy being told his first fairy tale. I tell him about Demi and Michael. Here he seems not to believe me.

"It's all right if you did kill her," he swears, squeezing my hands so the whisky sloshes in the bottle. "It's all right!" And I feel a rush of gratitude followed by a dart of uncertainty: What kind of man thinks that's all right? Money forgives everything, but this might be too much. "It's beautiful," he insists, kissing my temple. "Everything you did. Everything you had to do. It makes you so goddamn beautiful." When I'm finished, he extracts the bottle from my fingers, places it on the bedside table. He sets me underneath him, arranges me like a doll, brushes my hair, kisses my forehead. "You're the most gorgeous thing I've ever seen." His voice is blue and reverent. "Can I make love to you?" He kisses my neck. "Please?"

It feels so good just to be touched. And he is so handsome. And so, so rich. And I need money even more than I need forgiveness.

The next morning, I wake up alone in the presidential suite, redeemed. I don't go back to the guesthouse. I don't want to ever. I don't even leave when I'm supposed to check out, although it grinds through me: *Checkout time is eleven o'clock.* Other people can check out. I won't. I am the fucking president.

I order room service. Strawberries cut into heart shapes. A bottle of Moët. God, I can still feel him inside me. I have no past. I am all future.

LYLA

I wake up and have a glass of Moët. It's not a party if you're not drunk. Graham wasn't in the living room when I came in, which doesn't surprise me. He is probably at a private doctor getting his hangover drained from him on an IV. He'll show up for the party immaculate. He's going to be so impressed.

I sit with my Moët at the edge of the house, looking out through the glass at all of Los Angeles, spread like a dead flower below. My back is to the fountain but I see it in my mind's eye. I am trying to puzzle through all the things I learned but it's like the pieces don't go together.

The front door lock clicks and my housekeeper lets herself in. She starts to clean. The light through the windows makes everything glow white.

"This is embarrassing," I volunteer. "But I can't remember your name."

She stops cleaning. "Astrid." The star on her neck glints in the light, and I remember where I've seen it, where I last saw it. Winking around Elvira's dead neck.

"I really did adore Elvira."

"I know," she says. "She told me."

I sip my Moët. "Were you friends?"

She swallows. "Sisters." Her sister. Of course. I spoke to her on the phone. I try to remember her, but all I remember is her question: "You want to know why."

She nods once. Then her hand darts out to steady herself on the front table. The gun clatters in the silver tray. We both see it.

I sigh. "I can't tell you. There's no reason." My husband was bored. Bored and maybe more. Maybe he didn't like that Elvira was my friend. Maybe it bothered him that I loved her and she loved me back. Maybe he is incapable of love, like Margo said. Maybe it's not boredom but a wide, wild void. "Were you living in the van?" I say. "Did you break the gate? Did you . . . Bean?"

She doesn't answer. I can see the resemblance now. She and Elvira don't look alike, but I can see how they would be sisters.

"If you're trying to decide if you can trust me," I say, "I can tell you, you can't trust anyone. Not here." Still she says nothing. I have no choice but to change my tactic.

"That dog was Margo's life. . . ."

"It wasn't me." She grips the table. The gun hums in its silver plate. "It was the man downstairs, Michael."

"Michael?"

"The man you saw in the courtyard. He's living with the woman downstairs. He gets high and goes into the gardens. He's the one who broke the gate. He's been robbing houses up and down this street. He killed the dog. He was in Margo's garden and the dog found him, was barking at him. He said it was the dog or him. He broke its neck. He put the body in your courtyard to scare you."

"Sorry — I'm still . . . There's a man living downstairs?" I'm going to need more Moët.

She shakes her head. "You don't know anything that happens. None of you pays any attention to anyone else."

"I have a lot on my plate right now. This party." I sigh. It's not important now.

"I want things to be fair," she insists. "I want there to be consequences."

I grip my glass. "These people can't give you fair. They can only give you money."

She looks down at the gun and then, cautiously, like she can't quite believe she is doing it herself, she picks it up. She points it at me. "What happened to my sister? I don't believe she killed herself."

It's more depressing than I would have expected, being held at gunpoint. It's disappointing. Maybe because I know, by the fear in her eyes, by the way she doesn't even touch the trigger, that she would never, ever shoot me.

"Tell me." Her voice shakes.

The truth throbs in my throat: *You're right. She didn't kill herself. Graham killed her.* If I tell her, what will she do? Kill me? Kill him? Go to the police? She couldn't kill him. And the police won't help her. The house always wins. That's why I play for the house.

"You should leave this place. It's not . . ."

I try to organize my thoughts, but the gun is distracting. I stand up. I cross the room toward her. I take the gun from her hands. She lets me. The safety is still on. I am inches away from her. I can smell her breath. It smells like Elvira's. The scent damages me. It tricks me into believing she's here in the room with us. The star around her neck winks. I sigh all through my bones and I tell her, "If you're looking for fair, you won't find it here. If you're looking for peace or happiness or some kind of resolution, you won't find it with these people. The only thing rich people have is money."

She sets her jaw. "I'm not leaving." I see myself on my wedding day. The gown with lace all the way to my chin. The train that dragged along the floor. My still, determined face.

"What's your number?" She says nothing. "I can't give you back what you've lost. I can't bring Elvira back. I would if I could. For you, for me, I would give everything back. But I can't do that. All I can do is make a transfer. And make sure you never have to worry about these things again."

She tells me her number.

As I walk down the stairs to the guesthouse, I consider how lucky Astrid is to get to walk away. I gave her that. My one good deed. If I could go back to my wedding day, back to that room and that question, would my answer be different?

I think of Elvira and the answer is yes. I would take the money. I would leave the life. If I could, I would.

But it's too late now. I knock on the door, but no one answers. I have a key. It's been a long time since I've been in the guesthouse. It wasn't like this. There's a tent in one corner, a cardboard rug, a stack of penis collages.

What the fuck is Demi playing at? Who is Michael? Her boyfriend? Her patsy? Her strategy?

I don't have time to figure it out. I have to plan. I have a party to attend and a person to kill, and what does it matter who she is or what she's done? It doesn't change the game. I have to win so I can keep playing. If I lose, no amount of money will bring me back. I have to win, or the game will end for me for good.

LYLA

Every rich person has at least one Versailles-themed room. Margo's is the ballroom. It's where she hosts her most important parties and it's where I host Graham's birthday dinner. The dinner party guests are reflected again and again in Margo's Ballroom of Mirrors. And because it's Margo, it's done with a twist — emphasis on "twisted." Hung among the mirrors are macabre works of art: *Judith Beheading Holofernes, The Massacre of Standing Creek* and a larger-than-life portrait of Marie Antoinette dressed in her most frothy, flounced pastel gown, holding her own bloody head on her lap.

Normally I find this room a little gauche. But tonight, it's perfect. Normally, I would serve Graham's favorites, but because I respect his perverse streak, I make a meal of everything he hates: caviar, truffles, brussels sprouts. I make sure that everything tastes divine.

He doesn't seem to notice. I placed seating cards, but Graham ignored his and sat next to Demi. He leans over to whisper something in her ear. She blushes. Her neck twists in his direction and I see Elvira's neck. How did he kill her? Did he plan all along to make it look like an accident?

Posey moves her place card next to me.

"I'm excited for the game!" she says too loud.

I don't want Graham to hear. I want it to be a surprise. Not that he's paying any attention to me. He caught my eye on the way in. His face was a persistent blank, so I know he remembers what he told me last night. Knowing this scares me.

Graham is sick but he doesn't like to be seen that way. He doesn't like to be seen for what he is, which is possibly the only human thing about him. Maybe that's why he's turned on me, turned away from me. Not because he's bored with me but because he doesn't want to be known, especially not to himself.

Demi's already wearing the black dress I bought her, even though we were supposed to change after dinner. There's a little tracking device sewn between her breasts that connects to an app on my phone. I don't want to kill her. But I don't have a choice.

It's her or me. There's no other way out.

I turn to Posey. "You're not playing. Only the men are."

"You're playing." She stabs a truffle. "And Demi is."

"Shut up." I elbow her. "You're going to spoil the surprise."

"I'm just saying." She gulps her Moët. "Equal rights."

Mitsi and Peaches and Grenadine and Margarita are all sitting together, gossiping like this is any other party. Their husbands, who are mirror images of them, are talking loudly in their section, swearing and making inappropriate jokes, competing to see who can say the most outrageous thing.

"That Marie Antionette is fit. Would you fuck her?"

"Head off or on?"

"Wherever you want it."

Watching them, I feel the fluttering of anticipation. I can't wait for them all to get shot.

"Fine," I snap at Posey. "You can play if you want to, but you'd better not shoot me."

"A game's a game." She shrugs and tops off her glass.

After dessert, and drinks, and cigars, the other ladies go home. I lead all of our players into the foyer to explain the game. The gaslight fixtures flicker pleasantly. I wanted the lights to be dim. I want it to feel surreal. It will only make my job easier.

"Everyone, listen up!" I wait for the boys to stop talking. Then I give up. I raise my voice so it is magnified in the stone foyer. "This is important: The boundaries extend across the entire grounds, all nine levels of the garden. The only portion of the house that's out-of-bounds is the west wing, where Margo is staying. You'll see it marked off with a red rope. There are staff members stationed everywhere to make sure no one cheats." I don't mention that these staff members are armed with Simunition, too, and under orders to shoot anyone who cheats. Except me. I have paid and instructed them to look the other way so I can hide in the west wing until I see my opening.

"What are we playing?" Graham asks drolly. "Tag?"

Behind me is a long table covered with a velvet cloth. I remove the cloth. Twenty-seven handguns glow on the table.

"Those are real guns," Mitsi's husband, Mark, observes.

"Real guns," I explain. "Fake ammunition. We're using Simuniton. It's what police officers use to train."

"Isn't that illegal?" Nigel says.

"Don't be silly! That's the fun part!" Tony laughs.

"Shouldn't we be wearing pads? I'm pretty sure cops wear pads."

"Has anyone tested this out?" Henri sounds genuinely scared.

Graham's dimples are showing. He's not smiling and he's not smirking. It's the same face he made when I showed him Elvira's body.

I swallow hard and continue. My voice wavers with the light. "They're each loaded with six rounds. If you need to reload, you can find more on a table in the gallery, but you'll have to be careful. There's no time-out, no safe zone."

"What about other weapons?" Mark asks, eyeing up a sword on the wall. "Couldn't someone just grab a knife from the kitchen?"

"The point is to shoot them," I say. "You'll know when they're dead. It's a special kind of Simunition. I hope you all don't mind getting a little dirty." Posey whoops. "Once you die, you can head out to the terrace for drinks and to wait out the game."

"What do you get if you win?" Mark asks.

I catch Demi's eyes. They glimmer in the half-light. "To keep playing."

Graham whispers in her ear, flirting. She flirts back. He gets the last word, then leaves her side and crosses to me so abruptly, I feel myself wither. He slings an arm around my neck, rank with testosterone, kisses my cheek. My stomach drops. I feel sick, and not the good kind. "This is a brilliant idea, darling!" He leans in closer; his voice drops so it hums against my ear. "Is this my present?"

I extract myself. "You'll know it when you see it."

He chuckles, like he is in on this and every joke. Then he strides to the table, selects the best gun, turns off the safety. He points it at Henri. "Shall we test it out? Make sure it's safe?"

Henri tugs his collar. "Might as well just start the game."

Graham smirks, brings the gun in, blows on the muzzle. "Happy birthday to me."

LYLA

Everyone selects a gun from the table. I explain the start. A member of the staff stands at the top of the stairs, holding a gun. One shot to run. One minute. Another shot and the game starts.

First shot at midnight. We wait, nervous. Little groups of men form to discuss strategy.

"It's better to form alliances!"

"No, it's better to go it alone. You can't trust anyone."

"It doesn't seem fair," Henri says, fiddling with his gun. "They know the house best."

"It's just a game."

Posey is fooling around with her gun, flipping it in the air and catching it. "This is going to be *so much* fun!"

At 11:59, the group falls silent. The staff member steadies their hand. *Five, four, three —*

Bang!

They fire early, and not into the air, like I expected. They fire at the chandelier. Gold dust and glass explode across the floor. I'm furious, but I don't have time to scold them.

I have a feeling this game could get out of control fast. I have to remind myself that's what I want.

Everyone is frozen, temporarily shocked. Graham is wondrous. I did good, but I don't feel good. Yet.

"Run, you fuckers!" Mark says. One group races toward the garden; another goes deeper into the house. Graham goes directly toward the gallery. Of course he does. It is not enough to have the advantage. He has to rig the deck. Demi goes outside. I am following her for a second.

Now, I think. *You could do it now. She's right there!* But it's too soon. I would be seen. I want Graham to know it was me, but I have to make sure no one else knows.

I split off, taking the back route to the west wing, where I have paid a staff member to let me in through a side door. She is there when I arrive, holding her gun. I pass through the door as the second shot goes off, too early.

Bang!

"The game hasn't started, fuck face!" someone shouts.

Bang!

This is going to be chaos.

I reach my out-of-bounds safety spot. It's a little alcove, like a box at an opera house with a bench. It's surrounded by curtains I can peek through. It's where the staff hides so they can be unseen. As such, I can see everything from here: the red foyer below, the arched entrance into the gallery, the stairs to the west wing, even a corner of the terrace outside.

I check my app. Demi is in Purgatory. She's still in the game.

Bang!

Bang!

Bang!

Bang!

Bang!

Five shots go off in quick succession. A real bullet waits in my pocket to be loaded into my gun. This is going to be a long night.

I watch from above as the foyer is destroyed. I should have known these boys would take any opportunity to make a mess. They seem more interested in destroying the house than in killing one another.

They form alliances and wander around in packs, taking shots at paintings and chandeliers, then covering one another to reload. The idea was to have people take a round at a time, but Graham and Mark, who have teamed up, decide to take all the bullets they can carry. Someone shoots a member of the staff.

"Sorry. Just wanted to test it out!" I hear their protest.

The air fills with gold-tinged powder. It has a weird metallic odor that probably isn't safe to breathe. The lights are out except for a few flickering gas lamps that bounce off the mirrors and reflect in the windows. My heart is pounding, even though no one can see me, let alone shoot me, up here.

Demi is still in the garden. She must be hiding in Purgatory. There is a gazebo there. She's probably made it her fortress. I wonder if she is out there alone, or if she joined up with Posey or one of the men. I think she must be alone. She's always alone.

I should go out there and take care of her, but there are still too many players in the game. I didn't think this through, didn't re-alize how chaotic and scary it would feel. I might not be able to get to her. I might get shot. I feel as if anything could happen.

Henri starts up the stairs leading to the west wing. He's alone. No one wanted him on their team. If he gets to the top of the stairs, he might see me. I don't know why he's going this way. It's a dead end. There is a red rope strung across the top of the stairs. It's obviously out-of-bounds. He's probably trying to cheat. I should shoot him before he sees me, but then he might realize *I'm* cheating. He is so the type who would rat me out.

I will him to stop but he keeps going. He reaches the rope. He's about to duck under. I back inside the curtain. He's been to the house many times. He might know about my spot. He might want it for himself. I tighten my grip on my gun. He's going to take me out of the game.

Bang!

A bullet hits him square in the back. "You fuck!" He trundles around, then slips. He tumbles down the stairs, then lands on the marble floor with a sickening snap. His leg is bent at an odd angle. I think he broke his fucking ankle.

"You fucking — What?" He tries to sit up, screams. "I think I broke my fucking ankle!"

"Oh, shit, oh, God. I'm sorry!" Nigel appears from behind a pillar below me. I didn't even know he was there. "You're not serious, are you? You're okay —"

Bang!

A bullet slams Nigel in the back, shooting him forward. He staggers, nearly tripping over Henri. No one appears to claim the shot.

Nigel finds his balance and wheels around. "That's not fair! I was trying to help him!" His voice echoes through the hall. Henri whimpers on the floor. "You're all a bunch of dicks," Nigel spits. "Come on, let's go," he snaps at Henri, helping him up. "I'll get someone to take you to the fucking hospital. Where is the staff?"

"I think they shot you," Henri says, stumbling up beside him. "I think they're playing, too."

"What, really?" Nigel says. "Well, thanks a fucking bunch for breaking your goddamn leg. We're going to miss all the fun!"

Their voices echo down the hall as they head toward the terrace.

I check my app. Demi has left the garden. I jump when I see where she is: right behind me. I swivel my head, searching for her. I order myself to be calm. She's not here, but she's close. I use my fingers to zoom in. Inhale sharply. She's worse than close; she's in Margo's room.

Bang!

The chandelier rattles over my head.

LYLA

Demi is cheating. She is clearly out-of-bounds. She's in the west wing. No one is stopping her. Henri was right: The staff is playing, too. There is no one to stop her. What is she doing in Margo's room? She must be checking in, getting her instructions. They must be plotting to take me down. What if tonight is the night? It's Graham's birthday, after all. What if I am *their* present? I have to get to her before she gets to me.

Down below, another group races through the foyer. The shots are less frequent now. I can't see into the gallery but I'm guessing the ammo has all been taken. When the foyer is empty, I peek down, stretching to see all the gold splatters on Margo's walls. It's kind of beautiful, a work of the avant-garde. She could sell it like this: *Very Bad Rich People.* She could turn the whole house into a shrine.

It's finally quiet. I could go after Demi now. It would be the perfect time, but she's with Margo. I can hear the flutter of voices from the terrace bragging about how good they were, how crazy, how dangerous, like it's all real.

"I shot three people. Then I got shot in the back!"

"The chef shot me — it wasn't fair!"

Suddenly, I see Graham cross into the foyer. I would recognize the cut of his suit anywhere, even in the dark. He's alone. He has gold rounds looped over his shoulders. The real bullet pulses in my pocket. I could load my gun. I could shoot him. It would take ages in all this chaos for anyone to realize he was dead.

Is it really her or me, or could it be me or *him*?

My hands move, shivering as if from affection. I don't think about what I'm doing. I just do it, step by step.

I slip the bullet from my pocket. I pop open the chamber. I remove the gold Simunition. I replace it. My fingers shake so badly as I close the chamber that the gold bullet drops. It makes a tiny sound — *plip!* — as it hits the floor.

Graham hears it. His chin darts up. His eyes are on me. He sees me. I feel it all the way down to my toes. He's going to kill me.

I don't move, don't breathe, don't swallow. I wait for my death. Then he looks away. I'm safe.

He's dead.

I have a loaded gun in my hand. One shot. I could kill him.

It hits me like a revelation: That is the only way to end the game. Graham is the game. It ends with him. I lift my weapon. *Ready, aim . . .*

Then I remember: Margo. But she is right behind me. I shoot him; then I shoot her. But I have only one bullet. Who do I kill?

My gun wavers. I could shoot him and then I can strangle her. I can smother her. I can batter her with one of her statues; she likes poetic justice. This is my chance, my *only* chance, to end the game for good.

I can do it.

I shut my eyes, order myself to stay calm. I picture Graham crossing the red room below me. I imagine myself shooting him. He explodes like a piñata, only money comes out.

I open my eyes. He's gone. I start to stand, search for him. I take a step. My toe catches on the gold bullet. I slip on the marble. My hands dart out to catch myself on the curtain.

Bang!

Pain echoes with the sound through my breast. I forget for a moment it's not a real bullet. I forget I'm not really dead.

"You killed me!"

"Cheater," a woman's voice says. "You were cheating!" Posey appears at the bottom of the stairwell. I train my gun at her, forgetting it's really loaded. "Come on!" She laughs. "Don't be a sore loser. You were cheating. You're out of the game." Graham appears from behind a pillar. Posey gasps. She points at me. "Lyla was cheating! She's out!"

His voice is stone-cold. "So are you."

Bang!

It's small consolation that I get to watch Posey die.

I have no choice but to go to the terrace with Posey. We have every drink imaginable and exquisite canapés, but no one to serve them.

"You shouldn't have given the staff bullets," Nigel advises. "They've all gone feral."

"Don't be soft. It makes the game more fun!" Thomas argues.

I pause for a moment to look at the sky. All the stars are out as if they were hiding all along.

"Who cares?" I say, taking a spot at one of the tables. Posey joins me with a bottle of Moët and two glasses. I hate everyone here, so I might as well sit with her until I can find a way to sneak back into the game. "Who's still in?" I ask Greg. He has drawn a chart on a napkin. "Mark, Ferro, the Italians, and that girl. What's her name?"

"Demi." I set my gun on the table, then slip my phone out and check my app as Posey pours me a glass. Demi has left Margo's room. She's in the gallery now. She must be looking for more bullets. I wonder if Graham will shoot her. Who am I kidding? Of course he will.

"I can't believe Graham shot me." Posey pours herself a glass. "I mean, I *can,* but still." We clink glasses. "You *were* cheating."

I roll my eyes. "Everyone's cheating."

Bang!

"They'll run out of bullets eventually," Nigel says.

"They've completely destroyed the estate. Have you seen the carnage in the garden?"

"It's brilliant. Best party ever!"

"Anyone fancy a bet against Graham? We might as well get involved."

"Ha-ha."

Posey puts her glass down thoughtfully. "I'll put a bet down. On Demi."

"What, the little girl?" Thomas says.

"I saw her take out, like, three of you in the garden." Posey says, grinning pleasantly. She's the type who thinks a win for one girl is a win for all. I guess I am, too. I hope Demi kills every last one of them.

"She shot me, too," Greg volunteers. "It's not fair. She's so small."

"She's a little animal."

"Wonder what she's like in bed?" someone *has* to ask.

"You really think she can take out Graham?" Nigel asks Posey.

"Absolutely," Posey answers with relish. "I'll always put my money on the woman in a game of life or death."

"I'll bet on the staff. Can we just count them as one? Margo's staff is brilliant at being invisible."

"That's a good bet!"

"How much?"

"A grand?"

"Let's make it something that matters."

"Thirty?"

I don't want to kill Demi. I want to see her win. Maybe this game will be enough to satisfy Graham. Maybe I don't need to kill her after all. Maybe I was taking things too far. Maybe it's a place I can't come back from. I think of how I shook loading the gun for Graham. Do I really think I can point it at Demi?

"No one's going to beat Graham," someone says. "If they do, he'll probably have them killed for real."

Posey meets my eye. She leans in close, says quietly so no one can hear, "How are things with Graham? We never talk about him."

"Why would we?"

"I know him pretty well —"

"I married him."

"It's not a competition."

I shrug. "Everything is."

She leans back, turns something over in her mind. "You know I broke up with him, right?"

I didn't know that, but I nod because I'm too proud to admit it. "But I don't know why." I need to know why.

She arranges the artful folds of her dress, and when she looks up, her eyes bore into mine. "Because he's a bad person. I think he's attractive. I think he's rich. But he's a bad person, you know?"

I do know. And I never thought that could mean more than his most stellar attributes. He is beautiful. He is rich. What else is there? And then I see Elvira's smile and I think, *There is one good thing. One genuine thing.*

I never believed there was such a thing as a good rich person. It seemed like a contradiction in terms, a conflict of interest. But this morning, I wrote Astrid a check. I could have fired her. I could have ruined her. I had all the money. I had all the power. And instead, I warned her. Instead, I let her go. Maybe there are good rich people. Maybe I could be one of them.

There's just one problem. The rich people I know won't let me go. I was complicit. And all the money in the world isn't enough to pay for it. "And Graham just let you walk away?" I ask her.

"No." She lifts her glass. "He found you."

I hesitate, then reach for mine. My heart skips a beat. My gun is gone. "Where did my gun go?"

"What gun?" one of the men says.

"You don't need it," Posey says. "We're out of the game."

"It was here on the table. I need it. Who took it?"

"It was probably one of the players or staff or something."

I stand up. "I need my gun back." I'll never find it. I'll never see who took it. Then I remember my app.

I see Demi's red light blinking away from me. It was her. She took my gun. She went to the gallery to get more ammo. When she couldn't find any, she came for my gun. I could leave it, let her shoot someone. That would destroy her life. That would win me the game. It's actually better than my original plan; there's less chance of it coming back on me.

It's perfect. It's fate. I win.

"Where are you going?" Posey says. My feet are moving. "You can't go back in the game. That would be cheating."

"Everyone's fucking cheating!" And someone might get killed.

Demi

I go straight from the hotel to Graham's birthday party, slightly tipsy. I take a car so I don't have to see too much of the city. I wear sunglasses. I have little glimpses of the places I used to know — the street corners and the underpasses and the swap meets — but they are the ghosts of a dead woman's life and I'm free. I am free and forgiven.

I have never been to Margo's house before. I have seen only the glint of the tower from below, the back side of the palace from the gardens. It's a house that was made to be entered from the front, crammed with glass windows, buffeted with turrets. It spins with the drive. It looks like a lion preparing to pounce, the way all its muscles are tight and coiled as the engine purrs closer.

Lyla greets me on the stairs. "Your outfit's in the anteroom." Like I know where that is. Like I know what that is.

Someone hands me a drink. I ask where

the anteroom is and they give me directions. I walk down a hall of mirrors, see myself reflected a million times. The faces don't match. I shiver, stop looking.

I find the anteroom and put on the dress Lyla selected for me. I get this peculiar feeling in the pit of my stomach. I slept with her husband. Now I'm wearing her dress in their house. But I won't let it ruin tonight. I've never been to a party like this. I've never been inside a house like this. Lyla said that wealth is access, and the higher you get, the more you unlock. Somewhere someone is even richer than this, in a bigger house with sharper glass. Why stop here? Why not go all the way to the top?

I might be a little drunk.

I am wandering back to the party when he finds me. He's in one of his soft midnight blue tailored suits.

"Happy birthday," I say. He toasts me. "Are you excited for your party?"

His dimples show. "I'm glad you're here."

I look around the house, confusing my reflection everywhere for other people, but we are alone. "Did you grow up here?"

He grabs hold of me suddenly, puts his hand around the back of my neck, pulls me against him and kisses me. It's like kisses used to be, sparkling and surprising.

When he pulls away, I wobble uncertainly. Off-balance. "Thank you for not saying anything."

He squeezes my hand. "It's my pleasure."

The dinner is obscene. Waiters set fire to our fish and it melts into caviar eggs. They spray pansies so they change color. Pour *jus* over sprouts and turn them bloodred. Every dish is dressed like something else. I guess I fit the theme.

Graham sits next to me, whispers in my ear rude comments about the most expensive food I've ever seen: "Looks like something you'd find at the bottom of a lake" and "Smells like cat litter."

After dinner, we all follow the staff into the entryway, where there is a long table beneath a velvet cloth. Lyla explains the rules of the game. I heard about it at the drinks with the girls, but Graham is hearing about it for the first time.

He grins from ear to ear, then leans over my shoulder. "Do you think you can win?"

"I know I can," I tease playfully.

He leans closer. His voice drops to a growl. "Let's make it more interesting. If you win, I'll give you anything you want. If not, I hand over that bag of yours to the police."

My throat starts to close. He's joking, isn't he? Who would say something like that? Who would do something like that? Put my life on the line for a game.

"I —," I start, but it's too late. He moves easily away from me, crosses to Lyla, throws his arm around her. "This is a brilliant idea, darling!"

His dimples are like burns in the side of his face. His teeth glint. He's joking. He has to be. No one could be that cruel. He doesn't even catch my eyes again.

It's like I'm nothing but a game to him.

DEMI

I race to the garden as soon as the game starts. It's darker there but I figure it's the most secure. There are uneven stairs, trees and brush for cover. Natural obstacles like walls and moats and gazebos.

I sight my first kill, one of Graham's friends creeping down the stairs.

Bang!

"No fair!" he barks, dusting the gold from his belly. "The game hasn't even started."

Bang! Off in the distance.

"Well, fuck it!" He toddles back up the steps. This is going to be easier than I thought. These men are weak. Their instincts are shot. They have never had to fight for anything. I was made for this.

I go to the gazebo, because it's higher up but enclosed. I am tempted to run into the house and take them all out one by one, but my instincts know this is the better way: to wait it out, let them kill one another first.

Then I will go in. Graham is the only one I'm not sure about, the only one with teeth. I don't know if he was joking. As long as I win, I'll never have to find out.

I am standing at the ready when I see a tall head towering above the flowers. I aim my gun. He puts up his hands. They're filthy.

"Michael!" I lower the weapon.

"You trying to shoot me?"

Bang!

He jumps down, covers his head.

"It's just a game. We're playing a game."

He rises carefully, rubbing his head. "Funny game."

Bang!

He flinches but stays standing. "I heard the noise. Thought they were all killing one another."

I explain the Simunition to him. "You should leave. They've all gone crazy."

"Are you kidding? This is the perfect time to go up to the house. See what's not nailed down."

I am about to tell him he can't, like I always do, but this time I stop myself. I step aside. "Knock yourself out."

He salutes me with pride, like I've passed some test, then hurries up the stairs.

Bang! Over our heads as I watch him van-

397

ish. Suddenly I don't want to wait out the game. I want to play it. I want to have fun. I want to enjoy the game.

I follow the path at the back of the house until I find an open door leading into the far section of the house. It's quieter here. There is a stairwell that leads to the overhang above the entryway. I could take a spot up there, shoot them all down like a sniper.

Or there is a servants' stairwell, darker and narrower but hidden, more secret. They will never see me coming.

I bound up the steps. They lead me into a dark hallway. I hear shots firing, but the sounds are far away, muffled. Still, the paintings rattle on the wall. The hallway is cluttered with dozens of oil-paint portraits, not of a person but of a red dog. The same dog I saw out walking every day. The same dog I saw dead on Graham's front stoop. Margo's dog.

The shots are sounding farther and farther away and I slow. I don't want to leave the game. I'm going the wrong way. I am about to turn around when I hear a voice. "Hello? Viola? Where did you go? I need you. I need help!" I follow the voice to a gilt door cracked open at the end of the hall. That's when I realize I am out-of-bounds. I am in

Margo's room.

She is perched in a bed as big as an ocean and just as turbulent. Frothy white blankets roll like waves across its surface. The room is a maze of mirrors. This house is like a fun house. I slowly step back. "Wait! I see you!"

I could run, but if she yells and someone comes, they will know I'm out-of-bounds. I'll be thrown out of the game. I have to win.

So I freeze, straighten my dress, set my gun down on the side table.

Bang!

I put on my most subservient expression. "Can I help you, ma'am?" I step into the room. A portrait hangs over her bed, this one featuring a much younger Graham grinning with the red dog in a choke hold.

"Viola was supposed to rub my hands," Margo protests, wringing her wrinkled palms.

I recognize Margo from the street. She was the woman who kept smiling at me. She doesn't recognize me. She looks older, frailer than I remember. She has one of those faces that's made for makeup, and without it she looks pinched and undefined.

"Where is everybody?"

This whole house is hers. And the one below and the guesthouse. All the houses and everything in them. Even Graham.

"I think they're helping with the game," I say. "I'd better get back to work."

"Wait!" She frowns. "Who are you? I don't remember your face."

"I'm just here for tonight. Lyla asked me."

Bang!

She covers her ears. "I can't stand all this noise!" She shakes her jeweled hands. The noise stops for a while, long enough for her to catch her breath. "You'll rub my hands, won't you?" She stretches her fingers like claws. "I'm in the most terrible pain. And it's always my hands that get it. All of my pain goes right to my hands." She clenches and unclenches her fingers.

"Okay." I need to leave, but I can't run now. As I cross the room toward her, my nostrils fill with her heavy scent. It's like a body in a bath of milk. It's like death but more expensive. Up close, her face is a mask of fillers and stiffeners, swollen as a stone balloon. But her eyes are extraordinary. Even watery with age they have a purple cast.

She holds out her hands. "Help me. It's all in my hands." I reach for her and she grunts, "The lotion." There is a bottle of Crème de la Mer on her bedside table. "Don't be stingy."

I scoop up fifty dollars' worth. She takes off her rings one by one. They are as thick as teething toys. I rub her hands. They are old and crinkled, strung with bones. She deepens her breath. "Yes, that's better. Can you believe my son is thirty today? I never thought he would live this long." Her voice is low, confidential, like we are on intimate terms. Her staff is her best friends but also totally interchangeable. "You won't believe the trouble it took to get him here, a boy like that! But he's special, very special. He's not like other people."

"No —," I gasp.

"His father, you know, he ran off with the maid. *My* maid, if you can believe it. And Graham is like him —"

Bang!

"He has a great love of poverty. He's a great connoisseur of it. When he was younger, he used to — Oh!" Her eyes expand with delight. I think she's high out of her mind, sitting alone on her diaphanous bed. "We would find him asleep out in the garden and he would say" — she puts on a voice — " 'Oh, Mummy, I don't need a bed! I don't need a house!' "

Bang!

"He used to blame me for not allowing him to struggle. He said, 'Mummy, you

401

ruined me!' But I made him. I made him better than other people. He's like a god. Nothing touches him. It's the poor that are the real monsters."

Bang!

"Saddling everyone with their needs." I squeeze the space between her fingers. "That's too hard! Not so hard!"

Bang!

She grunts, shifts in her bed. "Have you seen the people out there?" She indicates the window with her hand. "Living on the streets? *For free* — Well, not for free because *I* pay for it. I pay for it dearly, having to see all this hideousness every goddamn day."

Bang!

"I'm convinced they killed my dog. Some poor person! They probably wanted her to eat!"

Bang!

Her knuckle cracks beneath my fingers. I want to kill her. I think how easy it would be. A silk pillow. No one around. Why should I be a good person when nobody else is?

Instead, I release her hand. She grunts, "You're not done yet."

"No, I am done." I stand. "I don't work for you. You don't know me, so let me tell you who I am: I'm poor. And last night I fucked your son. And you know what? It was strictly ordinary."

DEMI

I am going to kill them all. I don't care if it's just a game. I am low on bullets, so I head toward the gallery.

Bang!

I am going to take every last bullet. I'm going to cheat — so what? They all do all the time and no one says a word.

Bang! Bang! Bang!

I pass through the hall of mirrors and see Demi over my shoulder, just out of reach, running away from me. I spin and fire in one slick movement.

Bang!

I shoot myself in the mirror. I wasted a bullet on my own goddamn reflection.

This place is like an empire crammed into a house: armor and art and artifacts now lit with gold vomit. Someone to my left.

Bang!

"Bitch."

"Give me your gun."

But he doesn't. He just frowns and runs off, gold paint bleeding down his pant leg like piss.

My temple throbs. I wish these were real bullets. The house is dark. It throbs with my head. I feel a line run down my forehead and think its blood. I wipe it away. It's sweat.

The closer I get to the gallery, the more gold paint oozes down the walls. The party guests seem to have taken special care to destroy anything valuable, so all the paintings, all the statues, weep gold. One of them, I'm sure, is a Monet. Another could be a Rembrandt. My heart is pounding in my ears. I grip my gun.

I see the house I grew up in, how cluttered it was with furniture and cords and electronics, a tangle of wires on the floor. I trip. My hands are sweating. I can feel my breath pull through my lungs like I am threading a needle. Someone to my left.

Bang!

"Ack! You nearly took off my finger."

I don't apologize. "You're out of the game." My voice is a husky whisper. Every kill brings me closer to him, to Graham. What do I want from him: his money, his love, his head?

All my life I believed, I bought into this idea, that I was somehow worthless. That I

should apologize for the tragedy of my existence while these people —

Bang!

— while these *people* —

Bang!

— blew my life to pieces. His money. His
love. His head. It's like a game of Russian
roulette. And I'm down to one bullet.

The entryway blasts open, a vast chasm of
gilt-laced ceiling, domed so it could be a
stunt double for the sky.

"Hey —"

Someone to my right.

Bang!

He gags and grabs his throat. Gold paint
lashes his face, burns in his eyes. He rubs
them, blinded. "I was going to ask for a
truce!" he says. "I was going to call a truce!"

I duck into the gallery. There is a long
white table. There are no bullets. They took
them all. Of course they did. That's how
they get you. That's how they win.

I am out of bullets. All I can do is die. But I
won't. I refuse.

I need to come up with something. If only
the men I shot had surrendered their bullets. One of them had a whole belt tied
around his waist. That's it! The dead all have
their bullets at their little garden party. I

will take their ammo. I will take their guns. They'll never see me coming. They never do.

I make my way to the edge of the party. I spot Lyla and her friend sitting at a table, guns tilted beside them. I wait until Lyla is looking the other way, caught up in conversation with the other woman. Then I slip in behind her, slide the gun from the table. It feels heavy. It's probably still fully loaded. I want to get more but there are too many dead. Someone might see me, so I take Lyla's gun and hurry back toward the garden.

I stop to check how many bullets it has, but I hear footsteps behind me. I see Lyla chasing after me, her dress a gold explosion. She's out. What is she doing? Can't she just let me have this?

"Wait!" she calls. "I need my gun!"

Can't she just let me win?

I grip the gun and run away from her, bound down the stairs and race deeper into the garden. She keeps chasing me, flinging herself down the stairs.

I spin around, turn the gun on her. "I'm not in the game!" she says. She puts her hands up. "Look at me! I just need you to give me my gun back."

Is she kidding? "No."

"But it's —" A figure rises from the bushes

beside her. I tilt the gun. She puts her hands over her face. "Wha—"

Bang!

Dark blood slaps Lyla's white face. Not gold. Not paint. Blood.

LYLA

The body is surrounded by jewelry: thick diamonds, fat ropes of pearls, a sapphire, two emerald earrings. Blood runs beneath them, setting off their sparkle. And I see the silver star around Elvira's dead neck.

Demi is frozen, still gripping the gun.

All the stars are out, burning holes in the sky. What a crock of shit.

"Who is it?" I ask. She stays frozen. I step forward gingerly, tilt the face with my spectator shoe. I recognize him. He's the man from the courtyard, the one with the eternal struggle on his face. Michael. The man she's been living with, keeping secret all this time.

Bang!

A shot blast from far up above makes me jump. Demi meets my eye. Her hair is tangled. A light dusting of gold has settled on her skin, giving it a St. Barts glow. Her eyes are wide. Her chest is pumping. She's so alive. I didn't kill her.

"You knew there was a bullet," she says.

"I tried to stop you."

"Why is there a bullet in your gun?" She pops open the chamber to check if there is another one. There isn't. The rest are Simunition. I only had one bullet.

I look at the body. In movies, dead bodies always look peaceful. Or at least they look dead. But all the bodies I've seen — Elvira and now this one — still look like they're in pain, like they've been wrenched from life. "We need to get him out of here."

"I asked you a question," she says, closing the cartridge. I tee up to his shoulders. He's tall but thin. We could drag him, but where? "What are you doing?"

"I'm trying to help you." I grip the shoulders of his coat, pull. My fingers slip and burn. The body doesn't move.

"This is your fault," she says.

Bang! From above.

"I know," I admit. I feel this lightening sensation, like I'm the one bleeding to death. Every time a privileged person takes ownership, an angel gets its wings. I laugh. I think I'm slightly hysterical, but still . . . "I know it's my fault." She won't meet my eye. It might be too late for us to form any kind of friendship, but it's not too late for me to save her, to do what I should have done a million times. But especially one. "How do we get him out of here?"

She hesitates, analyzing her exits like always. She could run, she could hide, or she could trust me. "There's a gate." Her voice is deep; it grips the surface. She doesn't want to do it. She doesn't have a choice. "That leads down to the street. He broke the lock."

"Do you know him?" I know she does.

"Of course not." She goes to his feet, waits for my signal. We're really going to do this.

"Where can we take him?"

"Anywhere. We just have to get him off the property."

"You act like you've done this before." I smile, once, then bend down to lift him up.

"Hasn't everybody?" she says. I grunt and prop his shoulders up. "Don't get gold dust on him!" Her fingers close around his ankles.

"On three," I say.

"What. The. Fuck?" Graham's voice from behind me. I drop the body. The head lolls back. I turn to find Graham poised at the top of the stairs. He is laced with belts of gold bullets but his suit is hardly crinkled. His skin glows with gold dust and perspiration.

Bang!

Graham flies backward, landing on his ass. Gold dust has exploded across his chest. "Christ!" He looks up in shock.

Demi's gun is still smoking. The dead body is still on the ground. "Sorry," she tells him. "I have to win."

Graham's dimples show as he dusts off his suit, turning his palms gold. He pushes himself back up. He circles the body. He squats down and checks Michael's pulse. He gets blood on his hand. It mixes with the gold paint. He pulls his hand away, tries to shake it off, but it sticks. "Well, he's definitely dead. Who is he?"

"He was robbing the house," I explain. "You can see the jewelry."

"Who shot him?" he asks. Demi is still holding the gun. I am unarmed. He looks from her to me, doing a quick calculation. He knows she shot him. He knows I created the game. He knows I set her up. He smirks at me. "Is this my present?"

Demi's eyes are wide, blackish in the dark and filled with something: fear, like we have collided on a fast train. I remember the night I met her, out in the courtyard, trapped inside the gate, trying to get out. The way I followed her, my target. The tangled mess all leading to this: I won. I won the game. I ruined her life. She murdered a man, a man she was living with. I am the witness. Her life is over. I ended it.

It all ends here. If I tell him, *Yes, this is your present,* then my turn is over. We go back to how things were before. We go back to pretending. We go back to the appearance of perfection, which is the most important part. Maybe they move another tenant in; maybe they play another game, but I don't have to play. My only job is to let them. My only requirement is to look the other way.

I won. I'm free. It's over.

Except it isn't.

Except it never ends.

Except it's not worth it.

I turn to Demi. I see Elvira, see all the women and men who ever tried to live in that guesthouse, who ever tried to make it in this world before. "It's a game," I tell them. "You asked me why the gun was loaded. It's a game they're playing: It's you or me." She doesn't seem to understand until that last line: *It's you or me.* That is a line everyone seems to understand.

Graham presses his lips together. The gold paint on his suit bleeds down artfully so it looks intentional always. "Darling, you seem rattled. Why don't you go upstairs and join

the party? Demi and I will take care of this."
That's when I know I'm finished.

"It's you or me," I repeat to her, but I think she knows. Her face is closed. Her eyes are dark. It's her.

Graham sighs — the poor, beleaguered husband to this mad, mad woman. "It's all right, darling. Just go upstairs and have a glass of Moët. No one is going to get hurt. I'll call someone to escort you." He unsheathes his phone, frowns when his call isn't answered immediately. "No one's picking up. Fucking staff is all playing the game! I shot about twenty of them. Better call the police."

I give Demi one last look but she won't meet my eye. The game is over. It was her or me. She won.

I run.

It's the only choice I have. Down the stairs and out the gate. I reach the street, but it's dark and it's cold and it's empty and I'm tired. I'm so tired of playing games. Sometimes I just want to know how it's all going to end.

I walk down into the courtyard. The fountain is gurgling in the corner, like a body choking on its own blood. It's lit from underneath so the water glows an unnatural blue, turns my gold skin green. I watch the surface as it breaks over and over again. Then it starts to rain. Margo probably ordered it to muddy the evidence.

Later, a male voice calls down from above. Through the rain I see two big black umbrellas hovering over two men. They are saying something like "Stand down."

They start down the steps. One slips and catches himself on the railing.

They hold their umbrellas out over me. I smile when I recognize them. They are the daddy-baby cop combo who came when Bean died.

"You won't believe what happened," I say like we are all friends here.

"We'd like you to come with us," the daddy says.

"Where are we going?" The rain is soaking my dress, washing away the gold dust.

"Down to the station."

"Why?"

"You're under arrest." It makes sense. I didn't shoot Michael, but wasn't I, really, responsible? I played the game. I lost. He reels off my rights.

"Where's my husband?" I ask but I know where he is. He's upstairs drinking champagne.

The daddy cop doesn't answer.

"Cuffs?" the baby says. The daddy shakes

his head.

I stand up, follow them out of the courtyard. All the times I saw other people fall, I never thought it would be me. The mind is amazing for that, the way it can shape things so everyone is always someone else and never, ever *me*.

We reach the street. The cop car is waiting. It's lights spin in lazy circles. Laughter echoes down from way up high at Margo's place. Even the cops look up. It sounds like they're having a good time. They always do.

DEMI

Lyla races down the stairs away from us. Graham is still fucking around on his phone. The gunshots have stopped. I'm pretty sure the game is over. I'm pretty sure I won. Michael hasn't moved.

I tell myself it was an accident. I tell myself it wasn't my fault. I didn't know the gun was loaded. I never would have shot him. Lyla set me up — except she didn't. I stole her gun. She tried to stop me. But I didn't know. I didn't know the gun was loaded. I was just trying to win. I was just trying to save myself.

Michael's face is frozen in pain, the kind of pain he never showed in real life. He was always grifting, always trying; even when he was wrong, he was always trying to survive.

Now that he's dead, I remember only the good things about him: the tent he offered me, his advice, his Pixar movies and his penis collages. Who would protect them now?

Michael is dead. And what made it worse was that no one would care; no one would miss him. He was a bad person. He did bad things. But living the life he did, he should have been *all* bad and he wasn't. The good things he did meant more, because he fought to keep them. He had to fight to do good.

"I should check his pulse again." I start to bend down.

Graham puts a hand on my shoulder. "It's better if you let him bleed out."

"What?"

He waves his hand dismissively. "They always try to sue. It's better if he dies."

I bend down anyway. His body is so cold I gasp. It's like all of his life he was just waiting to die. "This is Michael." I can't find a pulse. I can't even find a hint of one. "The man I told you about." I shake the cold from my fingers.

"Ah, the murderer! Even better."

I brush Michael's hair out of his face. I wish he looked better. I wish he didn't look so rough, because I know that's all they'll see.

"You really shouldn't touch him," Graham observes.

"I killed him. Not Lyla."

He tips his chin. "The gun is in your hand."

"Then why are you —"

"You won the game. You shot me over a man's dead body — that's commitment!" He offers an exuberant smile. It looks cheap on his expensive face. "I always pay off my debts. I assume this is what you want, but I can always give you something else. Maybe a yacht? A small island?"

"What's going to happen to Lyla?"

"The man's obviously homeless. He was trespassing. She'll probably get a slap on the wrist and a few months in prison, but you, darling" — he rests his hand on my shoulder — "will get taken in, identified and pronounced alive."

A loose chill rocks my shoulders. He's right. I put my ID next to Demi's body so she would be mistaken for me. If they realize I'm still alive, they might look into her death. They might look into me.

"But Lyla is your wife."

"Yes." He shrugs. "I'll admit it is convenient for me, too." He dials 911, holds the phone up to his ear. "Yes, hi. This is Graham Herschel. I'm at number One Herschel Drive. . . . Yes, my mother changed the street name. . . . Do you have the address?

Good. I'm calling because my wife has killed a trespasser. Yes, he's definitely dead." He doesn't even look. "She's run off but she won't have gone far. She's probably just downstairs. It's my birthday, you see. We were having a party, so of course we had a bit of a target on our backs." He bends down and arranges the necklaces so they lie symmetrically. "I'd very much appreciate if we could keep this discreet. My wife is in a very delicate mental state. Yes, of course. We won't touch a thing. We'll meet you at the top of the drive. I'll make sure the gate's open." He ends the call. I set the gun on a low wall. Graham scoops it up and wipes it with his pocket square. "You'll feel funny for a while, but it will go away." He angles the gun, searching for fingerprints in the light. "Every feeling goes away after a while."

"Have you done this before?"

"Certainly not this *exactly*." He smirks and says nothing else. "You shouldn't be morose about it, darling. You've won. Very few people win. Would you rather lose?"

"Lyla will tell them it was me. It's her word against mine."

He shakes his head. "Lyla is smart. She knows when she's been beaten. She'll go along with the game. Come on." He reaches out his hand. "Let's have a drink before the police get here. I wish you would be more appreciative, darling. My mother always taught me to say thank you. Manners are the only thing that separates us from the animals."

"Thank you."

"Good girl."

I take his hand. Michael doesn't move. I follow Graham up the stairs to the party.

LYLA

Three months into my stay, a name shows up on my visitor list: Helen Peters. I don't recognize the name, but I approve it anyway. Maybe it's someone I knew in school. Maybe it's the new tenant, onto Margo and Graham's game. I don't care who it is. I am so bored in prison. I have a roommate, so it's kind of like college but the girls are meaner. They play games where no one wins. I will be out soon. I'm looking forward to it but I'm also afraid. A life is such a dangerous thing to have. I'm surprised everyone gets one. Most people don't know what to do with it.

I take my spot at one of the tables. It's my first time having a visitor. My parents are happy with their wedding present. Post–prison sentence, they probably feel only more justified in choosing money over me. Posey sent me a postcard from St. Barts: *I can't believe you're in jail! Graham is such an asshole!* I pinned it to my wall. Who would have thought that Posey would be my only real friend?

This is a low-security prison. It's like a country club without champagne. Visiting hours seem like a chance for prisoners to ream out their loved ones. One woman is mad that her husband doesn't visit enough. Another is pissed at her son for getting a tattoo. Another one is crying because her family couldn't bring their dog in.

I am watching the door when Demi walks in. My stomach drops. She is dressed all in white. What a bitch; that's Margo's color. It makes me like her. No, it makes me love her.

A genuine smile spreads across my face as she takes the seat across from me. "Helen Peters?" She shrugs. "You look good." Who wears white to prison? Rich people. People so out of touch they don't realize how bad it looks.

"Thank you," she says, shifting in her seat. Her eyes narrow as she takes in our surroundings, always analyzing. Always looking for a way out. "I wanted to thank you for . . . for what you did."

"It's nothing." I toss my hand. Nine months in prison? Easy. I do it all the time. "I've done a lot of bad things. I deserve to be punished for something, even if it's something I didn't do."

"I appreciate it."

I don't say anything. It's a power move. Pathetic but it's all I have.

"Do you have anything you want to ask?" she finally says.

"You came to me." She shifts, uncomfortable in her white linen. "I'm guessing you're starting to see what I was dealing with. The games these people play. I could have warned you."

"Why didn't you?"

"Would you have believed me?"

"Yes."

"I'll be out soon. For good behavior."

"Graham wants to have you committed."

"You won't let that happen, will you?" I stand to leave, rap the table once with my knuckle. It's the only card I have left to play.

DEMI

I am living in the glass house. I'm not happy. I'm not sad. I'm rich.

Graham works all the time, and when he's not working, he goes on his golf trips. I am almost always alone. It is perfect. I sit on a chair next to the door so I can see the whole house, the way the floor stretches on and on, stops just short of forever.

The castle above us is being renovated. Margo is on vacation, a pilgrimage through Spain in Bean's honor. She still doesn't know who I am. She doesn't even know she's met me. I skipped her farewell party. I convinced Graham it was better that way. The fewer people who know the truth, the more secure my position. Graham is a problem, I will admit. He's obsessed with me now, but I have a feeling he'll get bored.

One Friday night, he comes home early, finds me in my spot, drinking Moët and watching the sky fall.

He kisses my temple. "Hey, I had an idea." He perches on the arm of my sofa. He is dressed in one of his ridiculous three-piece suits, like he might be asked to stand in on a period piece at any minute. "I wanted you to come on one of my golfing trips."

I wrinkle my nose. "I don't like golf."

"Neither do I." He smiles without teeth.

We pack nothing but a set of clubs, one fresh set of clothes. "You're going to love it," he promises. And then he drives me in his Rolls-Royce Phantom to a bad neighborhood. It's not the neighborhood I grew up in, but it could be. The streetlights are out and have probably been out for a long time. The glass windows are broken. Someone somewhere is screaming. Someone somewhere is crying. They are both far away and right beside us.

The Phantom rolls to a stop in front of a cracked red curb. Graham puts it in park. He shuts off the engine.

My heart itches. "What are we doing?" I can see a broken window above us covered with a bedsheet. We used to cover our windows with bedsheets.

Graham puts his finger to his lips. "Just wait." His teeth are so white, it's sinister.

"For what?"

"Someone always comes out. To see the

car." He indicates the Phantom's slick gray surface. It looks like a spaceship. Like a silver dress — *the* silver dress that woman wore in a different life, the night I realized I was poor.

"Then what?"

He grunts, frustrated by my lack of enthusiasm. "They see what we have, and they try to get it."

"Then what?" My voice is steel.

"Oh, look!"

A little girl stumbles out of a front door onto a concrete stoop. She is dressed in too-small pajamas. Her eyes are wild, not with fun but with exhaustion. She doesn't look like me but I see myself — the way she stoops, ducks her head, embarrassed.

Graham presses his back against the seat, reaches toward the clubs.

"Stop!" I put my hand on his shoulder. "Are you fucking insane?"

He frowns. "It's just a game. God, don't be boring!"

The girl has stopped at the last step, is watching us. Her eyes are wide, taking everything in. The silver car, the man in the blue suit, the woman in white.

Her lips part. "Can I see your car?" she asks like she's not already seeing it.

"We're just leaving!" I say to her as Graham says, "Of course you can, darling."

"What are you going to do?" I whisper in his ear.

He elbows me, calls to her, "You can touch it if you want."

I run through all the weapons at my disposal. I want to kill him. I want to take one of his clubs and split his skull open as she takes a step toward the car.

I lunge across his lap, turn on the engine and throw the car into drive. Hike up my leg, slam my foot over the center console and step on the gas. Graham gasps in surprise and grabs the steering wheel, keeps us from crashing as we stream off into the night.

"Don't ever do that again!" I say as the girl and the neighborhood disappear from view. "Don't ever do that again!"

He just makes a face. "I didn't do anything." He takes a gold cigarette case from his pocket. "What did you think I was going to do? Murder some kid? God." He lights a cigarette. "It's just a game. We're not playing for your fucking soul."

"Don't do that," I say again. I sound unhinged. He slouches moodily and keeps driving. And he will. I know he will. I am beginning to realize that I can't even fathom all the things that he's done, all the terrible things, all his life. All the terrible things he's gotten away with, will keep getting away with. Unless somebody stops him.

All I ever wanted was for things to be easy. I wanted to stop suffering. I never considered that it was a trade. That it was me or them.

I thought I wasn't rich because I didn't deserve it. I never considered that it didn't deserve me. Michael was right. Money is immoral. I don't want to be rich. It's not enough. I want more. I want what I deserve.

Some people deserve to die. And I deserve to kill them.

DEMI

I visit Lyla in jail to thank her for what she did. I want to tell her about Graham, about the golf trips. But when I see her, scrubbed of makeup but glowing with life, I realize I don't need her permission. She saved my life. It's my turn to save hers.

When I get home, I make him dinner. I was never a good cook but he likes my simple, plain food. It's exotic to him. He comes home from work and he asks where his kiss is. I kiss his dry cheek. My nose crinkles at his animal scent.

The floor stretches all the way to the glass so it seems to go beyond that, way out into the sky, where we live. I hear the scratch of the new tenant downstairs.

"Should we celebrate?" I hold up a freshly opened bottle of Moët.

He's been edgy ever since that night, unsure about me. "Celebrate what?"

"Nothing," I say. "Isn't that what we

celebrate?"

"Pour me a glass." I do. Mine is already filled and on the counter. He lifts his glass. "To the new tenant."

I clink his glass. "To the game."

He takes a sip, makes a face. "I hate Moët."

"Me, too."

We eat at the dining table, him on one side, me on the other. As he eats, he tugs at his collar. He breaks a sweat. "I feel very . . . peculiar." He coughs. "All of a sudden." He pushes his plate away, takes another gulp of champagne.

"You've hardly touched your food." I turn mine over on the plate.

"Yes." He gags, pushes his chair from the table so it scrapes the floor. Coughs. "Did you" — cough — "poison my dinner?"

"Of course not." I take a big scoop of potatoes. "I'm eating it, too." I stuff it in my mouth.

He grabs his champagne but his hands are shaking. The glass drops, shatters on the floor.

"Can I get you another glass?"

Our eyes meet. "The Moët." He fumbles in his pockets for his phone. On the other side of the table, I hold it up.

He smiles. Sweat is dripping down his

431

face. He coughs. "I knew you were the woman of my dreams." He starts across the house, toward the door, toward Margo's house. He won't make it. And even if he does, it's empty, hollowed out, midrenovation. His knees are starting to buckle. I finish my glass and follow him out to the courtyard. The air is crisp and cold. "You'll go to prison." He collapses by the fountain, coughs blood into the water.

"You're the only person who knows I'm not Demi." Him and Lyla, but he doesn't know that. And I trust her. We were victims of the same game.

I sit on the edge of the fountain as he pulls himself up, sits heavily beside me.

He tugs his collar so hard, a button pops off. "What did you poison me with?"

"Flowers. From your mother's garden."

"Shit. She loves poetic justice." He coughs and blood spurts down his suit. "How long do I have?"

"Too long," I snap.

Weak, he puts his head on my lap. "Can you tell me one of your stories?" Cough. "Make it a good one." Choke. "A real struggle."

It takes him forever to die. I keep thinking he might survive and sue. I tell him my stories and I pet his wet hair. He's a good sport about it. I don't think he was ever a great fan of living.

When he does finally die, its chilling how beautiful he looks. Even dead. It's all really just so fucking unfair.

LYLA

There is blood in the fountain turning the water an eerie rust color. I call someone to drain it.

I lead him to the fountain, at the center of the stone floor. It gurgles, desperate, like a person drowning. I stand over it, see my gray cashmere tinged dark in my reflection. "I want you to drain the fountain."

He steps forward, almost timid. His face wavers in the murky pool. "What is that?" He reaches with his hand, dips a finger so it undulates the surface, then brings it to his nose.

"How should I know?" I cross my arms. "I just want it out."

"It smells like blood." He shakes the water from his hand. His tool bag slips from his shoulders. It hits the ground with a crack. The tools rattle together. The sky is blue and glazed with clouds and there is blood in the fountain and I want it out.

"I don't know what it is."

"This is your house, isn't it?" He unbuttons each sleeve, rolls them slowly past his elbows. "Got a wall around it." He nudges his chin at the walls on all sides, high walls, the kind you can't see past.

"I don't see what that has to do with anything."

He snorts.

"It's not my house, as a point of fact. It's my mother-in-law's house. Margo. She lives above us, see? With the pointed roof." I indicate the tower, whittled to a point like a thorn crown. You can see it from our house. You can see it from almost anywhere.

Margo is not there. She is on a self-designed religious pilgrimage. She is finding God, *but make it picturesque.* She has left the upper house exactly as it was. She has left everything exactly as it was. I think she believes that once she finds Him, she will pay Him to give everything back.

"You live here."

I could go somewhere else, start over. I think about it sometimes. But this is good for now. A future is a valuable thing. I don't want to spend it all at once. I want to invest, save it for later.

I shrug. "Just because I live here doesn't mean I know every little thing that happens here. It was probably an animal. There are animals everywhere in the hills."

He grasps around the pool, then grunts, removes his arm from the water, shakes it out. Little droplets sting my flesh.

"You really think that I've had someone murdered, don't you?" I perch carefully on the edge of the fountain, close enough to smell his backwater scent. "And I've called you here, because I know you'll never do anything about it. Because even if you can see it, even if you can say it, you can never believe that someone you know could kill another person."

His skin crinkles as he tries to look at me but is blinded by the sun. "I don't know you."

"No." I flick the water with my index finger. "You don't."

The plumber finishes his work and I sit on the edge of the fountain, lost in the glow, when I hear footsteps coming up the stairs.

"Oh!"

I turn and see the new tenant standing at the top of the stairs. She has coltish legs, a neat gray shirt. Her hair is tangled and flecked with paint. "Sorry." I stand, move away from the fountain. "I hope I didn't scare you."

She steps toward me gingerly. "Lyla, right?" I nod. "Are you sure it's okay for me to be here? With everything that's happened?"

"Of course." I smile. "I'm happy to have you."

We could be friends. We could be whatever we want.

What do we want?

ACKNOWLEDGMENTS

This book literally wouldn't exist without my editor, Jen Monroe, who provides the perfect combination of trust and encouragement.

Thank you to my agent, Sarah Bedingfield, and the team at LGR, for unending support.

To the team at Berkley: Loren Jaggers, Stephanie Felty, Fareeda Bullert, Natalie Sellars, and Candice Coote.

And special thanks to the benefits system in England, for supporting my late husband and, consequently, me. These systems save lives and are desperately needed everywhere.

ABOUT THE AUTHOR

Eliza Jane Brazier is an author, screenwriter, and journalist. She currently lives in California, where she is developing her books for television.

The employees of Thorndike Press hope you have enjoyed this Large Print book. All our Thorndike, Wheeler, and Kennebec Large Print titles are designed for easy reading, and all our books are made to last. Other Thorndike Press Large Print books are available at your library, through selected bookstores, or directly from us.

For information about titles, please call:
(800) 223-1244

or visit our website at:
gale.com/thorndike

To share your comments, please write:
Publisher
Thorndike Press
10 Water St., Suite 310
Waterville, ME 04901